Married or Not

by Annette Broadrick

ᕫᘛᕫ

Why did her ex have to still be so attractive?

He made her motor run non-stop whenever he was around. Right now, she couldn't afford to be tempted.

"Don't worry about helping me," she said. She could sense his reluctance. "I changed clothes earlier this evening."

"All right. At least let me put you on the bed before I leave."

Before she could protest, he picked her up as though she were weightless and sat her on the side of the bed.

"I'll see you in the morning," Greg said.

She nodded. He continued to stand there. She closed her eyes. It would be so easy to forget what she'd gone through and accept the here and now…

Ian's Ultimate Gamble
by Brenda Jackson

ᘒᢊᡞᘐ

"Mere friendship between us just won't work."

"You don't think so?"

"No." Ian's voice was clipped and confident.
"And since things can never be like they
were, we need closure to the relationship, a
permanent end."

Brooke knew that what he was saying was true,
but hearing him say it hurt her deeply.

"So, how do you suggest we go about finding
this closure?" she asked. "Do you want me to
leave?"

He stared at her for a long moment before
answering. "No. I don't want you to leave.
What I want, what I need, is to have you out of
my system once and for all. I know of only one
way to make that happen..."

Available in December 2008 from Mills & Boon® Desire™

Married or Not?
ANNETTE BROADRICK

Ian's Ultimate Gamble
BRENDA JACKSON

🌀™ MILLS & BOON®
Pure reading pleasure™

*First published in Great Britain 2008
by Harlequin Mills & Boon Limited,
Eton House, 18-24 Paradise Road, Richmond, Surrey TW9 1SR*

The publisher acknowledges the copyright holders of the
individual works as follows:

Married or Not? © Annette Broadrick 2007
Ian's Ultimate Gamble © Brenda Streater Jackson 2006

ISBN: 978 0 263 85921 8

51-1208

*Printed and bound in Spain
by Litografia Rosés S.A., Barcelona*

MARRIED OR NOT?

by
Annette Broadrick

Dear Reader,

Families have an enormous influence on who
we are and how we make our way in the world.
I find the dynamics within a family interesting
and often entertaining. Other times I grieve
for all the lost opportunities that might have
salvaged a relationship.

I hope you enjoy *Married or Not?* and find
yourself rooting for each character in his or her
struggle for love, happiness and peace.

Sincerely,

Annette Broadrick

ANNETTE BROADRICK

believes in romance and the magic of life. Since 1984, Annette has shared her view of life and love with readers. In addition to being nominated by *Romantic Times BOOKreviews* as one of 1984's Best New Authors, she has also won the following awards from *Romantic Times BOOKreviews*: a Reviewers' Choice Award for Best in its Series; a WISH award; two Lifetime Achievement awards, one for Series Romance and one for Series Romantic Fantasy.

One

If Sherri Masterson had had a crystal ball when she woke up that Friday morning in the middle of May, she would have turned off the alarm and stayed in bed. Instead, she followed her usual routine. She got up and showered at the apartment she shared with Joan Price, who was a school-teacher. The automatic coffeemaker had her morning beverage waiting for her when she walked into the kitchen. She read the paper, nibbled on a piece of toast and drank her coffee before leaving for work.

Sherri loved her job as a technical writer. She worked in Austin, Texas, with a bunch of brilliant geeks who dreamed up new software for consumers. It was her job to translate computer-speak into plain, everyday language, so that a computer user would have no trouble understanding what the software had to offer and how to use it. She'd worked for New Ideas, Inc., for three years.

When she arrived at the office everyone she met was discussing plans for the weekend.

Her plans were the same every week: do her grocery shopping, take clothes to the dry cleaners and pick up last week's and return home to wash a week's accumulation of clothes, towels and bed linens.

Saturday was the big night of her week when she and her cat would curl up in front of the television and watch a movie rented from Netflix.

She looked forward to her weekends so that she could kick back and enjoy her time off. She wasn't interested in dating, which she had trouble getting across to Joan, who was always trying to fix her up with someone: a fellow teacher, a friend of a friend, even one of the single coaches at her high school.

Sherri wanted none of it: the dating, the possibility of falling in love…again. Getting her heart broken…again. Been there. Done that. Barely survived the aftermath.

However, the point was, she *had* survived. It seemed to be Sherri's lot in life to lose the people she loved and depended upon. She'd discovered that, despite the poet's comment, it was better *not* to love at all than to love and lose.

Sherri had learned that life could be unspeakably cruel three weeks before her fourteenth birthday when she'd been told that the plane carrying her parents home from Greece had crashed.

She'd been staying with her aunt Melanie at the time, and was eager to see her parents again, looking forward to enjoying their photos and, of course, presents and souvenirs they had picked up for her.

She'd talked to her mom every day and lived vicariously through the descriptions of their travels. It had been the first vacation they'd taken on their own. Aunt Melanie had teased them about taking a second honeymoon since they hadn't been able to go anywhere right after their wedding.

When her aunt told her about the crash, Sherri refused to believe that her parents were gone. She'd spoken to them earlier that day. They'd missed her as much as she missed them and finally the separation would be over.

The message must have been wrong. It had to be wrong.

But the crash was covered by all the news networks because the majority of the passengers were Americans and no one survived.

Sherri had little memory of attending the memorial service. Only vignettes of scenes had stayed with her. Her mother's best friend holding her and crying while Sherri stood there, dry eyed. The display of photographs of her parents that her aunt had put together. Her dad's boss telling her aunt that her father had substantial life insurance and a pension plan and that he didn't want Melanie or Sherri to worry about finances.

As though money could begin to replace what she had lost.

She'd been so angry…at everyone: classes that had prevented her from going with her parents, the airline for allowing the plane to crash, and especially her mom and dad for dying and leaving her on her own. She had wished she'd been with them. At least they would all have been together.

Sherri had watched as her home, most of the furniture and furnishings and both cars were sold. She'd told her aunt she didn't want anything from the house, but Melanie knew better and had saved many of the personal belongings that Sherri later came to treasure.

Sherri eventually worked through her grief, but at a price. She learned to keep people at a distance and to refuse offers of help, because depending on others who might leave her was too painful to contemplate. If she didn't let anyone too close, she didn't have to suffer the possibility of enduring another debilitating loss.

She had learned to survive whatever life threw at her without whining and to make tough choices, even if there was a price to pay. Her one attempt, after she'd become an adult, to allow herself to get close to someone had turned out to be a disaster.

Now Sherri concentrated on being an exceptional technical writer and was happy to forgo the painful pleasures of a relationship.

She was engrossed in finishing the technical manual she was working on—the one that had to be at the printer next week—when she heard that her boss, Brad Horton, had called a meeting for ten o'clock that morning.

Nobody seemed to know why. They generally had their meetings on Mondays. She looked at the manuscript with yearning. She was so close to finishing. With any luck the meeting would be short and she could spend the rest of the day finishing and polishing her work.

When she arrived in the conference room, there were fifteen other employees there. Why would Brad call a meeting for a few of them and not the entire work force? Was there some kind of rewards announcement he planned to make?

Sherri looked around the room. There were people from her department as well as from other sections of the company. Maybe all their hard work had paid off. Maybe Brad planned to give them midyear bonuses.

Yeah, right.

None of them had any idea why they were there and the room was buzzing when Brad strode into the room.

"Thank you for being here," he began, his hands clasped behind his back. "As you know, we've been having difficulty meeting our quarterly sales projections. Management has spent considerable time and effort to come up with a solution and we have had to face the reality that the best thing for the company is to lay off some of our employees."

A collective gasp swept the room. Sherri's heart stopped before it began to race. Was he talking about her? She glanced around the table and saw that everyone was looking at him in various degrees of shock.

"I want you to know that none of this has anything to do with your performances," he continued to say as her heart sank. "Each and every one of you is excellent at what you do. It's just that we're being forced to cut costs and unfortunately, this is the only way we can do it."

She was horrified. And embarrassed. No matter how Brad phrased it, each of them was being fired.

Sherri struggled to come to grips with the whole idea. She had never been fired before. Sherri had always received praise for the work she did. Why would they choose to let *her* go? She understood the economics, but why was *she* one of the employees chosen to be laid off?

Her thoughts were bouncing around in her head and she broke out in a cold sweat. What was she going to do? How was she going to face Joan and tell her she'd lost her job? The reason Joan had asked Sherri to be her roommate was because the rent was too much for Joan by herself.

"To make the transition a little easier for each of you…" Brad continued. Sherri forced herself to listen. She had to concentrate. She couldn't display her despair in front of everyone. "…you will each receive a check for two weeks' salary and any vacation leave you have coming.

"You're talented people. Remember that. This is strictly a business decision."

He looked around the room. "Any questions?"

No one spoke. Finally Sherri raised her hand.

"Yes, Sherri?"

"Uh, Brad, you know the manual I've been working on? I've been getting it ready for the printers next week. Do you want me to finish it before I leave?"

He shook his head. "I appreciate your offer, but no. We'll have to deal with this without you." He looked around the room. "Any others?"

No one said anything.

"In that case—" He reached into his coat's breast pocket and pulled out a sheaf of envelopes. "When I call your name please pick up your check from me. There will be someone waiting at your desk to help you clear out your things."

The ultimate humiliation. She would have to clean out her desk while someone looked over her shoulder to make certain she didn't take something that wasn't hers.

With all the dignity she could manage, Sherri walked to the head of the table when her name was called, took her check and returned to her desk. A smile was beyond her.

No one was talking. Those remaining with the company had their heads down, working. Had she been in their place, she would no doubt have done the same. She was now separated from them. They worked here. She didn't.

Numbly she found a box and began to strip her desk of reference books and other odds and ends she'd accumulated over the past three years.

She was escorted out of the building and once in the parking lot, Sherri hurried to her car, at the moment the only escape and sanctuary she had. The inside of the car steamed with heat and she quickly rolled down the windows while she placed the box on the backseat. Inside the car, Sherri placed her hands on the steering wheel and stared blindly through the windshield.

What did I do wrong? I was rarely late and always called in. I didn't take sick days like some of the others. Maybe I shouldn't have skipped that meeting a few weeks ago in order to meet a printing deadline.

Panic surged through her. What about her part of the rent and utilities? She had money put away for emergencies, but nothing like this. She'd have no income to take care of bills.

The money left for her by her parents had enabled Sherri to pay for her college education and to buy herself a car. She'd been thankful not to have to worry about student loans and very grateful for their foresight.

What was she going to do? She had to get another job, but where?

She'd have to go through interviews, which she detested. She'd have to tell them she'd been laid off. Would that be a black mark against her?

Her eyes finally focused on a few people standing near their parked cars, discussing what had happened. She didn't want to discuss what had happened with anyone. What she wanted to do was go back home and hide under the bed, or at least hide her head under her pillow.

Her life had been so carefully structured. She'd believed that working hard and honing her skills would protect her.

Tears trickled down her cheeks. She turned the car on and waited for the air conditioner to blow some cool air before raising the windows.

She couldn't sit in the parking lot all day. She had no place else to go but home. Thank goodness school was still in session. She wouldn't have to face Joan until later today.

Joan planned to spend most of her summer with three of her teacher friends traveling around Europe. They were leaving the latter part of June.

Sherri knew she was being cowardly, but she wished that this could have happened after Joan had left. She could have used the time to pull herself together and make some kind of plans.

She felt sick to her stomach. She had to get through this, somehow.

Sherri flipped the visor down and stared at herself in the mirror. "So. What do you intend to do now?"

The image in the mirror, with its dark-brown hair, green eyes and pasty white skin stared back blankly.

"Try not to panic. You can do this."

She flipped the mirror up and eased the car forward. As she pulled out of the parking lot, Sherri thought of one positive…at least her car was paid for. That was one less worry. It was a few years old but she took good care of it. She only prayed nothing major broke down until she had a steady income once again.

She glanced back for a moment before getting on the access road of the freeway. Happiness was *not* looking in your rearview mirror to see the building where you no longer worked.

Sherri followed the access road until she could merge with traffic on the highway. She glanced at the car clock, amazed to discover it wasn't even noon yet. Had it only been a few hours ago that she'd been home sipping coffee and reading the paper?

She shook her head. There was definitely a time warp going on. Nothing seemed real to her.

Once on the highway, Sherri headed for home. Traffic flowed smoothly at this time of day, which was a blessing. She had to force herself to focus on her driving.

After a few miles of traveling at seventy, she realized that, once again, luck was against her. Brake lights showed up ahead of her and she began to slow down. There must be an accident up ahead.

Out of habit, she glanced in her rearview mirror and froze.

A tractor-trailer rig had suddenly appeared at the top of the rise behind her and was bearing down on her.

Couldn't he see all the red brake lights ahead of him? Couldn't he see that she had come to a complete stop?

Time slowed down for her as she watched him attempt to slow down his rig. She could hear his brakes screaming as he moved inexorably toward her.

Sherri felt a certain calm fall upon her as she waited for him to hit her. Maybe this was the way her life would end. At that moment, she really didn't care.

The last thing she remembered was the sound of screeching metal as the rig plowed into her car.

Sherri roused at some point, wondering where she was. She felt as though she were floating. She vaguely heard voices that didn't seem to have anything to do with her. Excited voices. She lazily wondered what they were excited about.

A voice near her head yelled. "This one's trapped in her car. We've gotta get her out of here. Now!"

"Is she alive?"

"Can't tell. I can see her, but can't reach her.

She wondered who they were talking about.

Loud sounds echoed around her, which was irritating. How rude. Couldn't they see she was trying to rest?

She faded away, the voices in the distance, until she felt a hand at her throat.

"There's a pulse. Let's get her out of there."

The seat shifted. Why was she under the dash? Compact cars were too small to be playing games.

Then more hands touched her, moving her.

She screamed and blacked out once again.

Two

Greg Hogan was returning to the police station when dispatch called him to come in. As a homicide detective, he spent as little time at the station as possible. As it happened, though, today he needed to run some information through the station's computer. He was investigating the murder of a young photographer, and evidence he had gathered pointed to a person who knew his victim well enough to have invited him into his home. He had a couple of suspects in mind. Now he had to follow up on some leads in order to get the necessary evidence for an arrest.

He wondered why he'd been called in. Maybe he'd irritated the captain. If so, it would only be the third time this week. The captain didn't like Greg's attitude toward work. He wasn't a team player. He was a maverick. The problem was, Greg solved homicides and the captain had trouble arguing with his success.

Not that Greg's success ever stopped the captain from

griping at him. Greg had grown so used to it that he'd long ago tuned him out, figuring that while the captain was going after Greg, he was leaving the others under his command alone.

Last week Pete Carter had pointed out how altruistic Greg was, protecting the other men from the captain. Pete was a sergeant on the force and had been around longer than any of them. Greg promptly suggested that since all the men were better off with him taking the brunt of the tongue-lashings, they owed him a beer. And darned if they hadn't taken him out one night and wouldn't let him pay for anything.

Greg smiled at the memory.

He pulled into his parking space at the station and got out of his car. The parking space was one of the perks he'd received with his promotion to lieutenant a few months ago, despite the prickly relationship he had with the captain.

Life was good.

As soon as Greg walked inside, he knew something was wrong. There were more men standing around in the bull pen than usual. And all of them looked grim. Greg put his hands on his hips.

"What's going on?"

Pete walked over to him and put his hand on his shoulder. "Greg, I'm afraid I have some bad news for you."

Greg looked around the room and frowned. "What happened? Did one of the guys get hurt? Who?"

"No. It's Sherri."

"Sherri? What about her?"

"She was in a multicar accident this morning. They airlifted her to the hospital...alive when they got her to the hospital, but I heard she was in critical condition."

Greg was thankful there was a chair nearby. His knees

shook so hard he sank into the chair before his reaction became apparent to everyone. He clenched his jaw.

"I figured that since the two of you had some history together that you'd want to know," Pete went on, sounding sympathetic.

Greg shook his head, feeling dazed. He pushed his hand through his hair and forced himself to look at Pete. "They're sure it was her?"

"Yeah. A semi jackknifed when he tried to stop on the freeway and he plowed into her. She was in the last car of a string of them that were stopped due to an earlier accident. Six vehicles were in the smash-up and there were serious injuries in several of the cars, but she caught the brunt of it."

Greg closed his eyes. Sherri? Near death? Couldn't be.

"What hospital?" he finally asked.

Pete told him.

"Thanks for letting me know," Greg said, and left.

He drove to the hospital on autopilot. He parked near the emergency entrance and strode across the parking lot. Inside, the place teemed with people; doctors and nurses moved among patients with various injuries. It looked like a war zone, with some of the injured on stretchers and others in chairs. The Emergency Medical Technicians from the various ambulances outside were working on those victims not as severely injured as the ones they'd brought in.

He quickly checked each stretcher and when he didn't see her, went over to the nurses' station.

"I'm looking for one of the accident victims who were air-lifted to this hospital. Sherri Masterson Hogan."

The harried nurse said, "Sir, you can see that we're overwhelmed with all the injuries here and—"

"Just tell me where they took her and I'll be out of here."

She hurried past him, shaking her head.

He turned around and faced the noise and confusion around him. He knew he wouldn't get any answers here.

Greg continued down the hallway, ignoring signs that read Do Not Enter and shoving doors open, looking into each cubicle for signs of her. A member of the hospital staff stopped him. Greg checked his name tag, which read Dr. Luke Davis, and figured he was one of the doctors on duty.

"Sir, I must ask you to return to the waiting area. Someone will help you as soon as possible."

Greg said as clearly as he could with his jaws clenched, "Dr. Davis. I'm looking for Sherri Masterson Hogan, who was in that six-car smash-up. I'm told she was airlifted here and I intend to find her."

The doctor nodded. "I see. Are you a family member?"

"I'm her husband."

What difference did it make, anyway? He was determined to see her, regardless of their relationship.

"Hold on. I'll see what I can find out for you," Dr. Davis said, striding down the hallway, the tails of his medical coat flapping around him.

Greg paced back and forth, dodging carts, beds and medical personnel until the doctor returned.

"She's in surgery."

"What are her injuries?"

Dr. Davis shook his head. "You'll need to speak to the surgeon about that."

"Where can I find him when he gets out of surgery?"

"You can wait for him upstairs, in Intensive Care. He'll look for family members when he finishes."

Greg swallowed. "I want to see her as soon as possible."

"The surgeon will discuss that with you."

Greg nodded, turned on his heel and headed toward the bank of elevators.

"Good luck," Dr. Davis said behind him.

Greg rode the elevator to the next floor where the ICU was located. It was quiet on the ICU floor, which was a relief from the pandemonium downstairs. He pushed through double swinging doors and found the nurses' station.

"Sir," one of the nurses said, "you can't come in here."

"I'm waiting for Sherri Masterson Hogan to come out of surgery."

She looked down at the desk and riffled through some files. She read some of the files before saying, "We have a Sherri Masterson who has been recently admitted."

So she'd taken back her maiden name. Why wasn't he surprised?

"Are you family?"

He'd already lied once. "Her husband."

She nodded. "Good. We need to get more information on her."

He took a deep breath. "Okay."

She went down a list, asking questions. He knew her age, birthdate, even her blood type, but he had no idea where she lived these days, so he rattled off his own address.

After answering the rest of the questions, Greg wandered down the hallway to the ICU waiting room with the nurse's promise that the doctor would be out to speak with him as soon as he was out of surgery.

Greg hated sitting around, but he had no intention of leaving the hospital until he knew more about Sherri's injuries.

He wondered why he cared. He hadn't seen or spoken to her in almost two years. Eighteen months, six days, to be precise.

She'd asked him not to contact her once everything had ended, and he'd determinedly followed her instructions. He'd almost convinced himself she was part of his past. He was so over her. Then what was he doing here? Why had he panicked at the thought that she could die?

For one thing, she was much too young, six years younger than his thirty-two years.

Just because she wanted no part of me didn't mean she deserved to die.

The last six months they were together had been filled with so much tension that it had become a third party in their marriage. She'd withdrawn into herself. When he asked what was wrong, she told him that he was too secretive about his past and his background. She said she didn't really know him at all.

Okay, so he wasn't the most talkative person in the world…especially about his feelings. He'd never been good about opening himself up and sharing his innermost thoughts and emotions with anyone.

When they'd first married, she had asked him all kinds of questions…about his childhood, his family, why he'd chosen to be a cop. He never liked talking about his childhood or his family and admittedly he was less than forthcoming. As far as he was concerned, all of that was in the past and had no bearing on who he was today. He'd just had trouble explaining that to Sherri's satisfaction. He'd finally stopped trying.

He shouldn't have been all that surprised the day he got home to find every last trace of her presence in his apartment gone. She'd left the key to his place on the counter with a note telling him that she was getting a divorce and to contact her attorney—she also left the attorney's business card—if he had any questions.

Hell yes, he'd had questions! How could she just move out like that? She'd kept asking him to talk to her about stupid things, but that was no reason just to walk out on him. He'd loved her and she'd thrown his love back in his face. Why else would she have hired an attorney before she'd even bothered to tell him she wanted a divorce?

He'd been furious with her. He'd waited three days to calm down enough to call her attorney, who had told him that since they'd acquired no property of significance during the three years of their marriage, Sherri wanted to keep what was hers and let him keep what was his.

He hadn't argued because he knew there would be no point. She'd obviously made up her mind and his opinion didn't matter.

He'd tried to be what she'd wanted in a husband, but he hadn't really known what she expected a husband to be. He'd been alone for most of his twenty-seven years before they'd met. Of course there had been adjustments to sharing a place with her. However, he'd loved her and showed his love in every way he knew how, but his love hadn't been enough. He knew, was absolutely convinced, that she'd loved him in the beginning. There was no way she could have faked her response to him. His off-duty hours had been spent in bed with her, making love to her, holding her, listening to her while she talked about her childhood and her family.

She'd had it tough and he'd told her that he would always be there for her, that he would never abandon her, or leave her to deal with life on her own.

And yet...

After a while she'd stopped talking to him as much and he figured that was because she'd told him everything about her past. She would ask him about his work, but once he was home he didn't want to talk about his job. He just wanted to be with her.

He'd always worked long hours during an investigation, but she'd known that. He might have rushed her into marriage a little fast, but he had been afraid he would lose her if he settled for a long engagement. He'd lost her anyway.

Well, he'd come to terms with the divorce. There wasn't much else he could do. He'd tried to console himself that cops had a higher rate of failed relationships than almost any other profession. Somehow, that hadn't helped him get over the pain of losing her.

And now she was seriously injured. Regardless of the circumstances, he could not leave the hospital without knowing how she was.

Greg waited three more hours before a weary doctor wearing scrubs appeared in the doorway. "Mr. Masterson?"

"Um, no. Greg Hogan. Sherri uses her maiden name." He had trouble talking around the knot in his throat. He finally managed to ask, "How is she?"

The doctor rubbed the back of his neck. "There was some internal bleeding and we had to remove her spleen. She's in stable condition. I think she's going to get through this with no problem. The airbag saved her life but there was some bruising. Her right arm is broken as well as her right leg, so she'll be slowed down for a while, but otherwise, I think she's in good shape, considering what she went through."

Greg's relief at the news caused him to choke up. He rubbed the bridge of his nose with his thumb and forefinger, trying to gain control over his emotions.

"May I see her?" he finally managed to ask.

"She's in recovery at the moment. Once they move her to ICU one of the nurses will come get you."

"Thank you." Greg held out his hand and the surgeon shook it before leaving the room.

Broken bones. Those would heal. The trauma caused by the surgery would also need time to heal. She was going to

be okay. He fought the constriction in his throat. He was tired,
that's all.

He glanced at his watch. It was after six and he still hadn't
followed up on the investigation he was conducting. The team
needed answers quickly. Law-enforcement personnel knew
that the first forty-eight hours after a crime was committed
were the most critical for gathering evidence. He needed to
get back on this one before any more time was lost.

He approached the nurse who had taken down the information on Sherri. "May I help you?" she asked.

"Do you have any idea when Sherri Masterson will be out
of recovery?"

"Not really." She shook her head. "They'll keep her in
recovery until her vitals stabilize."

When would that be? Soon, he hoped. He really needed
to see her.

"I have to get back to work right now, but I'll definitely be
back later tonight."

The nurse nodded and Greg headed for the elevators. He'd
started to shake once the doctor had left. Reaction and relief
that her injuries were no longer life-threatening and that she'd
made it through surgery all right had gotten to him.

There was nothing he could do for her at this point, a
feeling he'd often had when they were together. That didn't
mean that he could just walk away from her now.

Three

Greg returned to the hospital a little after midnight. Another shift was at the nurses' station.

He'd managed to get some work done on his latest investigation before he'd gone to find Sherri's car. What he'd seen had sickened him and caused him to wonder how she had survived.

"I'm Sherri Masterson's husband, Greg Hogan," he said quietly. "I haven't been able to see her since her surgery. Would it be possible to see her now?"

An older nurse came around the counter. "Follow me. Please don't stay long."

"Has she been awake at all since coming to the ICU?"

"For a few minutes when they brought her to her room. She's being given something for pain and is pretty groggy."

Greg hadn't known what to expect when he walked into her room. He hadn't seen her in almost two years, but nothing could have prepared him for the shock of seeing her lying there so still.

He wouldn't have recognized her. Her face was swollen, with cuts and bruises that no doubt occurred when her airbag inflated.

The hospital staff had her hooked up to machines and a bag of liquid. One machine monitored her heart, another kept track of her blood pressure and pulse and he knew the drip contained saline solution to keep her hydrated.

She was so pale that if it hadn't been for the steady beat of the machine, he would have thought she was dead.

He'd forgotten how small she was because she had loomed so large in his memory.

Her thick lashes lay on her cheeks hiding her amazingly green eyes. She looked peaceful lying with her arms beside her. Her dark hair framed her face and he realized she'd cut it. Now it feathered around her head. Her poor face was battered and she had a black eye but all of that would go away with time and rest.

He stepped closer to the bed and placed her limp hand in his.

"What have you done to yourself, Sherri?" he whispered. "What were you doing out on the highway in the middle of the day? Had you gotten sick at work and gone home early?"

She stirred and her lashes fluttered, but her eyes stayed closed.

The nurse returned to the room. "You'll need to leave now. I'm sure she'll be more awake in the morning."

The next morning Greg was at the hospital by seven o'clock. He found Sherri sleeping. One of the nurses came in.

"How's she doing?" he asked, his voice low.

"Remarkably well, considering. She roused a few times in the night while we were checking on her but went back to sleep. Rest is the best thing for her. "

Sherri heard people talking nearby. She wished they would go away and let her sleep. The alarm hadn't gone off yet to

remind her to get up. They continued to talk and Sherri could
have sworn she recognized one of the voices: a deep voice that
had always made her heart race.

"Greg?" she whispered. Surely not. Why would he—

"I'm right here, Sherri," he replied, picking up her hand and
bringing it to his lips.

She was probably dreaming, but why would she dream of
him?

Finally, she opened her eyes and stared at him. "Greg?" she
whispered in wonder. "Is it you?" She remembered now that
she was in the hospital. What was he doing there?

He nodded and flashed a brief smile at her. "How are you
feeling?" He sat in the chair next to her bed.

She looked at her hand still nestled in his. "Very strange. I
think I'm actually dreaming this conversation."

"No, I'm really here. I've been worried about you."

"I must be in worse shape than I thought if you're here,"
she said roughly, her mouth dry.

Without hesitation he reached over and handed her a bottle
of water with a plastic straw in it.

She sipped on the water, trying to bring her brain into
some kind of focus.

He brushed her hair off her forehead. "You cut your hair."

"Yes. It's easier to keep this way."

Neither one of them spoke after that. Sherri couldn't come
up with a coherent thought or question.

"Do you remember the accident?" he finally asked.

"No. I guess I got a little banged up."

"Some internal injuries and a broken arm and leg would
bear that out."

"The doctor said he had to remove my spleen and sew up
some tears inside." She paused before saying, "No more gym-

nastics for me, I guess." He didn't smile, which didn't surprise her. It was a lame joke.

"My guess is that the seat belt did its job and saved your life but caused damage of its own."

She had trouble keeping her eyes off him. Greg Hogan was there in the hospital to see her. They'd had no contact in years and yet, now he was here.

"This is too weird. Why are you here?"

"I told you."

"How did you hear about the accident?"

"At the station. That was one heck of a pile-up and several units were out there. Someone radioed in that your car had been sandwiched between an eighteen-wheeler and an SUV." He nodded toward the nearby table. "They brought your purse back to the station when they recognized you and gave it to me. I left it here when I checked on you last night."

She closed her eyes for a moment. "Sorry," she said. "I'm having trouble concentrating on anything. I feel like I'm floating."

"It's the meds they're giving you. You're going to be fine, you know."

"That's good," she murmured.

Greg watched her go back to sleep and smiled. He'd turned over his cases to some of the other detectives and asked for time off. He wanted to be here in case she needed him. She had no family since her aunt had died and he didn't want her to be alone.

Of course he knew he had no business being there. She'd made it more than clear when she left him that she no longer wanted him around her. He picked up on the fact that she was less than thrilled to see him there, honestly puzzled, and he couldn't explain to her what he couldn't explain to himself.

He just knew that he had to be there. He leaned back in the chair and closed his eyes. He hadn't gotten much sleep last night. Now he waited until she woke up again.

The next time Sherri opened her eyes and saw him, she frowned. "You're still here."

He nodded.

"I don't understand. Aren't you supposed to be at work?"

"I took some time off."

"You said you talked to some of the men who were at the scene of the accident. Did they say how badly my car was damaged?"

"There's not much left of it, I'm afraid. It's a miracle you survived. When I saw it, I didn't know how you could have come out of it alive."

"It can't be repaired?" she asked wistfully.

"'Fraid not." He rubbed her knuckles with his thumb. "I'm sorry. I know how much you loved that little car."

Tears welled into her eyes. "I'm being silly to cry over a stupid car. It's just that it was my very first car and I bought it brand-new."

"I spoke to your roommate a little while ago while you were asleep. She didn't know you'd been in an accident until late last night. When she called the hospital this morning to find out how you were, the nurse forwarded the call to your room. I guess the hospital will only give out information to family members."

"You're not family." Tears continued to slide down her cheeks.

"But the hospital doesn't know that. I told them I was your husband."

She started to sit up and then grabbed her tummy and winced.

"Easy. You've just had major surgery."

"Why would you lie like that?"

"Like I said," he began patiently. "The hospital won't give

out information on a patient except to family members. I needed to know how you were doing so I told them we were married. I had this same conversation with Joan. She'd never heard of me." He cocked his head and looked at her, his brows raised.

"I never told her your name. All she knows is that I'm divorced."

"I think she was surprised to find me here."

Sherri almost smiled. "I'm sure she was." More tears flowed. "I didn't get a chance to tell her."

"Tell her what?"

"About what happened. I lost my job yesterday."

"So that's why you were on the highway at that time of day." She sighed. "It was definitely a Black Friday for me."

She kept wiping away her tears. He took a tissue and wiped her cheeks.

"The important thing is that you're alive. You can always get another car and another job."

She glanced down at her body. "Right. With my arm and leg in casts, I have a hunch a prospective employer would not be impressed."

"You don't need to find a job next week, you know. You're going to need time to rest and recuperate."

She shook her head. "You don't understand. I'm obligated to pay half the bills for our apartment. Joan depends on me just as I depend on her."

"Joan wondered how you'd be able to climb the stairs to your apartment, which I think is a fair question. You can't handle crutches until your arm heals and that would be at least six weeks."

"Oh, no! I hadn't gotten around to thinking about that." She shook her head. "I can't believe all of this happened in one day."

"Did you get a severance check?"

She nodded toward her purse. "I hope it's still in there."

"May I look?" he asked, reaching for it.

She closed her eyes. "I suppose. I don't seem to have any secrets from you."

He saw the crumpled envelope just inside the purse. He handed it to her. "Is this it?"

She opened her eyes and looked first at the envelope and then at him. "With one arm in a sling and the other hooked up to a drip, I can't even take it."

"I'll put it in the bank for you if you like. I'll need a deposit slip."

"Also in my purse."

He found her checkbook and without looking at the balance, tore off a deposit slip and put it back in her purse.

When he looked back at her she was staring at him. She didn't say anything, just looked at him. After a lengthy silence, he finally asked, "What?"

"I still don't understand why you're here."

"I care about you."

She sounded frustrated when she replied, "I don't understand why."

He smiled. "I've gotta admit, it surprised me, too."

Her eyes drooped.

"Get some sleep. I'll come back later."

"You don't have to. I'm okay."

"Yes, I know. Just humor me, okay?"

Her eyes closed and he waited for her to say something, but she didn't. She'd fallen asleep.

He stroked her hand as he studied her. He was glad to see she had a little more color in her face.

Greg stroked her cheek and whispered, "Take care of yourself, little one," and walked out of the room.

Four

Two days later Sherri woke up in a panic. She'd been having a nightmare, or perhaps her subconscious had chosen to relive some of her worst moments. She looked around her room and saw that she was alone.

She realized she was holding her breath and let it out with a whoosh, her relief overwhelming. The nightmare had probably been the result of knowing that she was being released from the hospital today. Somehow she would have to navigate the stairs to her second-story apartment. Once there, she would be something of a captive until her leg cast came off.

At the moment, getting to her apartment wasn't her worst problem. How could she look for work like this? No one in his or her right mind would hire her. She wasn't even sure she could work full-time right away. She'd been in good shape, relatively speaking, but she was a long way from getting over the wreck. Her little car was gone. Her insurance would only pay a percentage of her hospital bills, which were going to be astronomical. For that matter, she might not have any insurance. Had it been canceled the day she was laid off? She hoped it had been in effect until midnight of that day. She'd paid her part of the insurance premiums for the entire month and, as if all of that wasn't enough to deal with, she also had Greg to contend with.

He'd come by to see her for both of the past two days. She didn't want him here. She'd hoped never to see him again. Why? Because she still turned to mush whenever she was around him. That was the reason she had asked him to leave her alone after the divorce. She could deal with the hurt and the pain of the divorce as long as it was a distant memory. As soon as she saw him she was instantly reminded of how much in love she'd been with him, and how much he'd hurt her.

One of the things she found attractive about him when they'd first met was that he was a man of action and didn't talk much. Clams were chattier, she was sure. She hadn't understood then that without open communication between them, their marriage could not succeed.

Granted, she didn't expect him to talk about his work. She understood that. Eventually, they didn't talk at all. She couldn't live that way. He knew her entire life history. She knew little about his background or past. She understood that there were people who hated to talk about themselves, but Greg had carried his reticence to an extreme.

What had ended the marriage as far as she was concerned was that she'd discovered he'd lied to her. Flat-out lied. The other things had been tough enough to deal with, but when she'd found out the truth about him and that he had hidden it from her for their entire marriage, she knew she could no longer live with him.

And yet… He'd heard about her accident and had come to see her. Okay. She could understand that a little. I mean, they had known each other intimately at one time. She supposed he could have been concerned about her.

However, she was at a loss to figure out why he came each day to see her. It was ridiculous. They had little to talk about. She certainly had no intention of getting involved in his life again.

Each time he'd left she'd politely told him not to come back. He came anyway.

Well, if he showed up today she'd give up the polite part and tell him to leave her alone. If he didn't show up, she'd be gone. As far as she knew, he didn't know where she lived— No. Wait. He'd said something about her living on the second floor. He couldn't know that if he hadn't been by there.

Well, when she saw him, she intended to set him straight. She did not want him in her life in any way. Thanks for the offer, but no thanks. She hoped that the meeting would happen later rather than sooner. She needed to get her strength back before facing him. Otherwise, she might end up throwing herself into his arms crying, "Save me! Save me!"

Not her style at all, but then whenever she was around Greg, she had trouble thinking coherently.

The aide came in with her breakfast. "The doctor wants to check to see how you are this morning. He's making rounds now, so it shouldn't be too long." She set the tray on the rolling table. "Enjoy."

Sherri looked at the tray. Enjoy. Right. Clear liquids. No coffee. She had to be on a special diet until everything damaged inside her healed. She'd have to give Joan a list of the things she could eat and have her bring them home. It would be good to get home and let Lucifer, her cat, love her.

Or rather push his head into her hand to love him. He was company, all the company she needed.

She began to eat, resigned to the diet for now.

Greg pulled into the parking lot of the hospital. Sherri was being dismissed today and he already knew she wasn't going to like what he'd done.

Too bad. Like it or not, she would have to accept that this was the way things would be for the foreseeable future.

Greg saw her doctor as soon as he stepped off the elevator. Dr. Hudson stood at the nurses' station, going over a chart with one of the nurses.

Greg waited until the two were finished and walked over. "Good morning, Dr. Hudson. I understand Sherri is being moved today," he said as he approached the doctor.

"Yes. I was just in there. She's doing well, considering, but will still need plenty of rest. The bones should knit back together with no problem. My only concern would be that she might start hemorrhaging. I wouldn't leave her alone for the next several days."

"No problem."

Greg nodded, his mind racing. He walked to the open door of Sherri's room and knocked on the jamb. When she glanced up, he walked inside, his hands in his pockets.

She scowled. "What are you doing here? I thought I made it clear that you don't need to keep checking on me. I'm fine."

"Ah. You must be feeling better."

"I am. In fact, I'm going home today."

"Good for you."

"So you don't need to worry about me."

"Okay."

"I'm waiting for the nurse to come help me dress. So if you'll excuse me…"

"Want me to help? I'm right here and it wouldn't be the first time I've helped you to dress…or undress."

Her sigh was filled with frustration. "No, Greg. I do not need your help to dress or undress. Thank you for coming but—"

"But don't let the door hit me in the—"

"Goodbye, Greg."

He shrugged and walked out of the room. Hoo-boy. His powers of persuasion better kick in really fast or he was going to be in bigger trouble than he already was.

He'd finally had to face his real motive in helping her. The fact that she had no family was part of the reason, but the hard fact was that he was in still in love with her. He was supposed to be completely over her by now. Instead, he hadn't wanted to leave her side since the accident. Once he realized that his feelings for her had never changed, he knew that he would provide whatever she needed to heal, whether or not she was comfortable with his help.

After signing her release papers, Sherri was placed in a wheelchair and taken to the lobby. When she looked outside, she didn't see her cab. Well, it should be here soon.

"You can leave me here by the door while I wait for my taxi," she said to the nurse.

The woman looked at her as though she'd lost her mind. "I don't think so," the nurse replied. As the automatic doors opened for them, the nurse continued, "You aren't going home in a taxi, honey. Your husband is taking you home."

The doors closed behind them as Sherri whipped her head around. She saw Greg, leaning against a black sports car parked at the front entrance, his arms folded over his chest, his ankles crossed. At the moment he was in profile, gazing across the parking lot.

Panic set in. "He's not my husband!"

The nurse chuckled. "Well, that's good to know. Then can I have him? Whoever he is, he's here to take you home, according to your discharge papers." She continued to push Sherri's chair toward Greg.

Greg saw them and straightened. He wore wrap-around sunglasses and still had on the dazzling white T-shirt and snug-fitting jeans he'd worn earlier. He'd finished off his haute couture ensemble with sneakers that might have been white in a far-distant past.

"What are you doing here?" she said.

"I am here to whisk you away in my chariot, milady," he said with a bow.

"That really isn't necessary," she said, looking over her shoulder at the nurse, intending to ask the woman to take her back to the lobby. The only problem was that the nurse was staring at Greg with a dazed grin on her face.

Sherri quickly ran through her options and realized that she had been outmaneuvered. She rubbed her forehead where an ache began to throb. "Great," she muttered, and said nothing more while Greg and the man-hungry nurse helped her into his car.

Once inside, she stared straight ahead pretending he wasn't there, which was a little difficult to do when he leaned over and carefully fastened her seat belt. "I know you're glad to be out of the hospital. No one can sleep well with all the activity going on."

She didn't reply. There was no way she could interact with him and keep her distance, and it was essential that she remain distant.

They'd been driving for about ten minutes when she broke her silence. "Wait!"

"For what?"

"This isn't the way to my apartment."

"I know."

"What are you doing, kidnapping me?"

"Nothing so dramatic. I thought you might like to go to Barton Springs and enjoy the sunshine."

"Greg, it's a hundred degrees today."

"We'll park in the shade."

The pounding in her head intensified.

He found shade and pulled beneath one of the huge live oak trees. He left the engine and air conditioning running while he removed his seat belt and turned to her.

"I know I'm the very last person you want in your life, now or at any other time. I get that. I just want to give you a chance to look over your options."

She sighed. "They're extremely limited."

"Not necessarily." He paused, cleared his throat and finally continued. "Please hear me out before you say anything. Okay?"

She just looked at him.

"I spoke to Joan a couple of days ago about your situation. We agreed that you can't stay at the apartment. With no elevator you would be trapped up there. It isn't safe and it could be quite dangerous."

She lowered her head, not wanting to look at him. "Then why didn't Joan tell me herself? I've talked to her every day."

"I asked her to let me talk to you about everything."

"You mean there's more?" she asked, wishing her voice didn't sound as though she were on the edge of hysteria.

"Yeah. There is. Joan will be leaving in a few weeks—"

"I know that! She's been planning this trip for two years!"

"Yes, well, then you probably don't want her to cancel the trip," he replied smoothly.

"Of course I don't. I don't need her to look after me."

"That isn't the point. Without your paying half the bills on the apartment, she'll need the money she set aside for her holiday to pay all of them."

Sherri slumped in her seat and closed her eyes.

"My suggestion was that she get another roommate, which she has done."

Her eyes flew open. "You did what? Are you out of your mind? I no longer have a job. I no longer have a car. And, thanks to you, I don't even have a place to live? Gee, thanks, Greg. You've certainly made my day. Maybe you'd better drop me off at the Salvation Army. I understand they look after the homeless with no jobs."

She hadn't realized how loud she'd gotten until she stopped. Her voice still rang around them. She took several deep breaths. *I can get through this. Somehow, some way, I can do this. I've got friends. I've got…what, exactly? A broken arm and leg and I'm presently recovering from surgery. Oh, yeah. I'm in really great shape.*

After a silence that stretched between them for several minutes, he asked, "Are you through?"

Oh, how she'd love to brain him over the head with her cast. With her luck, she'd probably break her arm again.

"Yes," she muttered, looking out the side window so he wouldn't see the tears that filled her eyes.

"What I think would work out best for you is to stay with me until, quite literally, you get back on your feet."

She whipped her head around to stare at him so fast she'd probably added whiplash to her other injuries.

Horrified by the suggestion, she could only stare at him.

So many thoughts raced through her mind that her head was spinning. The whole world had gone mad. Or at least her tiny part of it. Didn't he know it would be impossible for her to live with him again? Was he so insensitive to her feelings that he didn't understand how painful being around him would be for her?

She settled on one major objection that she'd already heard him explain about her apartment. "You live in a second-story apartment, too."

"I've moved."

"When? Yesterday?"

She saw his lips twitch. She was glad somebody was enjoying this nightmare.

"About three months ago."

"Good for you." She gazed out over the park. She could hear splashing from a nearby pool and saw people sitting in the shade. What she wanted to do was to get out of the car and walk away. And she couldn't.

She was well and truly trapped by her own circumstances.

"Not really."

"The move didn't work out the way you hoped?"

"My great-grandmother died a few months ago and left me her home."

"Oh, no! Millie's dead?"

"Well, she was in her nineties, after all. She didn't suffer. She just didn't wake up one morning."

"Oh, Greg. I am so sorry. You were so close to her."

"Yeah, I know." He waited a couple of beats and said, "Here's what I would like to do, if you'll allow it. As you know, there's plenty of room for you and me to stay in the same house and never see each other. Once your casts are gone you can get back some of your muscle strength using the pool.

"Your doctor said that it would be a while before you'd be able to get along on your own. It makes more sense for you to stay at my place until you're mobile. You'll be comfortable there and I'll be available if you need help."

She knew she would need help. She still had trouble dressing, and getting a shower would be a major ordeal. But there was no way she would accept that kind of help from Greg.

Sherri shook her head. "It's kind of you to offer, Greg, and quite generous considering the history between us. Sharing a place, no matter the size, would be tantamount to living together again and I can't do that." She looked away and repeated softly, "I really can't do that."

"Then where do you want me to take you?"

She rubbed her forehead where her headache had intensified. "I don't have any idea, but I need to lie down somewhere. I can stay at your place until I figure out what I'm going to do, I suppose." She'd be living a nightmare until she was able to find a place to rent. She had enough savings to pay for all the deposits and the first and last month's rent if she was very careful. After that, she'd be without resources.

"Of course," he said, pulling out of the parking space. "I know you've been through a terrible ordeal and this is far from being a perfect option, but it was the only one I could come up with for now."

"Having you come back into my life when I'm in this condition hasn't helped, believe me," she said, rubbing her forehead.

She saw his jaw clench, but she was too exhausted to care if she'd been too blunt. Her emotions had been all over the place since she had seen him standing beside his car today and had discovered that he wasn't going to be out of her life. At the time, she'd thought she could hold out another few hours. Not days or possibly weeks.

"Nice wheels. Did they come with the house?"

"The house came with a tidy sum from a trust fund."

"It must be nice having money," she muttered bitterly.

"Not necessarily," he said in response.

They rode the rest of the way in silence. She recognized the neighborhood and thought about the times they'd visited Millie when they were married. She'd thought Millie was the only family Greg had. In fact, he'd told her Millie *was* his only family and she had been able to relate to being raised without parents.

Once Sherri had left Greg, she'd missed seeing the elderly lady. It would be strange to be in her house when she wasn't there.

"Is Lorraine still there?"

"No. After Millie died, she said she wanted to retire. She'd looked after Millie for many years and Millie left her enough to live on in comfort."

They pulled into a long driveway that ended at a three-car garage behind the large home.

Greg walked around and opened her door. She hadn't thought about how she would get into the house because, frankly, too many other things were going on in her head.

He reached inside the car and effortlessly picked her up. There was nothing for her to do except put her arms around his neck. She was at the end of her stamina. All she could do was lie against his chest and close her eyes.

Millie's place was so beautiful with its colorful flower beds and shrubs. Once inside the gate between the high privacy hedges, the view opened up to reveal a pristine lawn spotted with large trees and an Olympic-size pool.

"Millie always enjoyed her pool," she murmured to herself. She closed her eyes again.

"She kept herself in great shape. Probably why she lived as long as she did."

A wide expanse of floor-length windows and French doors looked out over the vista. As Greg stepped up onto the redbrick terrace, a woman opened one of the doors.

"Ah, Hannah," Greg said, smiling. "Thank you for opening the door." He looked at Sherri. "This is Sherri. Sherri, Hannah."

So he was married. He could have mentioned that when she was going on and on about their living together. He must have found her quite amusing.

He could have told her at some point. It made no difference to their relationship, or rather lack of relationship. Sherri was glad to know that he'd found someone else. She didn't know why she was so surprised. He was handsome, well-educated and now could give any woman whatever she wanted.

Being this close to him was so disturbing. He wore the same aftershave, the one that had haunted her for months after she'd left.

Greg carried her through the wide hallway toward the front of the house. A wide, curving staircase went up to the second floor. Before they reached the stairs, Greg stopped in front of a closed door.

He gathered her closer, if possible, and opened the door. This had been Millie's room. She remembered it well. Millie's light perfume still lingered. A motorized wheelchair was near the bed. She wondered if Millie had needed it during her last few months. If so, Sherri knew Millie would have hated to be confined to a chair.

He carefully placed her on the bed and stepped back. "I'll be right back."

She closed her eyes and was drifting in a sea of pain when she felt something move on the bed. Her eyes popped open and she gasped. Two cats had jumped on the bed and were daintily stepping up to her.

"Where did you two come from?" she asked them in astonishment.

Greg said from the doorway, "When Joan mentioned that you had planned to take care of both cats while she was gone, I volunteered to keep them here, since she didn't want to split them up."

He handed her a glass of water and two capsules. She recognized the pain meds from the hospital.

"How did you know I was taking these?"

He shrugged. "I got a list of your medications from the doctor."

Sherri swallowed the capsules, chased them with the water and lay down again. She was grateful that these were fast acting.

After a moment of silence, Greg said, "I forgot to ask Joan their names."

"This is Lucifer," she replied. Lucifer reached her side and butted his head against her hand, purring all the while.

"So is this one Satan?" he asked with a teasing glint in his eye, a look she'd always loved.

"No. Angel." She glanced at Angel. He had lifted his back leg and was now engrossed in cleaning himself.

She scratched Lucifer's ears and under his chin until he settled in next to her, his front legs across her chest. Sherri looked up at Greg. "You hate cats."

He stood watching her from the foot of the four-poster bed, his hands in his back pockets. "Yep." He smiled. "Looks like he's missed you."

"Why would you accept the care and feeding of animals you don't like?"

He stood there and looked at her, as though he could see her soul and understood all her emotions. Which was impossible.

"Good question," he finally replied thoughtfully. "So far, I haven't found a sensible answer." He turned away and headed for the door. "Get some rest," he said over his shoulder, leaving the room and closing the door behind him.

When Sherri opened her eyes sometime later the room was in deep shadow. She noticed that the sun was beyond the treetops. She must have slept all day. She looked around her and saw the two cats still on the bed and sound asleep.

Lucifer enjoyed stretching out on his back as far as his long legs would go. Angel preferred sleeping in a ball. One was on either side of her.

A small lamp came on near the door and Sherri saw Hannah standing in the doorway.

"I'm sorry to disturb you, but you didn't eat anything at lunch and Greg said you need to eat something. May I help you into the chair?"

Sherri pushed herself up on her elbows. Hannah looked Swedish, with beautiful skin and flaxen hair. She was tall, almost as tall as Greg. They made a nice-looking couple.

"Thank you. I'd appreciate it."

After they maneuvered her into the chair, Sherri pushed a button and it moved silently across the room. Hannah opened a door. "This is your bathroom. Will you need help?"

Not in this lifetime.

"I'm fine. Thank you."

She managed to get inside and closed the door. The room was about the size of her bedroom in the apartment. There was a free-standing shower and a large tub with jets. A long counter and mirror stretched across the width of the room.

Sherri had never been inside this particular bathroom. She found a washcloth and filled the sink with water. She bathed herself as well as she could. Somehow she would have to learn to help herself into the shower once her dressing came off. When the nurse changed it that morning, she had used a smaller dressing, saying that the incision looked healthy and was healing. There was a built-in seat inside the shower, plus shampoos, conditioners and creams. The place could have been a five-star hotel.

After struggling to get her clothes off, she wet a washcloth and washed herself with soapy water.

Sherri was drying off when she heard a tap on the door.

"Yes?"

Hannah said, "I've laid out your clothes for you. Greg will check in on you in about forty-five minutes."

Sherri finished drying herself and opened the door. She looked at the clothes laid out for her. They were new. She moved to the closet and opened the door. The walk-in closet had all of her clothes and several new things that still had tags on them.

She spun her chair around and crossed the room to the dresser. When she opened the drawers, she discovered all of her things were here…plus several new items.

He'd certainly been confident that she would fall in with his plans. Why not? He'd made certain that she had no place to go except here. She hated to admit that he'd been right about everything. She really couldn't have taken care of herself. What she had trouble understanding was why he'd do this for her. He'd put himself out to see that she had every-thing she needed, including Lucifer. Which was another thing. He'd once mentioned that he was allergic to cats. She'd been disappointed because she'd always loved them and once she settled into her apartment she had found the kittens. Thank goodness Joan had wanted one, too.

Now here they were, content to be nearby. It was difficult to be upset with him; he'd done so much for her at a time when she'd desperately needed help.

She took underwear out of the drawer and with a great deal of effort managed to get the pants over her cast. She was already exhausted. Hannah had laid out a simple pullover dress that was new. Sherri slipped it over her head. She pulled the sling over her shoulder and slipped her arm into it.

She was as ready as she would ever be. She saw no reason to wait for Greg. With new determination to be nicer to him, Sherri left the room.

Five

Out in the hallway, Sherri went back the way she and Greg had come into the house. She stopped at the French doors and admired the view. Greg had been given a truly wonderful gift. She knew he must miss Millie very much. Sherri wished she'd stayed in touch with her. As the minutes passed, she began to relax. It was difficult to believe that such a pastoral place existed only a few miles from downtown.

She was startled when Greg spoke behind her.

"Ah, there you are. Enjoying the view, I see."

She turned and faced him. "Thank you for all that you've done, Greg. I'm sorry that I've been so rude to you. It's just that—" She couldn't find the words to continue.

"I know. You'd made a clean break, and I was the last person you wanted in your life."

She nodded, looking down at her hands folded in her lap.

"Understood," he replied tersely. "I know how difficult all

of this is for you. I just want you to know that you have a place to stay here for as long as you want it."

She gave a quick shake of her head. "Don't you think having me here is unfair to Hannah?"

He looked puzzled. "Why should it be? One more person in the house isn't going to make much difference to her."

She almost rolled her eyes at his obtuseness. "In my opinion, having your wife looking after your ex-wife is asking a lot of her."

He made no effort to hide his amusement. "It certainly would be…if she were my wife. But then, she'd be a bigamist and I might have to arrest her." He turned her chair and they went to a small dining area not far from the kitchen. It was a cozy area with a bay window that brought the beauty of the lawn into the home.

"Hannah is happily married to Sven and I'm happy to have both of them living here. Actually, they live in the garage apartment, but that's close enough." He looked past her, flashing his heart-stopping smile. "Looks delicious, Hannah, as usual."

Sherri glanced around and saw the tray Hannah carried. Behind her, a large blond man carried two wineglasses and a bottle of wine.

"Sven," Greg said, "this is Sherri. She'll be staying here until she literally gets back on her feet. Sherri…Sven."

Sven's smile dazzled her with its brilliance. Unfortunately for her, she seemed to be immune to all men but Greg.

"Pleased to meet you."

"Sven is one of the best landscapers in the area. He has a thriving business, including a nursery not far from here. He takes care of this place, but refuses to take money for it." Greg smiled at Sven. "Not a good way to run a business, you know."

Sven shrugged. "It's only fair. You don't accept our rent payments."

"I definitely get the best of that deal."

While the two men talked, Hannah quickly placed the food on the table, lit the candles and refilled the water glasses.

Sherri looked at her food and sighed.

"Something wrong?"

"I see that I'm on a soft-food diet. I suppose this is better than clear liquids."

"The doctor said to keep you on a soft diet for another week. If you have no problems, you could have normal meals again. Believe me, once you taste Hannah's cooking you'll know it was worth waiting for."

She looked at his plate. Mmm. Baked chicken, mashed potatoes and what appeared to be fresh green beans. She almost whimpered with longing. Oh well. She picked up her soup spoon and began to eat. Actually, the food was delicious, much better than the hospital's food.

The room was so quiet she could hear the soft tick of a clock somewhere in the house. She needed to get away from Greg for her own emotional preservation. Right now, though, she intended to enjoy her meal and being in Millie's home once again.

Once she finished her meal, she said, "This was so good. My compliments to the chef."

Greg grinned. "My secret weapon to coax you into continuing to stay here."

She looked at him and he met her gaze. "I don't understand any of this, Greg. Yes, we used to be married. It didn't work. We've both moved on. Why in the world would you decide to take over my life like this?"

"Is that what it looks like to you?"

"That's what it is. I'm pretty much confined to this chair until my bones heal." She paused and said, "Did this chair belong to Millie?"

Greg nodded. "She fell last year and broke her hip."

"I can see her now, zipping around the place. She was really something."

"Yes, she was. I miss her a great deal."

"So, why am I here?" She came back to her question. "And don't answer a question with a question, okay?"

"I was hoping that we could use this time together as a chance to deal with some of the issues that caused the divorce."

She frowned. "You're looking for closure."

He nodded slowly. "Something like that. You moved out without any warning. You gave me no chance to deal with whatever was bothering you."

"Why don't we leave it at this—I left you because I discovered that I didn't really know you at all. What I did learn while we were married was that we were too different. We wanted different things in our lives. The longer I stayed, the more painful it was going to be to leave you. I also knew that if I talked to you about leaving, you would convince me to stay."

"I would have liked the chance to know what in the hell I did to make you leave like that and refuse to communicate with me except through your lawyer."

"Do you remember how we met and how quickly we came together?"

His lips quirked. "Oh, yeah. I remember it well." His gaze was so heated Sherri felt scorched.

"Granted we had a great sex life, but—"

"Better than great, Sherri. Much better."

"Okay. However, we didn't take time to get to know each

other out of bed. You wanted to spend our hours together in bed rather than talk to me."

"And your point is?"

She shook her head. "This discussion is pointless and I'm tired. You've been a wonderful support since the accident and I do appreciate it, but this isn't going to change anything between us, Greg. Being around you is upsetting, which is why I didn't want to talk to you once I left."

"You make me sound like an ogre."

"You're not." She looked around the room. "I can't believe we're having this conversation. I'm really tired. I think I'll go back to my room."

Greg sighed and then stood while she backed away from the table, turned and rolled away.

He followed her to her room. "You're going to need some help getting ready for bed."

As tired as she was, she knew he was right. "Perhaps Hannah could—"

"She and Sven are off-duty. There's no reason to have her come back when I'm here to help you."

She looked at him and thought about changing clothes in front of him. That would be all it would take to get them into bed together, surgery or not, broken bones or not. Why did he have to be so attractive? He made her motor run nonstop whenever he was around. Right now, she couldn't afford to be tempted.

"Don't worry about it. I changed my clothes without help earlier this evening."

"All right. At least let me put you on the bed before I leave."

She rolled to her dresser and found one of her sleep shirts before going to the bed. She held up her arms.

He picked her up as though she were weightless and sat her on the side of the bed.

"I'll see you in the morning," Greg said.

She nodded. He continued to stand there. She closed her eyes and looked down at her hands. She was on the verge of tears and she didn't want him to know. She was so vulnerable right now in so many ways. It would be so easy to forget what she'd gone through in their marriage and accept the here and now.

She'd tried to make a clean break but fate was against her. She heard Greg leave the room and quietly close the door behind him.

Greg poured himself another glass of wine and wandered out to the back terrace.

He'd always loved Millie. She had been agile, both mentally and physically, all of her life until her fall. He'd spent as much of his childhood as possible in this home. His brother had refused to come for more than a couple of days at a time, saying there was nothing to do here. Kyle had found it boring and had preferred to spend his summers in Connecticut with his friends.

Millie was the reason he'd moved to Austin directly after graduating from the Police Academy. He had visited her as often as he could. She was the family he'd never had, she and Sherri.

There was no way he could get Millie back but he was going to do everything in his power to have a second chance with Sherri. He loved her too much not to try, and tonight he'd realized that she wasn't indifferent to him.

That offered him a sliver of hope.

Six

Five years earlier

Greg Hogan saw the flashing lights from police cars and an ambulance before he turned into the restaurant's parking lot. The yellow police tape already encircled the area behind the place and forensics was there gathering evidence.

A man had been murdered and it was Greg's job to find his killer.

He pulled up alongside one of the police cars and walked over to the area.

"What have you got on the guy?" he asked one of the men, pulling a notebook out of his pocket.

"White male, forty-two years old, Kenneth Allred, according to one of his driver's licenses."

"What does the other one say?"

"He had four—Kenneth Allred, Fred Conway, Ken Crosley and Jerry Allen."

"Maybe his prints will be on file somewhere."

"We have an approximate time of death, based on a witness's statement."

Greg looked around the parking lot. "Has he been questioned yet?"

"She. She told us a little but she was so shaken that we placed her in a squad car with one of our men. We got the call forty-five minutes ago and were here in ten. One of the officers on patrol answered the call. The woman had gone back inside the restaurant and told the manager, who called it in."

"Did she see the murder?"

"She said she saw two men running to a car from behind the restaurant as she was getting into her car. Their car left and she backed out of her parking space and glanced behind the building. That's when she saw the victim." The policeman nodded toward the floodlights at the back of the building. "She was able to see that he was covered in blood. That's when she ran back inside."

"I'll talk to her…see if she can describe the men. I wonder if they saw her? Whatever else we do, we need to keep her name out of the papers in case they saw her and go looking for her."

Greg spent the next half hour studying the crime scene, discussing the findings with the forensic team and studying the body. When he was through, he walked over to the police car where the witness sat in the front seat, staring out the windshield. He nodded to the uniformed officer who immediately got out of the car. Greg slid inside and looked at the witness.

The first thing he noticed was how small she was. She had thick, dark hair that tumbled around her shoulders.

"Ms. Masterson?" he said softly.

As though she were in a daze, she slowly turned to look at him.

"Yes?"

He held his hand out to her. "I'm Detective Greg Hogan." She hesitantly offered her hand to him. He wasn't surprised to find it cold. "Would you like to go inside and have a cup of coffee?"

Her husky voice intrigued him. She looked like a teenager and yet sounded like a seductive woman. "All right."

He walked around the car and helped her out. She was shaking. Scenes like these were rough on civilians.

The manager had closed the restaurant. When he saw Greg at the door, he came over and let them inside.

"Hi. I'm Randy Kramer," he said, offering his hand to Greg.

Greg shook his hand and replied, "Detective Greg Hogan, Homicide. Could we have some coffee, please?"

"Certainly. I've been sending coffee out to the men since they arrived."

Greg led her to one of the booths. After she slid in, he sat opposite her.

Under the lights, he could see that her eyes were green and she had the longest lashes he'd ever seen.

"I have some questions for you. I know you've already talked to one of the policemen. I just have some follow-up questions for you if that's okay."

Randy placed two mugs of coffee in front of them. The woman immediately wrapped her fingers around the steaming cup.

Finally, she nodded at him.

"Okay. Let's start with your name and address."

"Sherri Masterson. The address is 2610 Mockingbird Lane."

"Are you employed?"

"I'm finishing my last semester at the university. I help out on weekends at a pet store whenever I can."

"How old are you?"

"Twenty-one."

Greg concentrated on getting all of this on paper, but it was tough. He was having such a strong reaction to the woman…girl…that he was embarrassed. He had never met a woman who affected him so suddenly. Maybe he'd been working too many hours or hadn't been with a woman for too long, but something was going on that was interfering with his concentration.

He cleared his throat. "Let's go back a few hours and describe what you were doing."

"They needed me to fill in this afternoon at the pet store for an employee who'd gone home sick. After my eleven o'clock class I went in and worked the rest of the day. A friend called me and asked me to go out. We met and had dinner."

"Was he with you when you left?"

"No. He'd parked in front. He watched as I crossed the parking lot and waved when I reached my car."

"Did he see the two men?"

She swallowed. "I don't know."

"Okay. So you got in your car. Then what?"

"I dropped my keys and they fell beneath the car. I had to reach under the car a little to get them. When I stood, I saw those two men running to a car parked in back."

"Did you happen to notice the make or model of the car?"

She was already shaking her head before he finished the question. "I'm sorry, but I don't know much about cars. It was either dark blue or black." She closed her eyes for a moment. Then she looked at him. "I think it had four doors."

"Texas plates?"

"I didn't notice. Seeing two men hurrying to a car didn't set off any alarms for me. I figured they were late for something."

"Okay. Then what happened?"

"When they backed out, their headlights blinded me. I couldn't make out anything at all. Then they gunned the car and sped away."

"What did you do then?"

"I got into my car and pulled out, preparing to drive away. When I glanced around to make sure there were no other cars, I happened to see—" she swallowed again "—this, uh, this man and he was, uh, he was sprawled near the back door of the restaurant. The way he lay, and the sight of so much blood, made me think he was dead."

"So you came inside?"

"Yes. I told the manager, who called 911."

Greg leaned back in the booth and Sherri lifted her cup to her mouth, using both hands. She swallowed some coffee and carefully put the cup down.

"I know this is difficult for you." He looked at his notes deliberately so he wouldn't see the vulnerability in her eyes. It was all he could do not to move to the other side of the booth and put his arm around her for comfort. "Did you hear anyone say anything?"

"No."

"Were you in your car or still standing beside it when their lights blinded you?"

"I was standing beside it."

Which meant that they would be able to identify her. Great. Just great.

"Okay. I'd appreciate it if you could describe these men to

me…whatever you can remember. Were they tall or short, thin or heavy, move with a limp, anything like that?"

She clasped her hands and was silent for a moment. Finally, she shook her head. "I'm sorry. I know I'm not being very helpful, but I didn't see their faces. I really didn't pay much attention to them."

"But you did see them run. Long strides? Short strides? Athletic? Or laboring?"

"Oh. Well, I would say they were both agile. They practically sprinted. They were both tall, at least to me, but then everyone is tall to me."

"Can you guess a height?"

"Mmm. Maybe five ten, five eleven. How tall are you?"

He was startled by her question. "Six one."

"I guessed six feet, so I think I'm fairly accurate on their heights."

"Would you please give me the name of your friend, just in case he may have seen them?"

"Sure." She gave Greg the name and phone number.

"All right. If you don't mind coming to the station in the morning I'd like to show you some mug shots as well as get your written statement. I don't think it will take long."

"Okay."

They stood and he escorted her to her car. "I'd like to follow you home, if you don't mind. I'm somewhat concerned that the men you saw may start looking for you. Let's keep you as safe as possible."

"I'm all for that."

He walked her to her car, noting that the ambulance and the uniforms were gone. Only the yellow tape remained.

Greg waited until Sherri pulled out and headed toward the street and then he pulled in behind her. Once they reached her apartment building, he watched her until she disappeared inside, giving him a little wave as she did.

He needed to get his notes into the computer and get to work.

Sherri hurried into her apartment, closed and locked the door and turned on every light in the place. Then she went into the bathroom and threw up. After she washed her face and rinsed out her mouth, she went into her minuscule kitchen and got out a small carton of yogurt.

She turned out the living room/dining room/kitchen light and went to her bedroom. She glanced at her watch. It was eleven o'clock. She felt as though she'd been up all night. She sat on the side of her bed and finished her yogurt. Then she went in and took a long, warm shower.

When she finally crawled into bed and turned out the light her mind returned to the dead man. She shivered. She hadn't gone near him but she had seen what he looked like from her car.

Sherri wished she could remember more about those men. They had definitely got a good look at her. Would they think she could identify them? She sincerely hoped not.

When Sherri drifted off to sleep she didn't dream about the murder. Instead she dreamed about Detective Greg Hogan of Homicide.

In her dream something or someone was chasing her. She was in a panic because she couldn't get away. Next, Greg Hogan was there. She ran into his arms, knowing she'd be safe. He held her so close she could hear and feel his heart beating. In the next scene she was watching him slowly take off his clothes...baring his broad shoulders and muscled chest, slowly unfastening his pants and sliding them down.

She was mesmerized by his male beauty. He held out his hand and she took it, only then aware that she was nude.

He held her close and began to kiss her, which kindled flames of longing in her. He laid her on a wide bed and continued to kiss her as his hand stroked her body. She returned his kisses, feverishly wanting him to make love to her.

Sherri looked into his eyes as he moved away slightly and settled between her legs. Yes! This was what she wanted! She—

She woke up with a start. What in the world? She'd been dreaming about that detective. She sat up in bed and clutched her head. The dream had been so real.

How embarrassing. She had to go to the police station this morning to look at photos and to write out her statement. How was she going to be able to face him after having had such an erotic dream about him? How strange. Why would she have dreamed such a dream? She'd barely noticed him last night.

Liar. You were scared but not so scared that you missed his strong features, his sensuous mouth and his gentleness with you.

She went into the bathroom and took her shower, adjusting the water to be cooler than normal.

Seven

"Hey, Hogan, you've got a visitor."

Greg looked up from the file he was working on and saw Sherri Masterson standing just inside the bull pen area of the station, looking a little lost. He stood, once again irritated by his body's instant reaction to her.

Today she wore some kind of flowery dress. Greg forced himself to concentrate on why she was here while he strode over to where she waited.

Greg stuck out his hand, "Mornin', Ms. Masterson. Thank you for coming in. I know last night was very traumatic for you. Did you sleep well?"

His innocent question caused her to turn a fascinating red and she looked away from him. Now what was that about? Had she spent the night with her boyfriend? He didn't know why, but that thought bothered him.

"Mmm, yes, I slept all right…and please call me Sherri."

"Sure. And I'm Greg." He took her elbow and felt her stiffen. He immediately stepped away. "I've set up one of the rooms for us so we can have some privacy."

And she blushed again. What was her problem? He tried not to come across as intimidating, but she was definitely nervous around him.

He cleared his throat. "Would you like some coffee?"

She smiled. "Is it as bad as I've heard police station coffee generally is?"

He grinned. "Naw. We just want people to think that. Otherwise, we'd take most of Starbucks' business away."

She chuckled and he relaxed a little. Maybe this wasn't going to be as bad as he'd feared. His biggest concern was that she might be picking up his strong attraction to her. He was a professional and he didn't want anything to get in the way of obtaining this woman's help in solving a murder.

"Yes, thank you. I'll take some coffee."

He opened a door and motioned to the table. "Have a seat and I'll be right back."

He closed the door behind him and took a big breath. He was being absolutely ridiculous. Maybe he should get his partner to do the interview. No, that wouldn't work because he would somehow have to explain why he couldn't do it.

He poured two mugs of coffee and headed back to the interview room.

"Here you are," he said, setting one of the mugs in front of her and sitting down across the table. "I'd like you to write out your statement for me. If anything came to mind since we spoke, please let me know."

She sipped her coffee. "Okay."

He watched her write. She was a lefty. When she finally

looked up, she caught him staring at her. He quickly blinked and smiled.

"Finished?"

"I think so. I can't think of anything else."

She handed him the paper and he put it aside. He opened a file and pulled out a photograph. "Have you ever seen this man before?"

Sherri took the picture and studied it. This wasn't a mug shot. The man was smiling into the camera, his arms around two small children.

She looked up. "You know, I think he may have been in the restaurant last night."

"Really?"

"I wouldn't swear to it, but his smile reminds me of a man we passed as the hostess led us to a table. In fact, my friend teased me about it." She looked back down. "I didn't pay all that much attention to him, though. He left before we did. Is he important to this case?"

"He's the victim in this case."

"Oh, no!" She sounded horrified. "Are you sure?"

He nodded. "I spoke with his family this morning and they gave me this photograph."

"Are these his children?"

"One is. The other one is his nephew. We wanted to see if he'd been in the restaurant that night. His wife said he had a meeting to go to, although he didn't say where."

"I'm so sorry for his family."

"Was he alone when you saw him?"

She thought about his question before finally saying, "He was when we passed him. After that I had my back to him. All I know was that he wasn't there when we passed that table on the way out."

"We interviewed several people, including your friend, who were at the restaurant last night. You seem to be the only person who actually saw the two men run from behind the restaurant."

She shivered.

He moved his hand so that it rested on hers. "They have no idea who you are. You don't have anything to worry about."

She looked at his hand. He noted that his hand swallowed hers. She didn't pull away so he left it there. She looked back at him. "But they saw me very clearly. They saw my car."

"Unless they have someone in their pocket who can run a DMV check on you, they won't bother you."

She nodded. "Okay."

"Next, I'd like you to look at some of these mug shots to see if you recognize anyone. We're still investigating his possible contacts and hoping you see someone here that you recognize."

He opened the book and she blinked. "That's a lot of people. And I never saw their faces."

"There may be something that might trigger a memory...a tilt of a head, the shape of a jaw, that sort of thing. I'll leave you to look and will be back a little later."

He checked on her from time to time, but in the end she didn't recognize anyone.

"I'm so sorry. I know I'm not being much help," she said.

"Actually, you are. We know these guys weren't involved."

"We can hope. I should have been more aware."

Greg looked at his watch. "It's almost lunchtime. Would you care to go get something to eat? That is, if you don't have other plans."

She stood and stretched, causing her top to ride up and bare her midriff. Greg looked away but he was too late to stop his reaction to the sight. He had a sudden desire to kiss her right there.

"Actually, lunch sounds good. I sort of skipped breakfast this morning."

"Great." He opened the door and ushered her out of the room.

He drove them to one of the cafés where he generally ate lunch. It was a little hole-in-the-wall place that served the best hamburgers in town.

Once inside and seated, Sherri looked around the room in wonder. "I never knew this place was here."

He grinned. "Another top secret among law-enforcement guys. They're open all the time and there have been times when it was the only place where we could get something to eat."

"Do they have trouble with people dealing drugs late at night? I've heard that the places that stay open all night tend to attract them."

"No. They've made it clear to the people who come in that the place is frequented by off-duty as well as on-duty cops. Seems to work."

Once they gave their order, Greg leaned on his folded arms and asked, "Tell me a little about yourself."

She looked at him in surprise, obviously startled by the question. "Didn't you get all that information from me last night?"

He grinned. "This isn't about the case, Sherri. I've tried my darnedest to hide the fact that I'm attracted to you but I can't seem to be detached where you're concerned. This is just for my own information."

Her cheeks flamed. "Oh."

He lifted his shoulder in a shrug. "Of course, it may be all one-sided, so if you'd rather not—"

"Uh, no. It isn't at all one-sided."

He settled back in the booth with a grin and said, "Good. Let's hear it."

"My life is very ordinary. I've been in school most of my life, it seems. Right now I'm taking a course in computer software and technical writing."

"How about family?"

She shook her head. "No family. Parents died when I was fourteen. The aunt who took over caring for me died of cancer last year."

"You've had some tough breaks."

"Since I can't do anything about the past, I do my best to look forward to the future."

Their food arrived and they concentrated on their meal. Once they finished, Sherri looked at him and said, "Your turn."

He looked at her quizzically for a moment and then nodded. "What do you want to know?"

"How old you are...are you married...what about family? Those things. Oh, and why you decided to go into law enforcement."

"Are you sure you aren't writing my biography?"

"Depends on how interesting it might be."

"Oh. In that case, you'll be bored right away, so I'm safe."

He paused. He didn't like talking about himself. Hated it, in fact. However, if he wanted to spend time with Sherri...which he definitely did...he'd better give her some idea of who he was.

"Let's see. I'm twenty-seven years old, never been married, got a degree and immediately went into the Police Academy."

"Did you go to college here in Austin?"

Okay, no hedging. "Actually I, uh, no, I didn't. I graduated from Harvard."

Her eyebrows went up. "Really?"

"Yep."

"Are you originally from the East Coast?"

"I have to admit I'm not a native Texan, but I got here as soon as I could."

She laughed, which was what he wanted. "Have you traveled much during those twenty-seven years?"

"Some," he replied.

"What made you come to Texas?"

"Because my great-grandmother lives here."

"So what made you want to be a detective?"

"You know, there are times when I've wondered about that, myself. I guess I like the idea of being on the side of the good guys. I like challenges, solving puzzles, that sort of thing." He glanced at his watch and said, "Which reminds me that I need to get back to work."

They slipped out of the booth and he took her hand as though it was the most natural thing in the world. *Uh-oh, Hogan, better slow down.*

He paid for their lunch and they went outside. "I've got to admit, I'd rather run and play."

She glanced up at him and stole his breath away. He'd never been so strongly attracted to anyone. What was going on with him, anyway?

They drove back to the station in silence. Once there, he walked her to her car. He opened the door and said, "I'd like to see you again, Sherri."

Her green eyes sparkled. "I'd like that."

"Okay, how about next Friday? We can grab a bite to eat, maybe catch a movie if you'd like." And he would do his best not to seduce her. Unless, of course, she wanted him to.

"That sounds like fun."

He leaned down and gave her a chaste kiss. Anyway, it was supposed to be chaste, but when she responded so beautifully he might have lingered a little longer than he had intended. He straightened and placed his hands behind his back. At least he hadn't grabbed her.

She got into her car. "Friday, then."

"Around seven."

"See you."

He watched her drive away and already felt the loss of her company. Oh, brother, he had it bad. He'd known her less than twenty-four hours and he didn't want to let her out of his sight. Ever.

Eight

Sherri really didn't need the car on her way home. She could have floated there.

Greg Hogan had kissed her! He was practically a stranger and he wasn't one to talk about himself much, so she really didn't know much about him. Common sense told her that she needed to get to know him better before feeling so swept away by him.

She'd never responded to anyone the way she had to Greg. Of course, it could be a result of her dream. She certainly felt she knew him much better than she actually did. She got hot just remembering the dream.

What should she do? She'd said yes to seeing him again, but was that wise? She thought about it for a while until she came to a conclusion: she had no idea. All she knew was that she didn't intend to cancel their date.

He'd graduated from Harvard? He'd chosen police work

for a career? Greg Hogan was definitely a complex man…and so very fascinating, as well.

Once home, she forced herself to think about the homework she needed to finish before Monday. She was scheduled to work at the pet store this afternoon and tomorrow afternoon. Her plans had been to study after dinner last night, but her study schedule had been abandoned while she dealt with the horror of what she'd seen.

Once she got home, she immediately focused on her schoolwork. All week she could enjoy the anticipation of knowing that she would see Greg next Friday.

She began to hum as she opened one of her books.

He tapped on her apartment door the next Friday at seven o'clock. Sherri hurried to let him inside. She'd had a crisis when it came to deciding what to wear. She didn't want to dress too sexily in case he got the wrong idea about her. However, she did want to look attractive.

She was a little short on date clothes. She spent her time on campus hanging out with other students and had never worried about what she looked like.

Tonight she did.

She opened the door and her knees went weak. He grinned at her. She fought to regain some composure. "Please come inside."

He wore a sports jacket over a pair of khakis. The jacket looked custom-made and he looked delectable. She wanted to throw herself into his arms and dramatically cry, "Take me, take me. I'm all yours!"

He stepped inside her apartment and looked around. "I like what you've done with the place."

She looked at it more objectively and said, "Goodwill stuff, mostly."

"Did you do the refinishing on this table?" He rubbed his thumb along the surface. She was rather proud of that one.

"I've refinished and reupholstered most of the furniture I own."

He turned and looked at her. "You're quite talented."

She swallowed. "Thanks." Seen through his eyes, the place must look like a typical college girl's room, with the big colorful posters and some watercolors she'd painted once for a class. He was very much a sophisticated man about town, while she felt awkward and flustered.

He glanced at his watch and said, "Ready to go?"

Without a word she picked up her purse and turned to the door.

"How long have you lived here?" he asked, helping her into his car.

"Since I was a freshman. I preferred to get a smaller place that I could afford rather than have a roommate."

Sherri finally began to relax with Greg during dinner. He entertained her with various stories, all amusing, about work and his coworkers, but she idly noted that he didn't talk about himself at all.

They did compare their favorite movies and musicians and laughed about how diverse their tastes were. He liked thrillers and war movies while she preferred something light, like romantic comedies. However, the movie they decided to see was one she'd heard a lot about, and she was more than willing to see it with him.

"Just don't be surprised if I suddenly hide my face in your shoulder."

"Don't worry. I'll put my arm around you so you'll know you're safe."

Her dream popped up in her head and she recalled that she had run to him in her dream and felt safe in his arms. She felt she could trust this man who was more stranger than friend. It seemed almost as though she'd known him from somewhere long ago—a past life or something—and they had found each other again.

Sherri didn't dare say any of that to him; he'd think she was crazy. At the moment she couldn't swear that she wasn't a little insane to think they might have known each other before now.

They got popcorn and drinks and went inside the theatre. Sherri noticed that Greg caught every female's eye from little girls to octogenarians. She could certainly relate.

The movie was excellent, a thriller with one of her favorite actors in it. Greg had placed his arm around her when the movie started.

Once the movie was over, they left the theatre hand in hand and strolled back to his car.

"Would you like to stop somewhere for coffee?" he asked.

Okay. She'd been practicing and hoped she sounded casual when she answered, "Why don't we go to my place? I'll make coffee and I've got some bakery cookies if you want something more than coffee."

"I'm not going to touch that one," he replied wryly.

She laughed.

They pulled up in front of her apartment building and climbed the stairs to the second story. Greg was teasing her about staying in shape because of the climb when he came to an abrupt stop and grabbed her wrist.

She looked at him in alarm. "What?"

He nodded toward her door. She hadn't noticed that the door of her apartment was slightly ajar until he pointed it out. She froze. He put his finger to his lips and pulled her behind him.

She had no idea when he'd pulled a pistol. She didn't even know he carried one but there was one in his hand now.

"Stay here," he said next to her ear.

She nodded.

He moved closer and listened. After several moments he pushed the door open and waited.

Nothing happened.

Greg found the light switch just inside the door and flipped it on. She peered around the door and gasped.

"I told you to stay back there," he said gruffly. "I need to check out the rest of the place."

She nodded mutely, her fist to her mouth.

Someone had come in and destroyed her apartment. There was no other word to describe it. Every piece of furniture had been broken or ripped apart. Curtains hung in shreds, dishes were smashed and when she followed Greg into her bedroom, she saw that her closet had been emptied and her clothes ripped into pieces. She didn't need to check her drawers because they were broken and on the floor, their contents cut up.

Her bed had fared no better. Mattress stuffing littered the bed and floor, along with the remains of her pillows and linens.

Without a word Sherri stepped around Greg, who had put his gun away, and stepped inside her bathroom.

"Be careful," he said from behind her. "Shattered glass and pieces of the mirror are on the floor."

She didn't want to see any more. Sherri turned away and saw Greg using his cell phone.

"Get the forensic team over here now." He rattled off her address and hung up before looking at her. "We'll wait outside until they get here. I don't want to contaminate the scene."

Sherri looked around her. She felt violated. Someone had broken into her apartment and deliberately and systematically destroyed it. She had nothing left: no clothes, no place to sleep, nothing. The whole apartment had been defiled. She wrapped her arms around her waist and shivered.

Greg touched her shoulder. "They'll be here in a few minutes. Let's get some air."

Only then did Sherri notice the heavy scent of cologne from the broken bottles in the bathroom. Once out in the hallway he pulled her close to his side and continued to hold her as they walked outside and back to his car.

He opened her door and waited for her to slide inside the car before he carefully closed it and walked around to the other side.

The man who had taken her to dinner and a movie was gone. In his place was a frowning, tough and formidable cop.

Greg got into the car and turned toward her. "I would say that someone left you a very strong message."

She returned his gaze, her eyes dry. "I think I got that. It looks like every Friday is the thirteenth to me."

"Do you have any idea who might have done this? A former boyfriend, a jealous female?"

"I have no former boyfriend and if anyone is jealous of me, that's news to me. "

He took her hand and she saw a flash of the Greg with whom she'd spent the evening. "I'm so sorry you have to go through this."

She looked down at their clasped hands. "Me, too. It really is a bit much. Everything I own is destroyed as though a fire had swept through. Nothing is salvageable. The only clothes I have at the moment are what I'm wearing."

"I know. We'll deal with that a little later."

A couple of cruisers arrived and Greg got out of his car. He walked over and spoke to the driver of one of them. Two others got out of the second car and joined him. She recognized one of them whom she'd seen last week investigating the murder.

She shivered. What if— No, she didn't want to go there.

After several minutes the two men and a woman followed Greg back into the apartment building.

How did whoever had done this know she'd be gone this evening? Was she being watched? She glanced around the parking lot and quickly locked the doors.

Greg returned shortly and she unobtrusively unlocked the doors.

He got into the car and started the engine. Once out of the parking lot he headed away from the university area.

"Where are we going?"

"I'm taking you home with me," he said softly. "You'll be safe there, I promise you that. You can use my other bedroom until we get all of this settled."

She had no intention of arguing with him. "There is one thing," she finally said.

"Yes?"

"I need to stop at a store and get a few things."

"We can do that." He changed lanes and signaled to turn left. After a few miles, he turned into the parking lot of a large store that stayed open late.

There were few cars around. Not too many shoppers at close to midnight on a Friday night.

Greg parked across from the entrance and stopped.

"Thank you. I won't be long."

"Doesn't matter. I'm coming with you."

"Oh, that isn't—"

"Yes, it is. We're going to be joined at the hip until this thing is put to rest."

"You think it has something to do with the murder," she stated, suddenly feeling exhausted.

"That's one of the theories I'm working on. We hope to find some prints in that mess. If not, we'll continue to follow other leads. I don't want to take any chances where you're concerned. The men you saw could very well believe that you saw them and reported it."

"So they've been watching me?"

He nodded. "Has anything unusual happened to you this week? Besides your apartment being destroyed, I mean."

"Well, I don't know how unusual it is, but I've gotten several hang-up calls. Probably wrong numbers."

"Or checking if you're home."

She stared at him in surprise. "I suppose."

"My guess is that they're trying to scare you."

"They have definitely done that."

He groaned. "And I've made it worse by showing an interest in you. They think you're giving me additional information."

"That's a logical assumption."

"But we both know that isn't the reason I asked you out."

She bit her bottom lip. She refused to cry in front of him, but it was tough because he was being nice to her. It had been easier to hide her emotions when he was in his cop mode.

"Let's go shopping," he said, opening his door. She got out and met him in front of his car.

"From now on, you wait until I open your door."

"I've been opening my own doors for years. I'm sure I can handle it."

"So if a car happened to pull up beside you as you were getting out of the car, and a couple of men grabbed you and threw you into the back of their car…or van…you could cope with that?"

"Are you trying to scare me?"

"If it makes you a little less independent for a while."

"I've never been the damsel-in-distress type."

He took her elbow and guided her across toward the front of the store. "We'll have to do something about that."

Nine

Greg lived in a quiet, residential area, made up of several apartment buildings that looked so much alike Sherri wondered how anyone would know which one was his or hers.

He pulled into a covered parking area. "We'll get your car in the morning. I have two parking spaces."

Sherri had so little energy left she had to force herself to get out of the car and gather the sacks in the backseat that contained all of her worldly belongings.

Greg gathered the ones she couldn't reach from her side and, once the doors were closed, locked the car. Without a word, he led her across the driveway to one of the buildings, climbed two stories to the top floor and strode to the door of one of the apartments.

"Talk about getting your exercise," Sherri said in a strained voice.

"I like it up here." He opened the door and waved her

inside. Once he had turned the light on, Sherri looked around. The apartment was much larger than hers and had a nice view of the hills west of Austin.

However, the place was definitely a bachelor's pad. Newspapers were scattered around on tables and the floor, a pair of sneakers sat beneath the coffee table, a few dishes sat on the kitchen counter and more were in the sink.

"I could make excuses for the way the place looks," Greg said. He must have noticed her looking around. "But the truth is, this is cleaner…and less cluttered…than usual."

He continued toward the hallway and she followed him. He stopped midway and opened the door to a bedroom. "I'll get some sheets and stuff." He pointed to the door opposite. "That's the bathroom. It's yours. I have one off my bedroom."

Sherri walked into the room and looked around. The bed had no headboard, but there was a bedside table and a chest of drawers.

"I'm not sure what's in the closet, but whatever's there, shove it aside."

She turned and looked at him. "I doubt that I'll need much space." She laid the sacks on the bed. He dropped his beside hers and put his arms around her. He rocked her gently and after a moment she slipped her arms around his waist.

Sherri had no idea how long they stood there. When he eventually let go of her, all he said was, "I'll get the bedding for you."

While he was gone, she hung up the few clothes she'd bought, placed her underwear and a couple of sleep shirts in a drawer and took her toiletries across the hall to the bathroom.

When she came out she almost collided with Greg.

"Sorry," she said.

"No problem." He made short work of making the bed with her help.

He glanced over the room before looking at her. "If you need anything, just let me know."

She nodded.

"Good night," he said and closed the door behind him. He had turned on the lamp beside the bed when they'd first walked in and now it was her only source of light.

By now, she was too tired to think straight. She got her sleepwear out of the drawer and went across the hall. A warm shower helped to revive her a little. Once she'd brushed her teeth, Sherri stumbled back to her room, closed the door, turned off the light and dropped onto the bed.

The smell of freshly brewed coffee woke Sherri the next morning. She glanced at the clock and saw that it was almost ten. She didn't think she'd moved all night.

She quickly dressed and visited her bathroom. When she came out, she followed the scent of coffee.

Greg sat at the counter reading the paper, but looked up immediately when she walked into the room. She'd made no sound that she knew of. He wore battered jeans that clung to him like a second skin and an old sweatshirt with the arms cut out of it. The outfit on anyone else would look ratty. On him, it was sexy as all get-out.

"Mornin'," he said. "Ready for coffee?"

"More than ready," she replied, still standing in the hall doorway. "I didn't mean to sleep this late."

"You obviously needed it. Shock works that way on people sometimes and you've definitely had your share of that during the past week." He poured her a mug of coffee from the carafe by his elbow.

Sherri walked across the room and slipped onto the bar stool next to him, feeling his body heat beside her. She shivered and picked up the cup of coffee, inhaling the tantalizing scent.

"I'm afraid I don't have much here for breakfast…or any other meal, unless you have an addiction to sandwiches. I thought we could go out a little later for breakfast…or lunch…and maybe do some grocery shopping."

"Okay," she said softly.

They sat there in companionable silence. He offered her a piece of the newspaper and she took it.

When they were finished with the paper and coffee, Sherri asked, "How did those men find me?"

"A good question. We're looking for an answer to that."

"Did they think I'd leave town after last night?"

"At the very least, they were hoping to frighten you."

"Then their plan worked. Just thinking about what they did to my place gives me the creeps. I don't understand people like that. The destruction was so brutal and personal. Why would they destroy my clothes?"

Greg shook his head. "Once we know who did it, we'll find out why it was done."

"So you think you'll be able to find out who they were?"

"Generally speaking, people hired to do that kind of destruction aren't the sharpest blades in the drawer. Even if they wore plastic gloves there's a chance we can pick up a shoe print. There's always evidence to be found when we sift through everything. There's no need for you to be frightened. You'll be safe here."

She nodded and tried not to look at him. How was she going to make herself immune to his presence? She was already attracted to him more than she'd ever been to any man. Seeing him the last thing at night and the first thing in the morning, could become addictive and would play havoc with her peace of mind.

"So what next?" she asked after a long silence.

He looked at her and smiled. "What do you usually do on Saturdays?"

"Clean house, go shopping, pay bills, study." She shrugged. "I guess I don't need to worry about cleaning."

He laughed. "If you're afraid you'll get out of practice, you can always do something around here."

She glanced around the room before meeting his gaze. The teasing glint in his eyes was adorable.

"Ah, now I get it. I pay for my room by keeping the place clean, right?" She couldn't hide the amusement in her voice.

He sobered. "No, of course not. There are no strings attached to my offer, I promise."

"I have a hunch I'll get in plenty of practice getting my apartment cleared out and cleaned up.'"

"I hired a crew to go in and clean up the place and told the owner about what had happened. He agreed to let you out of your lease, given the circumstances."

"You've already done that this morning?"

"Yes. I also had one of the men tow your car over here. I didn't want it sitting over there any longer than necessary."

"I'm not helpless, you know," she said, feeling exasperated. "I'm perfectly capable of cleaning my apartment and of retrieving my own car."

"Okay. Sorry. I wanted to save you some of the grief. If you want to keep the apartment, you can let the manager know before he rents it out again."

She closed her eyes and rubbed her forehead. "I haven't thought that far ahead. I would have liked to at least save anything that was salvageable."

"The cleaners figured as much and will see what is fixable,

which they will save, and what isn't worth trying to put back together will get tossed."

"There's really nothing worth anything, even when it was whole."

As though unaware of what he was doing, Greg placed his hand at the back of her neck and massaged the bunched muscles there. The relief was immediate.

"Why don't we go get something to eat," he said after a while. "We both need some fuel."

"I think you're right. I'll need to go to the library afterwards. I need to replace some of the textbooks that were damaged so I can finish up my assignments." She got up and walked over to the window. When she turned around, she said, "I appreciate your offer of a place to stay more than I can say. You were right. I don't want to stay in that apartment, and your talking to the landlord in your official capacity no doubt saved me a great deal of hassle.

"I need to find my own place, though. I'll check the newspapers and see what I can find. You've been such a help and I don't want to take advantage of your kindness."

"Of course the decision is up to you. I have no problem with having you here. Until we get to the bottom of all of this, I'm a little worried about your living by yourself. If they found you so quickly once, they won't have any trouble finding where you've moved."

She allowed herself a small smile. "If they trace me here, they're going to wish they'd never bothered me."

He stood and stretched. "I almost wish they would. I'm getting hungry. Shall we go?"

"Let me get my purse." She hurried down the hall and into her bedroom. Tears filled her eyes. What would she have done without Greg these past several hours? He had stepped in and done what needed to be done.

She hadn't had anyone help her that much in years. The longer she stayed with him, the more susceptible she would become. Let's face it. She was already halfway in love with him.

Sherri grabbed a tissue and quickly wiped her eyes, checked her hair and lipstick, grabbed her purse and returned to the living room.

Greg had changed shirts. Now he wore a crisp, white T-shirt that set off his tan. He really was something.

She smiled and said, "I'm ready."

He stood by the bar, and when he saw her he picked up a key that had been lying on the counter. "I meant to give you this sooner. It's the key to the apartment. Since we're splitting up after breakfast, I want you to have a way to get in just in case I don't get here before you return."

"Thank you."

"I'd like you to keep very aware of your surroundings, including any cars that keep showing up wherever you happen to be. Watch the people around you, especially their eyes. Eyes generally telegraph what people plan to do. Key my cell phone number into your phone so that you can get me by a push of a button."

He put his hands on her shoulders and looked into her eyes. "I want you to be as safe as possible."

"I'll certainly do my best."

He draped his arm around her shoulders. "Good. Let's go eat."

Once inside the car, Greg reviewed what he'd done and said.

Meeting Sherri had been like being hit by a bolt of lightning. He'd been feeling and acting strange ever since then. Why else would he have brought her to his apartment?

He had never offered to share his apartment with anyone, no matter how desperate they happened to be. He liked his own space. He'd lived alone for a long time.

There was no reason why he couldn't have paid for a hotel for Sherri last night. He could have taken her to her room and made certain the room was safe before leaving her.

However, this morning he'd awakened with relief at the knowledge that he knew for certain she was safe because she was just down the hall from him.

He wished he knew why this particular woman had turned his life upside down and sideways. He had the insane desire to grab her and hold her and protect her from any possible harm. How unprofessional was that?

Then again, last night he'd been off duty and on a date with a delightful woman who took his breath away every time she flashed those green eyes at him. Even if the break-in had something to do with his case, he'd been first and foremost her companion last night.

What he had to do was to solve the murder. After that, his interest in her would in no way be professional.

His fear of getting involved with anyone had been overcome by the need to see Sherri as often as possible. He was now in unfamiliar territory because he'd never felt so strongly about anyone before now.

He'd didn't care for the vulnerability his feelings caused, but leaving her out of his life at this point would be impossible.

Ten

Ten days later Sherri let herself into Greg's apartment. She was relieved that he wasn't there. Of course, everything about the place reminded her of him but, when he was there, his force field pulled her to him like a magnet.

The only way she'd learned to deal with the tension between them was to spend as little time around him as possible. When they were in the apartment at the same time, he never came close to her, which was good, actually. If he'd ever touched her, she would probably have leaped on him and begged him to make love to her.

She had enough problems at the moment. She certainly didn't need to fall in love with her temporary roommate.

Too late. Way too late.

"Oh, shut up," she told herself. "It's just the situation. I'd feel the same way about any man I lived with under these circumstances."

Liar, liar, pants on fire.

"Would you please just shut up?"

Well, she was doing something about it. She planned to go apartment-hunting tomorrow. She'd finished her finals, thank goodness, and graduation was only a few weeks away. Hallelujah.

She had no reason to stay in Austin after that. She was as free as a bird. She could move anywhere she wanted. She could find a job somewhere else, although one of her teachers had mentioned that he'd had inquiries regarding the need for entry-level technical writers and he had recommended her to a couple of companies.

Didn't matter. She'd be much better off going somewhere new where there wouldn't be a chance of running into Greg.

They had reached a compromise after that first day. She would follow her routine during the day, but if she went anywhere at night, he would accompany her.

He'd suggested a movie tonight to celebrate the end of her finals. Not that she'd mentioned that she was taking them these past few days. Of course, it would be rudimentary detective work to figure out that she was doing a lot of studying, preparing papers and psyching herself up for the exams.

So. What the heck. They would grab a bite to eat and see a comedy. They would be coming full circle from the first date. A nice way to end things.

You are so full of it. You can't be serious.

She grabbed two handfuls of hair and tugged on them, trying not to scream with frustration…with the stupid voice in her head, with her not-so-secret longing for Greg and, to make matters worse, her steadily growing sexual frustration.

Seeing him every day, smelling the scent of his bath soap, his aftershave, even his toothpaste, kept her motor running.

She almost hummed with sexual tension. She saw him first thing in the morning and the last thing at night. Any red-blooded female living with a great-looking, charming and extremely sexy male would be frustrated.

He certainly wasn't bothered about being around *her.* He was engrossed in his cases. After all, hers wasn't the only one on his plate. Up until now, her studying had kept her busy. She wasn't certain what she would do with herself now. Get a job? Hunt for an apartment?

Everywhere she turned, it seemed, she was reminded of her feelings for Greg: If she did any reading…a romantic novel, or a suspense novel with some romance thrown in, or watched a drama on television that included love scenes, she pictured Greg in the leading man's role. When she saw couples on campus walking hand in hand, or with their arms around each other or kissing, she had the strongest impulse to yell, "Get a room!" at them. She needed no reminders, thank you very much.

Envy was not a pretty thing.

Yes. It was definitely time for her to move out.

She took the newspaper she'd picked up earlier into her room and slammed the door with a satisfying sound. After finding the Apartments for Rent section, she folded the paper and sat on the bed, propped up on her pillows.

She wasn't certain what part of town she should focus on. A job probably came first. The two companies looking for writers were nowhere near each other. She might have to wait until she had a job offer before making the decision about where would be most convenient area for her to live. Sherri tossed the newspaper onto the bed and rested her head against her knees.

* * *

"Sherri? Are you here?"

Greg closed the door behind him late that afternoon and looked around the apartment.

His place had never looked so good. The wood furniture gleamed with polish, the carpet had never been treated so well and there were no dirty dishes to be seen.

He appreciated the way Sherri had taken charge of the place, even washing his clothes. He had all the benefits of being married, except for one thing. That one thing was keeping him awake at night and causing him to take more cold showers than he'd ever had before.

The light scent of her perfume was everywhere. When he walked past the bathroom off the hallway, he could smell the shampoo she used. Each scent acted as an aphrodisiac on his system.

In other words, he needed in the worst way to make love to her, to drown himself in her scents and to keep her in bed for at least a week. He had a hunch that even a week wouldn't be enough.

Sharing the same apartment should have shown him her less attractive side. It was unfortunate that she didn't appear to have one. He would have expected anyone dealing with a break-in and losing everything she owned to show signs of stress and strain. Where was the short temper? The unreasonableness? The frustration about getting the matter settled?

Instead, she'd calmly and meticulously studied for exams without complaining or feeling sorry for herself.

How could he have fallen so hard so fast? If she had any idea of some of his more erotic thoughts about her, she'd be running down the street screaming for help.

"I'm here," she replied through the closed door to her room.

"I got some news about your case today."

She opened the door. "Really?"

She wore her school uniform of formfitting jeans and a top that was made out of some kind of material that clung to her, emphasizing her breasts and slender waist. He leaned against the hallway wall and felt himself going down for the third time.

"What is it?"

He turned away and headed for the kitchen. He got a soda out of the refrigerator. "Want one?" he asked over his shoulder.

"No, thanks."

She had followed him into the living room and now sat at the kitchen bar looking at him. "Tell me."

Greg stayed in the kitchen, resting against the back counter as far from her as possible. He drank some of the soda and tried to concentrate on the news he'd gotten earlier in the day.

"When forensics went over your apartment one of the men found a small shard of glass with blood on it. Otherwise, the place was clean. Whoever was there had obviously worn gloves. The glass must have slit the glove and nicked a finger. He may not have noticed in all the mayhem being created.

"Anyway, today we got a DNA match on the blood. We lucked out that he's already in the system."

Sherri looked relieved. "No kidding? Who is it?"

"A man who lives in Amarillo. That's why we didn't have a photo of the guy. We're going to need more evidence to arrest him but we're on the right track."

"What kind of motive would he have?"

"Our nice, charming family man who was murdered was shipping illegal drugs north. It's my guess he got crossways with his counterpart in Amarillo. He could have either stiffed him on the amount or the quality coming up from Mexico."

"That's horrible. His poor family."

"I know. The wife appeared to be stunned by that particular bit of news. After checking out her story we think she had no clue. His wife knew he was a successful businessman. What she didn't know was what his real business was."

"Why would some man in Amarillo worry about the possibility that I may have seen him?"

"Good question. But we know he was in your apartment. And we've been able to trace him to his boss in Amarillo, and he's the one we hope to get as well as the men who stabbed their Austin connection."

"What a relief," she said. Her look of gratitude flowed over him. *Remember, the look is only gratitude, nothing else.*

He nodded. "The local police in Amarillo told us that he has ties to individuals that the DEA is watching, so we're going to cooperate with the Amarillo police and the feds to build a strong case against all of them."

"I can't thank you enough for all you've done on this case."

"I can't take credit on this one. Most of the work was done in the lab. However, since we have two things to celebrate tonight I've made reservations at Henri's in town for us at seven. Is that okay with you?"

He was absolutely, positively irresistible when he grinned like that. She wanted to throw herself into his arms, hug and kiss him. Instead, she smiled and said, "Of course."

In anticipation of going out tonight she'd bought herself a new dress. She needed something to bolster her self-confidence when she told him she would be moving out. The red dress had tiny straps across the shoulders and hugged her body until it flared at her hips, ending above her knees.

He'd never seen her dressed up before and she definitely wanted to make an impression.

Greg finished his soda and said, "I'll see you later," and headed toward his bedroom, whistling.

At six-thirty Sherri heard his bedroom door open and his footsteps pass by her room. Without a mirror in the room, Sherri could only hope she looked all right.

Greg was thumbing through his mail and had opened a bill when he heard Sherri in the hallway. He glanced around and said, "It looks like—" His mouth dried up as soon as he saw her and every thought in his head left. He quickly checked that his jaw wasn't hanging open.

She looked up at him as she joined him in the living room. "It looks like what?"

"Uh. I don't remember. Wow, Sherri. You look great. I've never seen you in red before." What a stupid thing to say, but it was the most polite thing he could say as he took in her beauty. The dress showed off her shoulders and trim figure and she wore red strappy sandals that showed off her beautiful legs.

He glanced away and said, "If you're ready, we can go." His voice sounded hoarse. He now knew that he was a goner.

He'd booked a table at Henri's. Sherri looked around the room in awe. She had never been here before. A candle at each table created a series of oases in the otherwise shadowy room.

She and Greg followed the maître d' down the steps and to a table draped with a linen tablecloth. The maître d' pulled out one of the chairs and she slipped into it. Once Greg was seated they were handed menus.

A single rosebud in a vase sat next to the pillar candle.

The candle flame was reflected in Greg's eyes when he looked up from the menu. "Does anything look good to you?"

She avoided stating the obvious and forced herself to

look back at the menu that had no prices listed. "Hmm, well. I'm glad they put each item in English, even though it's in small print." How was she going to be able to order when she had no idea what anything cost?

"What would you like to have?" Greg asked.

She hesitated a moment and then said, "Why don't you order for both of us."

When the waiter appeared and introduced himself while filling their crystal glasses with water, Greg began speaking in what appeared to be fluent French. The waiter responded in the same language while Sherri looked on in amazement. The two men discussed the menu items; the waiter made notes on his pad and then left.

Greg smiled at her. "I hope you like seafood."

She nodded, hoping she didn't look as astonished as she felt. "You have all kinds of hidden talents, don't you?"

He looked at her and his ears turned red. He was embarrassed! How strange.

"Sorry. Guess I forgot myself there."

"You speak it like a native."

He nodded slowly. "I spent some time in France when I was younger."

"You keep surprising me, Greg. You talk so little about yourself."

"Because my life is fairly boring."

"Did you always want to work in law enforcement?"

"I played around with other options but I discovered I preferred detective work."

"Where were you born?"

"Connecticut."

"Really? Do you have any brothers or sisters?"

"A brother—Kyle."

"Do you see him often?"

"Um, no, I'm afraid not."

He looked relieved when their salads arrived and took the opportunity to change the subject.

Over dinner, Sherri said, "I feel like a princess. I've never been on a date like this before."

"I'm glad you're enjoying it. As a matter of fact, you look like a princess. All that's lacking is your tiara."

"Oh, darn. I knew I'd forget something!"

They shared a chuckle and continued with their meal.

By the time dessert and coffee arrived, Sherri knew that she'd never forget this night.

She decided to wait until tomorrow to tell Greg she would be moving out as soon as she found a job. She didn't want to be practical and prosaic and spoil the light mood and harmony they were sharing tonight.

"I propose a toast," Greg said, lifting his glass of wine. She picked up her glass and he said, "Congratulations for getting through finals without a nervous breakdown. I'm sure you aced everything."

They touched glasses and sipped on the wine.

"As long as we're making toasts," Sherri said, "thank you for helping me to deal with everything that's happened these past few weeks. Because I felt safe staying with you, I was able to focus and concentrate on finals."

They touched glasses once again.

"So," Greg said after a moment. "What next?"

She filled her lungs with air and slowly exhaled. "I'll be looking for a job and once I know where I'll be working, I'll find an apartment as near to work as possible."

"I've enjoyed having you with me."

She laughed nervously. "Oh, I bet. Having someone staying with you that you needed to babysit every night must have destroyed your love life these past few weeks."

He shook his head. "Not true. Mostly because I don't have time for a love life with the hours I work. How about you? Any boyfriends upset?"

"My group of friends understands why I've been staying with you and none of them are in the least jealous."

"If I was dating you, I'd be jealous as hell if you were living with another man."

His comment startled her. "You would?" Oh, my. He shouldn't have said that. Her body responded immediately and she could feel the heat in her face.

He reached over and took her hand, turning it over and tracing the lines on her palm. She had never thought of her palm as an erotic place until now, when steam must be coming out her ears.

"I know this sounds crazy to you, but I don't want to lose touch with you once you move away."

"Okay."

"The thing is, I've always been more comfortable on my own with no distractions. Until now. Now I want you in my life as much as you'll allow."

She closed her eyes, thinking she must be dreaming. When she opened them, she saw the heat in his and knew that he wanted her as badly as she wanted him.

"I'd like that."

He brought her palm up to his lips and kissed her. Sherri couldn't hide her shiver at the touch. "Do you still want to go to a movie tonight?" His voice sounded rough.

She could only shake her head.

"Me, either," he said with a wry smile. "What I want is to make love to you until we're both exhausted."

She took in a deep breath. Her fantasy and her dreams would be fulfilled if she only had the courage to agree. She turned her hand and slipped her fingers between his. "Let's go home."

Eleven

Neither spoke on the way home. Greg couldn't remember a time in his life when he'd been this nervous. But then, he'd never felt this way before. He was now operating in unfamiliar territory and hoped he didn't embarrass himself and offend Sherri.

Once home Greg helped her out of his car and offered her his hand, then the two of them climbed the steps to his apartment in silence.

He opened the door and, once they were inside, he closed and locked it.

He turned and saw that Sherri had moved over to the kitchen bar and put down her purse. Greg swallowed around the lump in his throat. She was so beautiful and he wanted her so much.

Sherri watched him warily. Who was supposed to make the first move? She'd imagined that as soon as they were alone they'd fall into each other's arms and let nature take over from there.

She'd obviously been reading too many romance novels. In those books passion overcame everything. Women didn't stand like ninnies and look at the men they were crazy about, waiting for some kind of a signal. She'd never been this intimate with anyone and she had no idea what came next.

He started toward her, which released her from her temporary paralysis. She met him halfway, and when he held his arms out she walked into the haven he offered. Greg leaned down while she went up on tiptoes and they finally kissed.

Yes! This was what she'd wanted since the one and only time he'd kissed her outside the police station. When he lifted her, she clung to him, her arms around his neck.

Greg wasted no time making his intentions clear. He ended the kiss and nibbled at her ear and neck before sliding his mouth back to hers. He vibrated with need and she clung to him, lost in the moment.

When he finally raised his head, Sherri discovered they were in his bedroom. She panicked. Of course she wanted Greg to make love to her. It was just that—

She closed her eyes. This was going so fast and she needed to— "Greg?"

He kissed her again. "Hmm?"

"I need to go to my room."

His head snapped back and he stared at her. "Now?" he said in disbelief.

"Uh-huh."

"Oh." He set her back on her feet and backed away from her as though he'd been burned. "Sorry. I didn't mean to—"

When he didn't say any more, she said, "It's okay," and almost ran to her room. The intensity of his lovemaking had overwhelmed her and she was on the verge of hyperventilating. How crazy was that?

I have to calm down. This is what I want. This is what I've wanted since moving in with him. She leaned her forehead on the door and took long, slow breaths.

When she could breathe normally Sherri undressed and waited until she heard Greg's door close before she went across the hallway to take a shower.

And think. Okay, so she'd overreacted. He must think she was a complete idiot.

She finally turned off the water and stepped out of the shower. After drying herself she wrapped the towel around herself and returned to her room. He was probably already asleep by now while she dithered about making love with him. Sherri looked in one of her drawers and pulled out a sleep shirt. Not a negligee, not even something slinky and sexy, because she didn't have anything coming close to that, but a sleep shirt—with kittens and puppies on it.

She pulled it over her head and carefully opened her bedroom door. She couldn't hear a thing.

He'd gone to sleep. She closed her eyes. She could not allow the evening to end on this note. If necessary she would go in there and wake him up. She'd tell him…something. Maybe confess her inexperience. She would also make it very clear that she wanted him very much.

Sherri walked silently down the hall to his door and was relieved to hear the faint sounds of the television. She closed her eyes and took several more deep breaths. She opened the door and stepped inside.

The only light in his room came from the television. He stared at her as though she were an apparition while she closed the door behind her.

She leaned against the door and looked at him. She was shaking and she was glad to have something to lean on.

"Either I'm dreaming or Sherri Masterson is now in my bedroom," he said, sounding wary.

"See what a great detective you are?" She attempted to sound sophisticated, as though she'd done this many times before. Her voice shook and didn't sound at all sophisticated.

He'd been propped up on pillows with the sheet at his waist and when she spoke he sat up. "I don't mean to sound crude or anything, but why, exactly, are you here?" He seemed to be having trouble with his breath.

She walked to the bed and sat beside him, so that their hips were touching. "I want to make love with you."

An eyebrow arched. "Are you sure? I got the feeling that you had changed your mind."

She shook her head. "It's just that…um…that I've never done this before and I'm a little out of my depth. So maybe, if you don't mind, you could teach me what—"

He interrupted her by grabbing her and falling sideways on the bed with her by his side. He turned to face her, his head resting on his fist. "You mean that you have never—"

"I know. It's ridiculous at my age."

"No, it's not," he said in a gentle voice, brushing a tendril of hair off her cheek. "You've been waiting and I don't want to do anything that would cause you to change your mind. We don't have to do this." He narrowed his eyes. "I mean that. I apologize for putting pressure on you."

"It's not that. Really. It's just that, if we could take it a little slower?"

He closed his eyes for a moment. "Are you really certain of that, Sherri?" he asked when he looked at her again.

She placed her hand on his chest and tentatively moved her fingers across his it. "I've wanted to touch you like this for what seems like forever."

"Be my guest," he said, his voice shaking.

She sat up and pushed him back on his pillow. Like a child with a new doll—a doll with an erection—she ran her fingers through his hair and trailed them down the side of his face and neck.

She leaned over and kissed one of his flat nipples and his body jerked but he didn't say anything. However, he was breathing harder. This time, she stroked his chest and continued downward, pushing the sheet away, revealing his engorged condition and that he slept in the nude. Her eyes widened.

She touched the drop of moisture with her finger and he grabbed her hand and pushed her backward. "Honey, you start that kind of exploring and I'm going to lose it, I guarantee you."

"Lose what?"

"Control. Do you have any idea how many walks I've taken at night trying to become tired enough to sleep while knowing you were just down the hall?"

She smiled. "I'm glad. Dreams about you have disturbed my sleep, too."

"Let me do the exploring," he said quietly. "There's just one thing that would help about now."

Sherri had trouble catching her breath. "What would that be?"

"If you'd remove your sleepwear. Take my word for it…you're not going to be sleeping much tonight, anyway."

She sat up and with jerky movements pulled the sleep shirt over her head, feeling awkward and exposed…until she saw his face. She allowed herself to relax and smiled at him.

Greg looked like a child on Christmas morning as he touched one of her breasts and watched the nipple draw into a tight bead. He leaned over and gently tugged on her breast with his mouth.

She could no longer lie still. When she shifted, he lifted

his head, cupped her cheek and kissed her with so much gentleness she thought she would melt.

He touched her tongue with his, thrusting and teasing before he pulled away from her. He cleared his throat. "Hold on. I'll be right back," he said and got up, striding to the bathroom. He was unconscious of his nude body—his beautifully proportioned body.

She heard him pull out a drawer and after a couple of seconds close it again. He appeared in the doorway—at full mast!—with a handful of condoms clutched in his hand.

He tossed them on the bedside table and was immediately back in his place. "Now, where were we?"

His teasing made her laugh. "I believe you were studying my body by Braille."

After that, her brain shut off. All she could do was feel and respond to his touch. He lightly pulled the tip of one breast into his mouth while caressing the other one. Eventually, he made a trail of kisses down her body, pausing to tongue her navel.

When he reached the juncture of her thighs, she stiffened and he sat up enough to move between her legs, where he knelt and looked at her.

"I don't want to hurt you," he whispered, running his hand across her curls and watching her response as his hand and fingers explored. She cried out and he increased the movement until she suddenly climaxed, calling out his name.

She couldn't believe the sensations flooding over her in waves.

Greg quickly put on protection and slowly leaned into her. She felt him touch her, slowly opening her to his entry. He moved forward and she opened up to him, loving the feel of his body on hers. Still caught up in new sensations, she lifted her hips to him, silently begging for more.

He took his time until he was completely sheathed inside her. "Am I hurting you?"

She shook her head, unable to speak at the moment. All she could do was to feel.

He continued to move, slowly at first until he let go of his strong self-control and let his needs take over. She climaxed with him this time. He dropped to his elbows, his forehead leaning against hers, breathing hard. He shifted slightly and rolled onto his side, gathering her in his arms.

Neither of them spoke for the longest time and Greg reluctantly moved away from her and went into the bathroom. She was too limp to move. She lay in the same place when he returned to bed.

He stretched out beside her and slid his arm under her head. She turned into him and placed her leg across his, settling her head on his shoulder. They lay quietly while the television made sounds in the background.

"Sherri?" Greg said after several minutes had gone by.

"Hmm?"

"I need to know something."

"Okay."

"Why did you make love with me tonight after waiting so long?"

"I've never met anyone I wanted to be with in this way until now."

"You continue to bring me to my knees. I've never wanted anyone the way I want you. I've never been so affected by a woman. You make me dizzy with desire, but that isn't all of it. You bring out feelings in me I never knew existed."

She turned her head and kissed him on the chest. "I'm glad. I feel the same way about you."

"I haven't been able to find a label to describe what I'm

feeling but I think all of that means I'm in love with you. Desperately in love with you. Can't-think-of-anything-else in love with you."

She raised her head and kissed him. When she finally pulled away, she murmured, "I feel the same way."

Without a word, he began making love to her again until they were both exhausted. They fell asleep in a tangle of arms and legs.

The next morning Sherri woke up alone in Greg's bed. She stretched and looked around. It was then she heard his shower going and she decided to join him.

She tapped on the open door and walked over to the shower stall. He stood with his head down, letting the water sluice over his head. He hadn't heard her. She opened the door and stepped inside with him.

They stayed in the shower until the water turned cold, dried off and went back to bed.

The next time she woke up she smelled coffee and opened her eyes. Greg stood beside the bed, watching her with gentle eyes and a slight smile on his face, holding two mugs of coffee.

She blinked and sat up to take the coffee. "You're dressed."

"Yep."

How silly was that, to state the obvious?

"Going to work?"

"Not today." He sat on the side of the bed and watched her. The coffee tasted as good as it smelled and she breathed in the aroma as she sipped. She didn't say any more because he didn't seem to want to talk.

She'd fallen in love with the tall, dark and silent type of male. He didn't make idle conversation. She could grow used to a hunk like that.

When she finished, he took her cup and set both of them on the table by the bed.

"I guess you know how I feel about you after last night."

"You also know how I feel about you," she replied and they both smiled.

"Here's the thing," he went on after a moment. "Given our feelings for each other, I'd like to get married. How do you feel about that?"

He was nervous. Didn't he know the answer to that?

"I'd very much like to marry you," she said softly.

He pulled her into his lap and hugged her.

"I need to put some clothes on," she said. "You have me at a disadvantage here," she added, kissing his chin. "We haven't known each other very long and I think we should wait a little while, don't you?" He let her get up. She wrapped the top sheet that hung half off the bed around her. "When did you have in mind? Late fall, early spring?"

"How about today?"

"Yeah, sure. I'm serious. We need to take time to get to know each other better. We've known each other for about two weeks. That doesn't give us time to—"

"Sherri, I'll get on my knees if I have to but I want us to get married as soon as possible. We know each other in all the ways that count. Regardless of the length of time, we've lived together, learned each other's habits. There's no reason to wait."

"Today?" she repeated slowly.

"Uh-huh."

"This is crazy, you know that."

"Don't I know it! I never intended to get married at all and here I am pleading with you."

His sheer physical presence was bad enough, but when

he spoke like that, there was no way she could resist him. "All right."

"Good. Get dressed and we'll go get our license. At least we salvaged your birth certificate from your wrecked apartment."

"What about your family? I don't have any, but didn't you once say—"

"I'll call Millie. I bet she'll let us have the service at her home. It's time you met her."

So Millie was his only family. How sad that they should both be without parents. Now they would have to form a family for themselves.

This marriage would work out. She would labor hard to make it do so.

Twelve

Sherri opened her eyes, feeling disoriented. She'd been dreaming about a time when she'd been married. She had gone into her marriage without a clue as to how to be a wife or what was expected of her. She'd tried to model the relationship on the one her parents had had, but it had been no use. Her dad had worked nine to five with two weeks off for vacation, a homebody comfortable hanging out with his family. Greg's personality couldn't be more different.

She looked around Millie's bedroom. She had loved that woman. She and Greg had spent any free time they happened to have with her. When Millie met Sherri for the first time and Greg told her they wanted to get married right away, Millie had asked her pastor if he would come to her home to perform the wedding service.

Sherri had thought about asking some of her friends to attend, but they had scattered after finals and wouldn't be back until graduation. She'd asked Greg if he wanted to invite friends or coworkers and he'd shaken his head no. "You're the only one that's important to me. If you're there, I'm happy."

The next several months had been fun. Sherri had felt as though she were playing house. She'd been hired at the place that had just let her go last week, and she'd made enough money that they didn't have to worry that she would bankrupt Greg.

They had kept separate bank accounts and shared expenses. Greg treated her like a princess. On their second anniversary he had actually bought her a tiara.

It was soon after that anniversary that everything seemed to fall apart.

She'd certainly grown up through the experience. She'd believed everything he'd said and implied...until she had discovered he had a life he'd never told her about. When she'd tried to talk to him about what she'd found out, he'd turned around and walked out of the room...or the apartment.

He hadn't trusted her enough to talk about his past, to let her in and help her understand him better. Knowing that was the beginning of the end. She'd distanced herself for protection and had been devastated by his lack of trust.

At the end she'd known she would have to get away from him, despite the fact she was still in love with him. He'd become someone she didn't know and she could no longer live with him. It had been too painful.

Now, here she was, living in Millie's home with Greg. What was she going to do? She needed to get well as soon as possible in order to get away from him.

It couldn't happen soon enough.

She got out of bed and hopped into the bathroom, hanging

on to whatever furniture was on the way. Her incision protested, so once she'd finished in the bathroom she took her time getting back to her chair.

She gathered her clothes from drawers and the closet and awkwardly got dressed. Once she got her arm out of its cast, she would be able to use crutches until her leg healed.

The doctor had mentioned putting on a walking cast in a few weeks. She'd be able to apply for jobs. She didn't dare rent anything until she knew what her salary would be.

Her situation mirrored what she'd gone through when she'd first met Greg. But she'd never dreamed that two years after her divorce she would find herself depending on him once again.

Yet here she was, in his debt with nowhere else to turn. She would have to be strong enough to see him every day without getting involved with him again.

Piece of cake, right? She knew better than that.

She steeled herself and went in search of coffee.

When she reached the large kitchen, Sherri saw Hannah preparing something that smelled delicious.

"Good morning," Sherri said, feeling awkward.

Hannah turned and saw her. "Why, good morning! You should have buzzed me and I would have helped you dress."

"I need to learn to take care of myself."

Hannah nodded. "I understand. Just don't forget to call me when you need a little assistance."

"What is that wonderful smell?"

"I'm making cinnamon rolls. Would you like some?"

"Yes, thank you."

"Coffee, orange juice and water are set on the table in the other room. I'll be right there."

Sherri paused in the doorway to the smaller dining room. Greg sat at the table where they had eaten the night before, his back to her, reading the paper and sipping coffee. She needed no reminders of his habits. After being married to him, she knew a great deal about his daily routine, his likes and dislikes, his hobbies and his favorite teams. She'd been so naive back then, thinking that it didn't matter that he didn't talk about the past. She'd presumed that whatever had happened had been traumatic and he didn't want to be reminded of it. She'd felt certain that their love for each other would be enough on which to build a strong marriage, but whatever they had when they married had been chased away by the tension between them.

Sherri moved toward the table on silent wheels. Greg glanced around and saw her. She'd never figured out how he could do that.

"Morning. Did you sleep okay?" he asked politely.

"I slept fine, thank you," she replied, equally polite.

It wasn't long until Hannah arrived with two plates, sliding them in front of each of them. Sherri had already drunk half of her coffee. "Thank you, Hannah."

Greg laid the paper aside. "Thanks, Hannah. I was going into withdrawal without these."

Hannah laughed and went back to the kitchen, leaving Greg and Sherri alone.

Sherri refilled her cup from the carafe on the table and then took a bite of the most heavenly cinnamon bun she'd ever tasted. "No wonder you go into withdrawal without these. They're delicious."

He smiled. After a moment he said, "I'm surprised to see you up this early. You were never a morning person."

"I don't know what time it is. I guess I must have slept all I wanted to."

"Are you feeling better this morning?"

"Much. I'm glad to be out of the hospital."

Greg glanced at his watch and stood. "If you need anything today, give me a call and I'll pick it up on my way home."

There were so many things she wanted to say. She thought it wiser to answer with a nod. She wanted to keep their present relationship polite, cordial.

She watched him leave the house and stride across the lawn to the garage. He disappeared around the tall hedge. A few minutes later she heard his car drive away.

They had gotten through another time together. Now she could relax until he showed back up sometime this evening.

Greg pulled up at the station and parked. Once inside, he relaxed a little. He was in his element here: doing his job, solving cases, testifying in court. These were things he understood.

Once Greg arrived at his desk, Pete came over and claimed the chair beside it. "How did yesterday go?"

"Mornin', Sarge," Greg drawled. "It's good to see you, too."

"Yeah, yeah. What did she say when you took her to your home?"

"About what you'd expect. She considers me to be high-handed and overbearing."

"Well, of course, that's to be expected, since you are. But besides that?"

"Nothing's changed between us, if that's what you want to know. She tolerates me, but that's all."

"Sorry to hear that. You guys were so happy for the first couple of years. I was sort of hoping that once you spent more time with each other again, you'd be able to work things out between you."

"All you need is a diaper and a bow and arrow, Cupid. But do me a favor—point that arrow at someone else, okay?"

Pete got up from his chair and shrugged. "All I know is that you've been miserable since the day she walked out. Maybe the two of you can at least bridge the chasm between you, even if you go your own ways afterward." He studied Greg for a couple of minutes, which made Greg nervous. He picked up a file and began to look through it.

"You know, Greg, you could have bought her a place and hired someone to look after her. You didn't have to take her home with you."

Greg didn't look up from the file in front of him. "Now why didn't I think of that?"

"I think you want her back and now's your chance while she can't get up and walk away. Of course, you're too stubborn to admit your motives."

Greg laughed. "You just keep thinking that, Cupid, while I get to work."

"You're a good man, Hogan," Pete said, turning away.

"Yeah? How about telling the captain that? He's on my case again."

"Nothing new about that."

Greg sighed and leaned back in his chair. "He can find the darnedest things to gripe about."

"He's afraid you're after his job."

Greg rolled his eyes. "Why would I want an administrative job? I enjoy working in the field."

"Buy him a Hallmark card to let him know he has your vote for remaining in his position."

Greg's answer was terse and unprintable.

Pete laughed and walked away.

Greg smiled to himself. Hadn't he been thinking earlier about being comfortable on the job? Well, putting up with the captain was part of it.

Pete was wrong. He hadn't been miserable with Sherri out of his life. A little bored, perhaps. She had added a sparkle to his life. But that was then. Now she wanted to be as far away from him as possible. She'd certainly made that clear. Yeah, he'd harbored some hopes that they could sit down and calmly talk about what had happened. The problem was that Sherri spoke in code. He didn't have a clue what he'd done that was so bad she'd chosen to end the marriage.

He would probably never know.

Maybe Pete was right. He might find a place for her to live. Tell her it's a rental, set the amount to something she could afford. He knew without a doubt that she would refuse to accept the place if she knew he'd bought it for her.

The thing he needed to watch out for was getting attached to her again. As long as she was as cool and distant toward him as she'd been during breakfast, he wouldn't have to make much of an effort.

Greg forced himself to focus on his job. No sense in giving the captain something else to gripe about.

Thirteen

Greg arrived home two weeks later to the sound of laughter and splashing from the pool area. When he stepped through the gate he saw Sven, Hannah, Sherri and a well-built man he didn't know gathered around the pool. Who was the guy? Not that it mattered to him. She could have a half-dozen men hanging around if it made her happy.

Hannah saw him and waved. "Come join us, Greg. We're celebrating."

He walked over to the pool. Sven and Hannah must have been in it recently because their suits were wet. Not a bad idea. The day had been a scorcher.

"Celebrating what?"

The man stood and walked over to him, holding out his hand. "Hi. I'm Troy. I'll be working with Sherri for a few sessions to help her strengthen the muscles in her arm and leg."

Behind him, Sherri held up her broken arm and he saw that

it was no longer in a cast. "I also got a walking cast on my leg. The doctor said I'm healing nicely."

She sat in one of the lounge chairs beside the pool, wearing—almost wearing—a bikini. Her body was exposed to everyone around and he hated the idea of other men seeing her like that.

He turned and walked into the house. He went to the refrigerator and got a beer. After taking a long swallow, he rubbed the cold bottle across his forehead.

Why not join them? After the week he'd had, he deserved to relax a little. With that thought in mind Greg went upstairs, changed into his bathing suit and grabbed a towel. He draped the towel around his neck and went back outside.

He walked to the small diving board at the deep end, bounced a couple of times and dived into the pool. The water caressed him like liquid silk. He swam the length of the pool underwater and came up near Sven and Hannah.

"Wow." He heard Troy's voice. Greg turned his head and Troy continued, "You're in great shape."

For an old guy, Greg finished what he hadn't said. "I swim a lot, mostly at night when I can't sleep." Which had been almost every night since Sherri came.

He glanced over at Sherri and was startled to see her staring at him with a heated gaze. He recognized her expression because he'd seen it often the first couple of years they were married.

The look had always turned him on, and today was no different.

He turned and swam back to the other end of the pool. The size of the pool was a blessing. As long as he stayed away from her she wouldn't be able to see how much she turned him on.

Now that she was more mobile it was time for him to look for a place for her to live, somewhere in another part of town so that he wouldn't be running into her at the local shops and post office.

He swam back and forth while Sven, Hannah and Troy stayed at the four-foot end. Eventually Hannah and Sven left. A little later Troy took his leave, leaving Sherri in the chair and making a date to come back in a few days.

And then there were two. Greg stopped in the middle of the pool and looked at her. She smiled.

"Do you realize that's the first time you've smiled at me in years?"

"I'm happy."

He swam over to her. "For good reason. Your doctor must be impressed with your improvement and so am I." Greg stood waist high in water while Sherri watched him. "Are you ready to go inside?" he asked, his hands on his hips.

She sighed with contentment. "All right."

Sherri waited until Greg pulled himself out of the water and pushed his hair back from his face. Once he was beside her chair he offered him her hand. He pulled her up, using enough momentum that she toppled into his arms.

"You've been driving me crazy in that poor excuse for a swimsuit. You know that, don't you?"

He kissed her. Not an exploratory kiss, but one of passion and need. He braced himself, knowing she would be angry. Instead, she eagerly returned the kiss. He stood there and kissed and caressed her until he knew he had to stop. Otherwise he'd be hauling her pretty butt into the house to make love to her.

He forced himself to step back, steadying her by grasping her upper arms. She looked away from him, breathing as hard as he was. Damn. He hadn't needed a reminder of how good she felt in his arms.

Without a word, Sherri reached for a cane that he hadn't

noticed beside the chair. He grabbed his towel, patted himself dry and wrapped the towel around his waist.

She started along the path toward the house. She was handling the cane with ease. "Why am I driving you crazy?" she asked over her shoulder.

He walked along behind her. "I thought I could have you here and not be bothered by your presence. More fool, I."

"I didn't ask to be here," she said quietly.

"I know."

She took the stairs to the terrace one at a time with little hesitation. Once inside, they moved toward the front hallway.

Sherri stopped in front of her room and turned to face him. "Thank you."

"For what?"

"For treating me with such courtesy these past few weeks. I'm sorry that it's been a strain on you."

"I'll survive." He walked away from her and trotted up the stairs. She watched him until he was out of her sight.

She'd almost come out of her chair earlier when she got her first glimpse of Greg striding across the lawn in his swimsuit. The man was too darn good-looking for his own good and hot, hot, hot.

And that kiss. She closed her eyes. She'd tried to ignore him while he was swimming, but her eyes had kept straying back to him. She really didn't need the reminder of what he could do to her with just a look. And a kiss? Mmm-mmm. She'd have to stay away from him for the rest of the day.

That evening they had dinner out on the terrace. Greg almost groaned out loud when he saw the table set for two. Was Hannah trying to play matchmaker? That's all he needed. He was already feeling vulnerable. How could he have been so stupid as to kiss her, no matter the provocation? All he'd been thinking about was the heated look in her eyes. Once he'd touched her, her response had made him forget everything but his need for her.

He went into the kitchen and got a beer. Hannah was placing the food on plates and it smelled delicious. He'd been too busy to eat lunch today and now his stomach growled in protest.

Hannah laughed. "I'm glad to know you're hungry this evening."

He looked at what she had made. "This is kind of a fancy dinner, isn't it?"

She glanced up. "Well, I thought it should be special for the celebration."

"What cele—" He felt like a fool. "Of course. Sherri is coming along nicely."

Sherri saw them in the kitchen and paused in the doorway. "I must have put on twenty pounds since I got here, Hannah. I'm going to have to go on a diet, but it will have been worth it. Everything looks and smells delicious."

Greg looked at Sherri but she wouldn't meet his eyes. "Wine?" he asked, holding up a bottle of her favorite.

She glanced at him nervously before looking away. "Yes, thank you."

Greg helped Hannah carry everything outside while Sherri trailed behind. "Oh! How lovely. You've really outdone yourself this evening, Hannah."

Hannah watched them as they sat and checked to see they had everything they needed before she said, "Thank you. Enjoy your meal."

After a couple of glasses of wine Sherri managed to relax. The food was out of this world and what could be better than the view of the back lawn, the pool and the blooming bushes and flowerbeds?

The two of them didn't have much to say during dinner and, after Hannah cleared everything away except for the wine bottle and glasses, she told them good-night.

Sherri sighed. "What a beautiful night. Look. The moon is just now appearing. Must be a full moon."

Greg didn't look at her or the rising moon. Instead, he finished the wine in his glass and poured another one.

"I have a question for you," Greg said into the quiet several minutes later.

Sherri turned her head and looked at him. "Is your question going to ruin the peace and quiet of this beautiful night?"

He didn't answer, which was an answer in itself.

Oh well, the wine had mellowed her enough, she hoped, to hear the question without getting upset.

"Shoot."

"That wouldn't be my choice of words," he replied.

"I'll rephrase, counselor. What is your question?"

"You're not going to like it."

"Yes, I've already gotten that."

"I was thinking about the day I came home and discovered that you had moved out of our apartment…without a warning, without an explanation, without a phone call. I've racked my brain in an effort to think about what had happened the day before, or even the week before, to cause you to walk out like that."

She held out her empty glass. "I need more, please," she said politely. He poured the rest of the wine into her glass without saying anything. She took it and sipped. Finally, she said, "Do you remember the evening when I first asked you why you never mentioned your parents?"

He didn't answer right away. "Not really."

"I didn't think it made much of an impression on you,

even though I tried to talk to you about them another time or two after that."

His face was in shadows. "You left me because I wouldn't talk about my parents?" he asked in disbelief.

"No."

"That's good to know."

"It was all of the things you never told me. You led me to believe your only relatives were Millie and a brother."

"I never said that."

"Correct. You never said anything. I was visiting Millie one afternoon and I asked her when your parents had died. That's when I discovered all kinds of things I didn't know before, such as that they were very much alive and lived in Connecticut. She mentioned that not only had you graduated from Harvard with a bachelor's degree, you had also graduated from Harvard Law School with top grades."

"And that's upsetting because…?"

"I realized that I really didn't know you at all. We'd been living together for over two years. I'd shared with you everything about my life, which I must admit wasn't as colorful as yours. You mentioned you'd been in France at one time. How about your lengthy stays in Italy and the U.K.? What upset me was that you didn't trust me enough to share any of that with me."

"It wasn't a matter of trust," he said tersely. "It was…" His voice faded away.

"Your past makes up who you are…your experiences, your traumas, your triumphs all contribute to the man you are today. Yet you chose not to share any of it with me. You were treating me like a live-in girlfriend who kept your bed warm at night, but who wasn't important enough to open up and talk to."

"You were very important to me. I loved you. I thought I made that clear."

"As long as we were only playing house together and I didn't make any waves. Do you remember the day I pointed out that we'd never talked about having children, and you said you'd make a terrible father?"

"Believe me, I would."

"Okay. But why had you never mentioned to me before that you didn't want children?"

"I guess because I never thought it was important."

"There were too many things that we didn't discuss before we got married that we should have."

"I don't get it. You left me because I didn't talk to you and tell you how I felt about everything?"

"About *anything*. The child issue was of real concern to me at the time because I thought I was pregnant."

Greg had been leaning back in his chair when she spoke and sat up abruptly. "You were pregnant?"

"I don't know. I missed a period. I wasn't just late. I missed it."

"Why in hell didn't you tell me!"

"The thing was, bringing up our views of a family was my naive way of broaching the subject. Since we'd never discussed it, I thought it was time."

"You should have told me anyway."

"By then we rarely spoke, unless it was about what to have for dinner or who was going to drop off the clothes at the cleaners. Sometimes we managed to converse about whatever was in the mail any particular day. I had already faced the fact that I didn't want to have a marriage like that, a marriage where certain subjects were not to be discussed. Even if I *had* been pregnant, I wouldn't have stayed, given your feelings about the subject."

Sherri discovered that she wasn't at all upset by discussing that time in her life. She'd worked through the pain; she'd dealt with the sense of betrayal. She'd even dealt with Greg's lack of trust. She felt as though she was talking about someone else who had suffered through that time in her life.

She finished her wine and yawned. "I'm going to turn in," she said to Greg as she stood.

"Sherri?"

She'd only taken a couple of steps when he spoke. She turned around. He stood, silhouetted by the strong moonlight. "I wish you'd told me back then," he said in a low voice.

"Would it have made any difference, or would you have brushed it all away as you had so many times before and told me that I was overreacting? Would we have ended up in bed together, as though lovemaking was the cure for everything that was going wrong in our relationship?"

"I never meant to hurt you."

"And I never meant to hurt *you*. My leaving was my way of surviving an untenable situation."

She turned around and walked inside. Looking back to that time in her life, she might have done things differently. She'd been so young and idealistic back then. She'd believed in all the love songs she'd ever heard. She'd believed in happily ever after. Eventually she came to understand that happily ever after could be living alone with her cat and not having to deal with continuing heartache.

Greg stayed outside. He walked over to the pool, stripped out of his clothes and dived in. He swam furiously as though all the sharks in the world were after him. When he finally stopped by the side of the pool he was gasping for breath.

The moon now rode high in the sky, casting its light.

He crawled out of the pool and, dripping water, gathered

his clothes and went inside. Once in his room, he tossed his clothes aside and went in to take a shower. With the heavy spray of water beating down on him, Greg finally allowed himself to think about what Sherri had said tonight.

There was very little emotion in the telling, that was the first thing he'd noticed. She'd loved him back then. He knew that. She did not love him now. It had been obvious in her voice and demeanor.

Like it or not, he knew that he didn't have a snowball's chance in hell of winning her back.

The next morning Greg went downstairs to find the coffee made but no sign of Hannah. That's when he remembered that she'd asked for the day off in order to help Sven at the nursery.

He'd spent a restless night going over everything that Sherri had told him last night. It wasn't that he hadn't trusted her. He had erased his parents from his life and saw no reason to discuss them. It hadn't been a lack of trust in her. No. He trusted her then and he trusted her now. But maybe he'd been a little high-handed with her.

She'd certainly been right about one thing: those last few months had been miserable. So maybe she'd done the right thing. She'd definitely done the right thing for her.

He knew what he needed to do. He'd go looking for a place to buy for Sherri. She didn't have to know he was the owner. He'd have a rental place take care of all that. He'd call a Realtor later in the morning to find out what was out there.

Without turning around, he knew that Sherri was nearby. He didn't really understand it, but he seemed to have an antenna that only worked where she was concerned. He turned around. "Coffee?"

She looked around the kitchen. "Yes, please. Is Hannah sick?"

"Uh, no. I'd forgotten until I came in here that yesterday morning Hannah asked for the day off. She's working with Sven today." He walked over to the refrigerator. "What would you like for breakfast?"

"I'll have toast. I can make it."

He poured two glasses of orange juice and carried them to the dining room table. When he returned to the kitchen, Sherri was buttering toast. Without saying anything, he picked up a tray and put the carafe, their two cups and her plate of toast on it.

"Do you want some?" she asked.

"Not now. It's nice to have the day off. I'll make something after a while."

They sat down and Sherri took a piece of toast and began to eat.

"Will Troy be here today?" he asked, breaking the silence.

"No. Monday. I have some exercises I can do." She looked out the window. "Looks like another nice day."

"Yes. I'd enjoy it more if it wasn't so blasted hot." So it had come down to talking about the weather. He supposed that was all they had left to discuss.

Sherri finished her toast and juice, then poured another cup of coffee. "I've made a couple of appointments this afternoon. I should have planned better. I think I've found a possible apartment. My problem is getting there."

"I can take you."

She smiled. "Thank you. I had planned to ask Hannah. She's run me to the store a few times. I should have checked with her first."

"No problem. I don't have anything else planned."

They looked at each other. He could see that she had no problem with moving out and she wasn't going to wait for him to buy a place. Probably just as well. She'd been right about something else. A clean break was the better way to leave their relationship.

Even so, there was no way he could have ignored the fact she'd been hospitalized because of a wreck. Everything he'd done after that was for her benefit, not his. At no time did Sherri give him reason to hope that she would come back to him. He'd been fantasizing. Now, he had to face reality.

"I've also managed to take a temporary job that I can do at home. That will bring in enough money to pay bills until I find a permanent one."

"You've been busy."

"I was waiting for the walking cast. There's really no need to take advantage of your hospitality any longer."

It was definitely time to cut his losses and get on with his life.

Greg heard the doorbell. He glanced at his watch. It was almost eleven. They'd both slept in this morning. Since Hannah was gone, he'd better see who it was.

The bell rang a second time before he reached the door. An impatient sort, whoever it was. He opened the door and his jaw dropped.

"If Mohammed won't come to the mountain, the mountain must come to Mohammed. Hello, darling."

Fourteen

Greg looked at the three people standing at the front door and cleared his throat. "What a surprise. Come in."

He stepped back and watched as his parents, Max and Katrina, together with Penelope, the woman his mother had wanted him to marry years ago, walked into his home.

His mother gave him an air kiss, his father lifted an eyebrow and Penelope threw herself into his arms. "Oh, Greg, I've missed you so much! It's great to see you after all this time!" She kissed him with exuberance. When he didn't respond she stepped back with an embarrassed laugh. "It's not fair that the years have merely added to your good looks."

He nodded to the living room. "Shall we?" he said to all of them in general. He escorted his unexpected and unwelcome company into the formal living room. "May I get you something to drink?" he asked politely.

Katrina said, "Iced tea, please."

Penelope nodded.

"Father?"

"Nothing for me." Max was making it clear that he had been coerced into coming by taking a seat as far away from all of them as possible. Greg and his father knew exactly where they stood with each other.

Instead of going directly to the kitchen—of all days for Hannah to be gone—he went back into the dining room. "Sherri?"

She looked at him in surprise. "There's somebody here for me?"

"You could look at it that way. As I recall from last night's discussion, you left me because I refused to discuss my parents with you. Well, here's your chance to find out all my deep, dark secrets."

She stood. "What are you talking about?"

"It seems that my parents have come for a visit. Now you'll be able to find out all about my 'other life' that you wanted to know."

Her jaw dropped. "Your parents? They're here?"

"Yes. I have absolutely no idea why they're here, but I'm sure I'm about to find out. I would like your help."

"Have they ever been here before?"

"No."

"What do you want me to do?"

"Be your usual gracious self."

"Now you're being sarcastic."

"No, I'm not. You've always been gracious. I need that today because it's next to impossible for me to be."

He walked with her into the hallway and said, "Hold on. I've got to get some refreshments."

She looked bewildered. "I really don't understand. How is my being here going to be a help to you?"

"I know I'm asking a lot from you, but will you please go along with whatever I say?" Greg spoke in a soft tone. "I will be eternally grateful if you will."

"Greg, I have never seen you this upset. What's going on?"

He clenched his jaw. "You'll find out soon enough." He went into the kitchen, filled two glasses with ice and tea and returned to her side.

Greg paused in the wide doorway of the living room. "Mother? Father? Penelope? This is Sherri Masterson. We were married five years ago." He didn't dare look at Sherri. The statement was a fact, after all. Instead, he handed Katrina and Penelope their drinks. They took them, both looking stunned.

Greg walked beside Sherri until they reached one of the sofas. He helped her sit and settled in beside her. "Sherri was in a bad wreck several weeks ago. We were both grateful she wasn't killed. It's a miracle she's alive today."

Katrina and Penelope were so much alike in their mannerisms as they looked Sherri over from head to toe with undisguised disapproval that they could have rehearsed the scene. He should be amused by their behavior, but he tended to lose his sense of humor where his family was concerned.

Sherri glanced at them and then at Greg. He casually put his arm on the back of the sofa behind her.

Katrina was the first to speak. "Did he say Masterson?"

Sherri nodded with a small smile on her face. The smile made him nervous. She knew she had him at her mercy. He could only hope she didn't decide that it was payback time. He sighed with relief with her short answer.

"Yes."

"What part of the country are you from?" his mother asked.

"I was born in Texas. I lived in a small ranching community in the Hill Country until I moved to Austin to attend university."

"Well," Katrina finally said. "I doubt that I know your family, then."

"No. My parents were killed in a plane crash several years ago."

Greg watched Katrina and Penelope exchange glances. This was so not amusing.

Katrina said, "You're looking fit, Greg." She paused, as though searching for words. "I suppose that marriage agrees with you."

He looked at Sherri and she grinned at him. She was actually *enjoying* his discomfort.

"Would it have hurt you to have told us about it? I'm surprised that Grandmother never told me."

"I understand that she rarely, if ever, heard from you."

Katrina's eyelids fluttered. "Well, I have such a busy schedule and Millie and I never had very much in common. I could never understand why you enjoyed visiting with her so much when you were a child."

He could tell her the truth, that Millie had been his escape from an oppressive household, but there was no reason to hurt his mother. She was who she was and was admired by many people. She'd just been a lousy mother.

"I liked her," he finally said. "She was fun to be around."

"Well," Katrina conceded, "she was always a little eccentric."

Greg laughed and looked at Sherri, who was trying *not* to laugh. "I'll have to agree with you on that."

Katrina looked at him with a puzzled expression. "I have never understood why you were so secretive."

Sherri's elbow connected with Greg's ribs and he coughed,

trying to cover the fact that he'd flinched. That had hurt. He took her hand and placed it on his knee and smiled at her.

"You know, that's an excellent question. I suppose it was because I wanted to keep Sherri all to myself." He leaned over and kissed her cheek.

Penelope cleared her throat and Greg glanced at her. "I'm sorry, Penelope. I didn't mean to leave you out of the conversation."

She did not look happy. "I probably shouldn't have come."

"Nonsense, dear," Katrina replied quickly, "I wanted you to come." She looked at Greg. "The reason we decided to come was to see if you would consider moving back east. Since Millie is gone, there's no reason for you to continue to stay here. I knew if I called to tell you we were coming that you'd put us off, which is why we decided to surprise you. Since Penelope had been asking about you quite a bit, I invited her to come along."

Penelope blushed an unflattering shade of red. Katrina looked at Sherri. "Penelope has been a close family friend since she and Greg were children. Her family owns the estate next to ours and the two of them often played together."

Katrina continued. "Penelope recently returned from living in Italy. She was married to a young man whose family can be traced back to the Middle Ages. Some kind of prince or count," she said airily, waving her hand in the air.

Penelope looked as though she'd swallowed something bitter.

Greg nodded and smiled at Penelope. She didn't return the gesture.

"So what's your married name, Penny?"

"Now, Greg," Katrina hastily said. "You know how she detests being called by that nickname, surely you haven't forgotten! Penelope took her maiden name back after the divorce."

Sherri squeezed his hand a little too forcefully. He brought it up and kissed her knuckles, giving her a loving smile and a narrowed gaze.

Greg glanced over at Max. "I'm surprised to see that you left your fiefdom. How in the world did Mother persuade you to come?"

Katrina trilled into laughter. "Don't be silly, Greg. Your father wanted to see you as much as I did!"

His mother was still living in her own fantasy world, it seemed.

"Do you have help to take care of this place?" she asked.

"Yes. She's working with her husband today. They have a nursery."

"Oh." Katrina looked at Sherri. "I suppose you have trouble being able to do much around the house."

"That's true," Sherri said blandly.

"Well." Katrina seemed to run out of things to say. She looked at Max, who sat with his head resting on the back of his chair and his eyes closed. "Max!" she said irritably. "I don't know why you don't sit over here and join in the conversation."

"I have nothing to say. As for my fiefdom, as you put it, Greg, I have a board of directors that somehow manages to keep me in line. Your brother is doing quite well in the company, by the way."

"Good for Kyle."

Katrina said, "Oh, Greg, you really must come back…at the very least for a visit. Kyle and Marsha have the smartest children. They're absolutely adorable." She paused and looked at Sherri. "I take it you don't have children, yet, do you? Marsha's the earth-mother type and enjoys rearing her brood."

Greg searched for something to say that wasn't impossibly rude, but before he could think of anything Sherri surprised him

by saying, "Oh, we don't have children, yet. I had just graduated from the university when we married," she said confid-
ingly, giving Penelope a quick glance. "We wanted a few years
together before we began our family. Although—" she paused
and gave Greg a melting glance "—we were just discussing
children last night, weren't we, honey? If I hadn't been
involved in that accident, I'd probably be pregnant right now."

Greg almost choked. Sherri looked at him and said, "I
know, sweetheart. I was disappointed, too."

Nobody said anything.

Not a thing.

The room resounded with silence.

Finally, Katrina said, "Well, I know you must have plans
for today and we don't want to keep you. We're staying at the
Omni while we're here and we'd like to take you out to dinner
this evening."

Once again, Sherri spoke before Greg could open his
mouth. "Why, that would be so nice, Mother Hogan. I hope
I can call you that." Katrina's face registered her distaste.
"Greg has told me so much about you and I would love to get
to know you better." She looked at Penelope and smiled
gently. "I'm sorry. I'm afraid he never mentioned his childhood friend. I'm looking forward to hearing all the stories you
must know about him when he was a child."

Max stood. "We'll see you tonight, then. Come to the hotel
at seven and we'll go from there."

"I'll see about reservations at one of the restaurants,"
Katrina added, also coming to her feet. Penelope looked as if
she couldn't wait to escape.

"Please excuse me for not getting up," Sherri said, smiling
at each of them.

Greg said, "I'm sure they understand, darling." He gave

her a brief squeeze and stood. He walked them to the door. "We'll see you tonight." His mother gave him another air kiss. This time, Penelope followed Katrina's example.

Once he opened the door, the three of them filed outside to the waiting BMW limousine. The driver hopped out of the front seat and went around the car, opening the doors for them.

Watching this activity, Greg thought, *I wonder if my father had the driver bring his limo down. Wouldn't put it past him.*

With a big sigh of relief he went back inside the house and headed to the living room. He and Sherri had a few things to discuss.

Fifteen

Sherri was coming toward him when he reached the doorway. She gave him a cheerful smile.

"Why did you accept that dinner invitation when you knew I didn't want to go?"

"Why did you never tell me that you came from money?"

They stared at each other. "It wasn't important."

"Essentially, nothing was important to you but getting me into bed."

"That's not fair! I—" He ran his hand through his already tousled hair. "To hell with it." He turned on his heel and headed upstairs. He heard Sherri's door close softly.

What an unholy mess. Sherri hadn't mentioned their divorce, but he almost wished she had. Or better yet, he shouldn't have had her meet them at all.

He hadn't been thinking straight. Sherry was no longer a part of his life, or wouldn't be in another week or two. He didn't owe his parents an explanation of his life. Just as he didn't owe Sherri an explanation—

He had shut her out in the same way he'd shut his parents out. He didn't like talking about himself or rehashing his past with anyone. Not just Sherri. Why couldn't she have understood that?

He'd fallen hard for her, had never felt anything like it before. He'd loved her to the best of his abilities and it hadn't been enough for her. He must be too much of a loner to have a relationship with anyone.

There was no help for it; he would be having dinner with his parents and Penny tonight. That one hadn't aged well. She was too thin and too tense. Of course, finding out he was married could have caused the last part. He smiled. It had been worth putting up with Sherri's crazy sense of humor not to have Penelope Prissy Pants, his childish name for her—which he'd wisely never said out loud—fawning over him all evening.

Greg and Sherri arrived at the hotel a few minutes before seven. Greg handed the car keys to the valet and helped Sherri out of the car.

She looked stunning tonight, wearing a dress he'd never seen before. Then again, there had been no reason for her to dress up before.

She'd chosen a green dress made of some kind of shimmery material that draped over her body in a very sensual way. Even using a cane and walking slowly, she caught the eye of every male nearby.

He took her arm in a possessive hold and they walked to the entrance of the hotel.

Once inside the hotel they crossed the lobby to the elevators. His mother had given him the room number this afternoon just before she got into the car. He kept pace with Sherri until they reached the elevator. Once it opened, Sherri stepped inside while Greg held the door for her.

He pushed the top button on the elevator and they rode up in silence. Why had his parents really come? Despite his mother's comments, he knew that his father never did anything he didn't want to do. He also knew that his father generally ignored his mother. So why cater to her whims now?

The elevator doors opened silently and they stepped into the hallway. There were only four doors on this level. Greg walked over to one and pushed a buzzer. Sherri had joined him by the time the door opened.

"Hello, Gregory," his mother said. "Please come in."

He motioned for Sherri to precede him inside.

"Hello, Mother Hogan," Sherri said with a smile. "I hope we didn't keep you waiting."

His mother didn't respond to the smile. She looked at Greg. "Penelope won't be joining us this evening," she said with barely concealed irritation. "She came down with a beastly headache and decided to stay here while we go out."

"Sorry to hear that," Greg said, suitably solemn.

"Yes, well," his mother said, turning away from them and leading them into a large room with a view of downtown Austin and the hills west of the city. "Max. Gregory is here." Since his father had already stood, her remark was unnecessary.

The four of them left the suite and took the elevator down to the lobby. Greg spotted the limo waiting for them near the entrance of the hotel.

His mother made a few remarks during the ride to the restaurant...about the weather—*beastly*—about Austin—*too provincial*—before she inquired about his job.

"It's fine," he replied tersely.

"Well, if you insist on doing police work instead of working with the company as in-house counsel, there's no reason in the world that you need to stay here in Texas." Her tone made her feelings about the state perfectly clear. "I'm certain that with your father's connections he could find you something back east."

He limited his reply to "I like living here."

Finally, his mother gave up and the four of them spent the rest of the ride in silence.

The limo pulled up in front of the restaurant. Once again Greg assisted Sherri out of the car while the driver assisted Katrina.

Max spoke to the chauffeur for a few minutes and then strode into the restaurant, Katrina hurrying to catch up with him.

"Do I have my cloak of invisibility on tonight?" Sherri asked in a low voice as she and Greg moved toward the entrance.

"Mother hopes that if she ignores you, you'll go away. You're standing in the way of her big plans."

"Then why don't you tell her the truth and call a taxi for me?"

"That would play right into her hands."

"So what? You're a big boy, Greg. You don't need me to protect you."

He almost smiled. "You're here so that my father and I don't create a brawl in a public place."

"Of course you're kidding," she said as he held the door open for her.

"Not in the least. I despise the man. The feeling is mutual."

"Okay. You've made that quite clear. What I don't under-stand is the fact that you've acted for years as though you had no family. Lots of people don't care for their relatives, but most don't erase them from their life."

The maître d' led the way to a corner table with Max and Katrina following behind him.

"Perhaps we could have this conversation at some other time," he said pleasantly and stepped back so that she could follow his parents.

Once seated, the four ordered drinks and studied the menu in silence. Greg glanced at his watch. He didn't want to wish anyone ill, but a call from the station about a new case would certainly be appreciated.

After they gave their orders to the waiter, Katrina turned to Greg and said, "I must say that I'm very disappointed you chose not to tell us that you were getting married. To think that you've been married for five years and I knew nothing about it! I really don't understand you at all, Greg. Why have you so stubbornly cut yourself off from your family?"

Greg took a swallow of his mixed drink, wishing he'd ordered beer, before answering her. "I don't think this is the venue in which to discuss my errant behavior, Mother."

Katrina looked at Max. "Can't you say something?" she asked in irritation.

Max had been gazing out the window until she spoke to him. He turned his head and looked at her. "Exactly what is it you expect me to say? You wanted to see Gregory. I brought you to see him. What more do you want from me?"

"He's our son! You treat him as though he were a stranger."

Max glanced at Greg for a moment. "I'm well aware of that, Katrina." With a half smile directed at Sherri, he added, "Although he looks just like I did at his age. Hardly a stranger."

Greg was relieved when their salads arrived.

His father had taken control of Greg's life at an early age. Because he wanted his father's approval so desperately, Greg followed his father's plans for him step by step. He'd gone to prep school. He'd spent three summers in Europe, learning languages and becoming familiar with other cultures. He'd graduated with honors from Harvard. He'd gotten his law degree and passed the state Bar. Then, he'd gone to work for his father.

Something happened to Greg when Max told him that he hoped to have Greg run for a political office in the state legislature once he had a little more seasoning. Greg had to face the fact that he wasn't living *his* life at all.

His escapes to Austin and Millie had been the only times when he'd truly been himself. Max had made no effort to hide his ambitions for his son. Max had money and power and having a son in politics would give him even more power. Greg knew that if he continued following his father's plans for him his father would control his entire life.

He'd been his father's puppet for most of his life and Max was only getting started.

He would never forget the day he'd told his father that he didn't intend to work for him anymore. That he had applied for a place at a prestigious police academy. He'd known his father would be upset with him and had braced himself to counter anything Max said to him.

He'd been the dutiful son all his life because he'd wanted his father to be proud of him. He'd always known that Max was grooming him to run his company.

The problem was that he didn't like the way his dad did business. His ruthlessness in acquiring assets and closing businesses without regard to the people who lost their jobs because of him was too brutal for Greg to stomach.

That meeting had opened his eyes to what his father was really like. He had viciously turned on Greg with such a personal attack that Greg felt he'd been annihilated. His blistering attack had caught Greg completely off guard. The names he'd called him and the threats he'd made to see that

Greg never had a decent job again had destroyed Greg's illusions about his father's feelings for him.

Greg hadn't seen it coming and knew he could never be a part of this family again. The man in a rage before him was contemptible in Greg's eyes.

He remembered turning around and walking out of the office with Max's words ringing in his ears. "You're no son of mine and you'll never get a cent of my money."

The lesson Greg had learned from that long-ago day was that his father had never seen him as anything more than his clone. Max had never bothered to get to know him. His father had certainly never loved him.

When Greg tried to explain to his mother why he was leaving she'd just looked at him in shock and said that of course he would do what his father wanted. It was his duty to honor his father.

Greg knew better than to continue any discussion with her.

He'd left soon afterward, and this was the first time he'd seen his family since. They hadn't even bothered to come to Millie's funeral.

After graduating from the police academy, Greg had accepted an offer to work in Austin as a chance to start over and to begin to live his own life. By the time he'd met Sherri, he'd put his family behind him. In his world, he didn't have family…except for his great-grandmother.

It was true that Sherri had asked him questions about his family but he'd put her off, not wanting to dredge up old memories. Now he was face-to-face with those memories and he knew that they had never faded.

During the course of the meal his mother did her best to keep polite conversation going, but she eventually accepted that the dinner meeting wasn't a success. After dinner they returned to the hotel and Greg signaled to have his car brought around.

"Would you like to come up for coffee?" his mother asked, making a last-ditch effort.

"Sorry," he said, helping Sherri into his car when it arrived. "Thanks for dinner." He gazed at his father. "Have a safe flight back home," he said, and walked around the car to get in.

When they pulled out of the driveway, Sherri looked over at him and said, "I don't know who you are tonight. You're definitely not the man I fell in love with and married. I have never seen anyone be so rude."

"That's why you left, wasn't it? You said I was like a stranger to you. So now you know the truth about me. I am an ungrateful son and I have no desire to spend any time with my parents. Or with Penelope. Or get involved in their lives. I have my reasons and I can live with them. You made the right choice, you know, about leaving. I'm not cut out for marriage, as you so firmly pointed out."

He pulled into the driveway of his home and drove around the house to the garage. He helped Sherri out of the car and followed her into the house. She continued through the house to the front hallway before she stopped, turned and faced him.

"Here's what I think. I think I knew parts of you better than you know yourself. You have a kind and gentle heart. You're full of compassion. You've rescued me during two very traumatic events in my life. You've been there for me. Whatever is going on between you and your father must have hurt you deeply for you to insist on locking all of your previous life away." She paused and just looked at him. "I can't help but pity you, Greg. You keep yourself bottled up so that no one can get close to you and yes, I gave up trying."

She turned and went into her room, quietly closing the door behind her.

Greg stood there for several minutes after the door closed.

He couldn't have been more shaken if she'd hit him with a two-by-four. She felt sorry for him! Why? Because he chose to live the life he wanted to live? To work in a profession that he enjoyed?

Okay. So he lived alone. Big deal. Everything worked out the way it needed to. He'd hated feeling so vulnerable where Sherri was concerned. He'd fallen in love for the first time in his life and he hadn't known how to handle it. He wasn't very good at compromise.

As though he heard a voice inside him, the thought came to him that he was, in fact, just like his father.

Sixteen

Six weeks later

Sherri heard her phone ringing as she put the key into the lock of her apartment. Whoever it was would have to wait until she got there. She didn't hurry for anyone. After getting the door open, she moved inside and closed the door behind her. She picked up the phone and said hello.

"Sherri? This is Greg."

Darn it, after she'd spent weeks dealing with her feelings for him and determinedly putting him out of her mind, he called.

"Hello, Greg."

"I was wondering if you'd have dinner with me tonight."

She took the phone away from her ear and looked at it. Finally, she said, "Why? Is this be-kind-to-your-ex week?"

He chuckled. "I don't know. If it isn't, maybe we can start a new trend. I'd like to see you."

She sighed. "Look, Greg, I know it got a little messy at the end of my stay with you and I apologize for the things I said. Your relationship with your parents is none of my business. Our pretending to be married was your idea and I went along with it, but we don't have to pretend to be friends."

"I don't want to be friends."

"Great. Look, I've got to go. I just got home and—"

"I've been doing a lot of soul-searching recently and there are some things I want to share with you."

She frowned. "Is this really Greg Hogan?"

"Oh, yeah."

"Did someone put you up to this? Is there a bet going or something?"

"Why are you surprised that I want to see you again? There's so much I want to say to you and I'd really like to talk to you in person. How about it? Will you have dinner with me tonight?"

She closed her eyes. She could see that if she said yes, she'd be putting her heart at risk again. "I don't think that's a good idea, Greg."

He didn't say anything right away. In fact, she thought he might have hung up. Finally, he said, "I really need to see you, Sherri." His voice barely audible.

Greg Hogan had never needed anything from anybody. He'd made that clear years ago. She couldn't help but be intrigued. Against her better judgment she finally replied. "All right. Where shall I meet you?"

"I'll pick you up at seven."

Not a good idea but she wasn't going to argue. "Seven," she repeated. "I'll see you then. Bye."

She hung up before her trembling became apparent in her voice. She had just agreed to do something that she knew was against her best interests. What was it about Greg that made her so weak-willed?

She had to be completely out of her mind.

Moving out of Greg's home had been as painful for her this time as it had been when they were married. Pretending to be his wife had come way too easily. She seemed to be jumping back into the fire without her asbestos suit.

She shook her head at her own foolishness. When would she ever get to the point where she could say no to Greg? Obviously not today.

Sherri went into her bedroom to find something to wear.

Greg arrived a few minutes before seven. Sherri had picked up the phone more than once to cancel the date. She would punch three or four numbers in before she'd hang up, feeling cowardly.

Now he was here. She went over and opened the door. Did he have to look so blasted masculine and mouthwateringly attractive? She would have to treat tonight as though it was routine to have a date with her ex-husband.

He nodded and offered a lopsided smile. "Hi," he said quietly. "Thank you for accepting my invitation."

"You're welcome. Come in."

He stepped inside and looked around. "Nice place. Looks comfortable. I like what you've done with it." He stuck his hands in his pockets and wandered around the room, looking at pictures on the wall. "Much nicer than the one you had when we first met."

He turned and faced her. "Do you like your new job?" he asked.

She'd never seen Greg so nervous before. "Very much."

"You're looking great, by the way."

The look he gave her was scorching. "Thank you." What had she gotten herself into? This man was not the Greg she remembered. He was far from at ease. Sherri still stood near the apartment door, watching him.

He cleared his throat. "Would you please relax? I'm not going to jump you. I would never do anything to you that you didn't want me to do. Surely you know that."

And that was her problem. After being around him this past summer, what ran through her mind was how often her dreams were filled with him making love to her. She hadn't needed the reminder.

"I know," she said slowly.

"Well," he said with a roll of his shoulders, "guess we'd better go."

He held the car door open for her. When he got into the car, he said, "Your leg seems to be fine."

"It still aches from time to time. It's more accurate than the weatherman at predicting a change."

"And your arm?"

"Good as new."

"I'm glad to hear it."

Sherri wasn't sure which one of them was more tense. She felt awkward around him now. On edge. She couldn't imagine how she would be able to eat a thing at dinner.

Once they were seated at the restaurant, Sherri felt a little better. A glass of wine helped. She ordered a salad and hoped she could eat it. Greg's appetite seemed unimpaired to judge by the meal he ordered.

When the silence between them got on her nerves, Sherri asked, "How's work? Still keeping busy?"

"Unfortunately, yes."

"How are Hannah and Sven?"

"Great."

They lapsed into silence once again.

She should have followed her instincts and canceled. Once their meals arrived, she set out to eat as quickly as possible so they could leave.

Greg asked for coffee for them once they finished eating. After the waiter brought their order, he picked up his spoon and turned it over a couple of times before nervously placing it on the table.

"I just want to say," he began and paused to clear his throat. "You didn't have to apologize for what you said about my relationship with my parents."

"Oh?"

"Yeah. Like I told you on the phone, I've done quite a bit of thinking about that situation as well as what happened to our marriage. I finally concluded that I needed to tell you some of the things I've faced about myself."

Sherri waited. His nervousness was contagious.

"It was a blow to me when I realized that I had treated you in the same way my father had treated his family. I've never heard him talk about his life before he married Mother. When I was in my early teens I asked my mother about him and she told me stories about their early marriage. She said that he'd become obsessed with making more and more money. Another time she commented that he was more comfortable in a work environment than he was in dealing with personal relationships. She said that he'd always been the kind of person who knew what he wanted and went about getting it. She'd been someone he'd wanted and he'd pursued her until she agreed to marry him."

He stopped talking and just looked at her. Sherri was blown away by his telling her all of this. She'd never heard him even touch on anything about his past.

When she didn't say anything, he said, "Does any of this sound familiar?"

"You mean because we'd known each other only a few weeks when you wanted to get married?"

"Yes."

"I suppose. So you think there's a pattern here?"

"A big one. I treated you the way he treats Mother. Even when he was home his mind was on his business. Mother learned to cope and chose to stay with him. You chose a different course."

She refused to feel guilty about her decision to end the marriage. "Yes, I did. I came to the realization that nothing was going to change between us. You had withdrawn into your work to the point where I decided that living alone was preferable to being married and being alone—emotionally, if not physically."

He nodded. "I can understand that. I guess what I wanted to tell you is that I have recognized that the very things I dislike most about my father are the traits I share with him."

What a revelation that was. She'd had no idea because she'd had no way of knowing the similarities between the two of them. Would it have made a difference in her decision? She would never know. At least Greg had been willing to share his epiphany with her now.

Knowing how much he hated his father, she knew that this realization was quite a blow to him. Impulsively she reached over and touched his hand. "That must have been hard to face."

He turned his palm up and grasped her fingers. "Yes, it was. All this time I've been feeling self-righteous and judgmental toward him. I've seen myself as standing up for what was right and going my own way."

"I take it he didn't want you to go into law enforcement."

"That's a part of it. Mostly, he wanted to be the one in control of my life. When I said no, he washed his hands of me. My father doesn't believe in making compromises."

"And neither do you?" she asked.

"Correct. When you told me the reasons you left me, I could have made changes and opened up to you then, but I didn't."

"And yet, you're telling me this now. Why?"

"Because I've been an absolute idiot where you're concerned and I miss you so much, I can barely function. I've slept in your room a few times since you left in an effort to feel closer to you. What I'm asking is whether there's a snowball's chance in hell that you might be willing for us to start over?"

No, oh, no. I can't go there again. It's too painful. Please don't ask me. Her heart beat heavily in her chest. Her fear of the pain she would feel if they tried to work it out and failed scared her to death.

Greg was watching her intently. "I remember you once said that all my past experiences had made me who I am today. I don't like myself all that much. I lost the woman I love more than anything else because I was too stiff-necked to realize what I was doing to our relationship." He looked away from her. When he looked back at her, his jaw had tightened. "I owe you so many apologies that I don't know where to start." He looked at their entwined fingers before adding, "I love you, Sherri Masterson. I never stopped loving you. And yet I did everything wrong when we were married."

She frowned. "That's not true. There were two people in the marriage, Greg. I was dealing with a lot of issues, too—the sense of abandonment was a major one. I had lost the people I loved most in the world and felt that I had lost you in all the ways that mattered, as well. A lot of my buttons were being pushed."

"Thank you for hearing me out this evening. You could have gotten up and left and I would have understood. But you didn't, and I appreciate your patience more than I can say. Do you think it's possible that we might be able to work things out?"

She stared into his eyes, knowing that this was the fork in the road of her life. Risk everything in hopes of gaining everything?

Finally, Sherri nodded. "I'd like to think so, yes." She smiled tentatively at him.

"I do have one other request to make."

She eyed him suspiciously. "And what is that?"

"Will you go to Connecticut with me? I want to go see my parents."

Seventeen

Sherri stared at him as though he'd started speaking in a foreign language. And maybe he had. Opening up to Sherri and enumerating his many faults had been the toughest thing he'd ever done in his life.

"You don't need me, Greg. You know that."

"Yes, I do know that. It isn't a question of need. I'm going to want your support if you're willing to give it. I have no idea how the visit will turn out."

"When are you planning to go?"

"Whenever you say."

"I can't ask for time off. I haven't worked there long enough."

"Okay. Then we'll do it on a weekend. Fly up Friday, come back Sunday."

"You're serious about doing this."

"Very."

"Let me think about it, okay?"

The waiter brought their check. Greg gave him his credit card and they waited while the waiter rang it up.

He couldn't keep his eyes off Sherri. Her hair had grown out some and she'd had it trimmed since he'd last seen her. Now it curved around her face, framing it.

After the waiter returned, Greg took Sherri's hand and they walked to his car. At least she hadn't said no. She'd given him hope, and he was determined to do everything he could to convince her that the two of them could make it.

He turned into the driveway of the apartment complex where she lived. "Did you get another car?"

"Not yet. I'm on one of the bus routes until I decide what I want. As much as I loved my little car, I want something larger—steel-plated, perhaps."

"I can understand that." They arrived at her door and he waited for her to unlock it. When the door opened, Sherri looked at him and said, "Would you like to come in for more coffee?"

He breathed deeply, not certain how to handle her invitation. Finally, he said, "I would very much like to come inside, but it won't be because I want coffee."

She nodded and went into her apartment. When she didn't say anything he knew that he was pushing a little too hard.

She turned and looked at him for a long moment. *Okay, here it comes.*

"Please come in, Greg," she said softly, a slight smile on her face.

She didn't have to ask him twice.

As soon as he stepped inside and closed the door behind them, he grabbed her and kissed her the way he'd been wanting to since the moment he'd first seen her tonight. He couldn't touch her enough, sliding his hand down her side and catching her knee. She responded by clutching his shoulders and hotly kissing him back.

He'd wanted her for too long not to know he wasn't going to last. He lifted her, turned and leaned her against the door, his hands feeling for her panties. She was moist and hot and he couldn't wait any longer. He tore her panties and dropped them to the floor, reached down and unzipped himself and plunged into her, frantic to be inside her.

Greg climaxed in an embarrassingly short time, his knees shaking as he clung to her. When he could breathe again he slowly lowered her until she was standing. "I am so sorry, honey. I didn't mean to act like a caveman. I just—"

She put her fingers over his lips. "Don't apologize, please." She leaned down and scooped up her torn panties.

He'd screwed up, big-time. "Look. I'll replace them. I can't believe that I—"

"Come on. I think we'd be more comfortable without so many clothes on." She turned and led him into her bedroom.

Greg wasted no time stripping off his clothes. She was reaching for the zipper in the back of her dress when he leaned over and quickly unzipped it. She shrugged and it fell off her shoulders and pooled around her feet. She hadn't worn a bra. None of it detracted from her beauty.

She glanced down at the scar from her surgery. "Not a pretty sight, I'm afraid," she said, and he realized he'd been staring at her.

"You're beautiful. I'm so sorry you had to endure all of that."

She ignored him and ran her fingers down his chest, pausing at the juncture of his thighs, her hand stroking him. "I'm happy to see you, too, big guy," she said, and leaned over and caressed him with her tongue.

That ended all conversation. Greg attempted to make up

for the time they'd been apart, or together yet not together. He brought her to a climax more than once before he let go and made a final surge within her.

He collapsed beside her and acknowledged to himself there was no way to catch up, no matter how badly he wanted to wipe out the last two years.

He dropped off to sleep and, when he woke later, realized he'd been asleep over an hour. Sherri wasn't there but he smelled coffee and knew she must be in the other room. Greg took a quick shower and dressed before going in search of the tantalizing scent.

He found Sherri in the kitchen, wrapped in a terry-cloth robe, pouring coffee into two mugs. She heard him and turned around. "I thought you might want some coffee after all."

Greg reached for the cup, chuckling. "Thanks." He took a sip before saying, "Guess tonight's my night for apologies. Sorry I fell asleep."

She leaned against the counter and watched him while she sipped on her coffee. "I didn't mind."

He sat at the bar and said, "I'd like you to move back in with me."

She shook her head. "Thank you, but no."

"No?"

"Greg, I'm no longer the naive twenty-one-year-old jumping to do your bidding. Give me a chance to deal with all of this. When I got home this evening, the very last thing I would have thought I'd be doing was not only seeing you but ending up in bed with you. I need a little space."

He shrugged. "I'm sorry. I guess I thought that—" He waved his hand toward the bedroom.

She smiled. "That all we needed was an evening of good sex to make everything all right?"

He felt sheepish. "I suppose," he said ruefully.

"I've discovered some things about me, as well, during these past several months. I know now that in the past I've made most of my decisions with my heart instead of my head."

"And your head is telling you…what?"

"To take this slow."

He smiled. "You call the last couple of hours taking it slow? I think I broke some kind of record racing you to the finish line!"

"What happened tonight has been building up between us since you came back into my life. Both of us wanted it and both of us are consenting adults. I'm just not ready to make a commitment to you at this point. I need to deal with some things that I harbored before I can be free of them. We have time to decide what we want in the future."

"I already know."

"But you don't really know me anymore. We didn't spend much time together while I stayed with you. I think we need to get reacquainted. I'd like to get to know this new, introspective person you've become."

"I'm still the same person. And you… I know you like I know my own body."

"Exactly. Physically, you know me well. However, in other ways you don't know me at all. I tried so hard to conform to what you wanted during our marriage that I became an extension of you. I won't do that again."

He ran his hand through his hair in frustration. Of course she was right. He just hadn't wanted to say goodbye tonight. He'd wanted to go to sleep with her in his arms.

"So. What next? We continue to date and have great sex?"

She looked at him, her amusement at his impatience obvious. Then she took in a big breath and sighed. "I love you,

Greg Hogan. I always have. Leaving you was hell. Seeing you again was sheer torture, reminding me of what I had missed in my life. Love wasn't enough to keep us together before. I think we need to take some time now to work out issues we may still have...that we've never discussed before...before we jump into something."

He finished his coffee and stood. "You're probably right," he finally conceded.

"Thank you for understanding."

He walked over to her and draped his arms around her. He scattered light kisses over her face. With a mock sigh he leaned back and looked at her. "Somehow, I feel so used. All you want from me is sex." Her mouth dropped open and he laughed. "Guess I needed to say that. I feel much better now." He gave her a resounding kiss and stepped back. "See ya around, kid. Gimme a call whenever you need a little tune-up."

"Greg!" She was fighting not to laugh. "Go home, get some rest. As long as you understand that you're my stud-on-call, we should get along great."

Darn woman. Always had to have the last word.

Eighteen

Greg drove home on autopilot. He'd been relieved when Sherri had agreed to have dinner with him. She'd understood how difficult it was for him to face his mistakes and admit them to her. She'd been open and compassionate with him, which he hadn't deserved but had desperately needed.

Sherri had made passionate love with him and he'd taken that as a signal that, with their new understanding, they would pick up where they'd left off in their relationship.

He'd never been more wrong. She didn't trust him. The realization had leveled him, but it wasn't the gut-wrenching pain he'd felt when she'd left him. At least she was willing to try. It gave him insight on how she must have felt when she didn't believe that he had trusted her.

He knew she was susceptible to him; she'd admitted as much. But something told him she'd resent him using her feelings for him to manipulate her into coming back to him.

You've got one chance, buster. Don't blow it.

Would he ever get enough of making love to her? He doubted that very much. So how did he handle the present situation? Somehow he didn't think she'd continue to make love to him without a commitment, one she wasn't willing to make right away, which meant...what?

He pulled into the garage and walked into the home that had seemed so empty after she'd moved out. He knew that when his parents were here, she'd been teasing him by telling them that they planned to have a family, but he was serious about having a home and children with Sherri. Even though he didn't think he'd be all that great a father—he certainly didn't want to be like *his* father—he knew that he would work at it by allowing himself to open up and love his children and, most of all, listen to them as individuals.

She'd been right. He had been closed off from her, arrogantly believing that she didn't need to know about his history with his family and why he'd cut himself off from them. So, yes, he'd withheld major parts of his life—and himself—from her.

He'd been an ass. Man, did he hate to admit that to himself. He'd been so blasted self-righteous. The consequence of his behavior was her lack of trust in him. Getting her to agree to marry him, to trust him, to believe in him, would be challenging, but he had no choice. He didn't want to spend the rest of his life without her.

Greg went upstairs to bed. Not that he expected to sleep. His thoughts would no doubt keep him awake for most of the night. He lay in the dark, his hands behind his head.

When the phone rang sometime later he immediately thought of Sherri. Was she lying awake, too?

"This is Greg," he said gruffly.

"Hello, Gregory. This is your mother."

"Well. Hello."

"I wanted to let you know that your father is in the hospital."

"What happened?"

"He was at the office talking with one of his aides when he crumpled. Thank goodness the aide stopped him from falling to the floor. They called an ambulance. I've been at the hospital all afternoon and evening. They're keeping him for the next couple of days. They want to run several tests to figure out what is going on. I just got home and thought I should notify you. I know it would be too much to ask of you to come see him, but I thought you would want to know."

"Is he conscious?"

"Oh, yes! And demanding to go home, threatening to fire whoever called the ambulance from the office."

Greg chuckled. "Sounds like everything's normal, then. As a matter of fact, Sherri and I were discussing coming to visit. She's working now and we won't be able to come until the weekend. Will that be all right?"

"Oh, Greg," Katrina said, her voice breaking. "Thank you. I know he'd be pleased to see you."

"Not a chance of that, but there are some things I want to discuss with him."

"Not if you're going to upset him. He doesn't need any more stress than what he's dealing with right now."

"Give me a little credit, okay? I'm not going to charge in there and tell him off."

"Well, since you haven't spoken to him in years, you may forgive me for my concerns."

Greg paused, trying to think of something to reassure his mother regarding his motives. Finally, he said, "I'd really like to see him."

"Shall I send someone to meet you at the airport?"

"No. I'll rent a car. We'll be in either late Friday or Saturday morning." He could only hope Sherri would be willing to go with him such a short time after he'd asked her.

"Well." His mother hesitated. "Just in case you decide not to come, I'll not mention the possibility of your visit to your father."

He grinned. The truth was that his mother didn't want to deal with his father's reaction to the idea of Greg showing up. He had no doubt that his father would not want to see him.

"Thanks for calling. I'll be in touch."

The persistent sound of a phone ringing somewhere nearby finally brought Sherri out of a deep sleep. She fumbled for the phone without bothering to turn on a light.

"H'lo?"

There was only silence.

Figured. It was either a wrong number or a crank call. "Hello?" she said again, ready to hang up.

"My timing stinks, I know. I'll call back in the morning," Greg said.

She sat up in bed. "Greg? Why are you calling?"

Again, there was silence. Finally, he said with obvious reluctance, "Do you remember the favor I asked from you at dinner?"

"We talked about a lot of things, Greg."

"About visiting my family."

"Oh. Yes. Do I have to decide tonight?"

"My mother called just now to say my father is in the hospital."

"Oh, no! What's wrong? Is he going to be okay?"

"They're running tests to find out. I told her I'd be up there this weekend. I'm hoping you'll go with me."

She dropped back onto her pillow. She was more than half-asleep and he wanted an answer *now?*

She sighed. She'd led such a calm, simple life before her accident. She'd felt in control of her life, content with her home, her job, her very existence. The only constant in her life since then was Lucifer, who at the moment was making it clear that his sleep had been disturbed and that he was far from happy.

She rubbed her forehead.

"Sherri? You still there?"

Oh, to heck with it. One more opportunity to learn more about Greg. "I'm here. And yes, if we can leave after work on Friday, I'll go."

He made no effort to disguise his sigh of relief. "I'll make the arrangements and call you with the information tomorrow."

"'Night, Greg."

"Thanks, Sherri. Go back to sleep."

She hung up the phone and did just that.

As soon as they left the airport on Saturday morning and headed toward Greg's former home, Sherri felt as though she'd stepped into another universe. She'd never visited the northeast before. It was nothing like Texas.

She gazed at the scenery and, after a while, at the homes. They were huge and each sat in solitary splendor. She couldn't imagine living in a home that could double as a hotel.

Greg slowed and turned into the driveway of one of those homes. The landscaping added to the overall sense of stately living and old money.

"How old is the house?"

"At least a hundred years. It was my mother's family home. Millie grew up here and lived here until she married. The family updated it periodically, adding all the latest conveniences."

"I thought your father might have bought it."

"Not a chance. He definitely married into money and never looked back."

"So your parents' marriage wasn't a love match?"

"It was definitely a love match as far as Mother was concerned. Who knows what Father thought or felt." He stopped in front of steps leading to the front door. "So. Here we are."

"How long has it been since you've been here?"

"Since I went into the police academy."

"You really were angry."

"I suppose. As far as I know, my father disinherited me once I left."

"You don't know?"

"I know my father. He never threatens…he acts. He said I'd never get another cent of his money. I believe him."

Sherri couldn't understand a family like that. She would have given everything to have her parents still alive. There was no way she could have gone so long without seeing them.

"How sad," she finally said.

He got out of the car and went around to open the door for her. He helped her out and said, "I suppose. I was just relieved to be out from under his thumb."

Once at the door, Greg rang the bell. When the door opened, he broke into a big grin. "Hello, Maribeth. How's my favorite girl?" He hugged the slim, elderly woman and gave her a smacking kiss on the cheek.

She stared at him as though seeing a ghost. "Gregory?"

"In the flesh."

"Come in, come in. No sense standing here with the door open. I can't believe my eyes," she said, closing the door behind them. While the two chatted, Sherri took the opportunity to survey her surroundings. The foyer was triple the size of the one in Greg's home, with priceless artwork hanging on the walls and sculptures on pedestals.

Greg said, "Forgive my manners, Maribeth. This is my wife, Sherri. Sherri, Maribeth practically raised me." He looked back at the older woman. "I am so glad to know you're still here."

"Where else would I be? My family has worked for yours for years and years. My granddaughter started working here in the kitchen just last summer."

"Amazing," Greg replied.

"Come. Your mother and father are in the dining room, having breakfast. Would you like something?"

"I'd love to have breakfast and lots of coffee. How about you?" he asked Sherri, hugging her to him.

He appeared comfortable pretending they were still married. She wished she could feel the same. "Yes, thank you."

"I'll get it ready," Maribeth said. "I believe you know where to find the dining room."

"I'll manage somehow." Greg took Sherri's hand. "Ready?"

"I suppose." She knew he recognized her reluctance.

He led her toward the back of the foyer and turned down a hallway. She'd better start leaving bread crumbs behind in order not to get lost. At last he came to a swinging door and pushed it open.

"Oh, good. Maribeth, could you bring us some—"

Katrina had her back to the door and only saw them as they came farther into the room.

"Dear God!" Max said. "I must be dying. Why else would you show up?"

"Nonsense, Max," Katrina replied. "Can't your oldest son come to visit you without a reason?"

"No." He pushed back his chair and stood. Greg walked over

to him and they shook hands. It was definitely a Kodak moment. "Sit down and have some breakfast," Max said. "I'll ring Maribeth and have her—"

"She's already on it. She answered the door when we arrived."

"Didn't hear the damn thing. My hearing must be going."

Sherri had been taking in the room. The place could be a museum. The table could comfortably seat five on each side and yet Max and Katrina sat at opposite ends of the table. They probably used cell phones to communicate with each other.

Sherri sat next to Greg, near his mother.

"The cast is gone from your leg," Katrina said, stating the obvious.

"Yes."

"Well…I'm glad to see you're well again."

Maribeth came in with two steaming plates and a large carafe of coffee on a tray.

She set the plates in front of them, placed the cups on the table and filled them with coffee. "Is there anything else you need?"

While Greg said no, Sherri stared at her plate in dismay. She could use a hollow leg or an additional stomach if she was expected to eat everything on the platter in front of her.

She had a choice of scrambled eggs, bacon, sausage, ham, hash browns and French toast.

Sherri glanced at Greg, who was eating from his similar plate with a great deal of gusto. She looked at Katrina's plate and saw that she had been eating toast and fruit. Did Maribeth think she was a lumberjack?

Sherri picked up her fork and made a valiant effort to eat as much as she could.

After breakfast, the four of them went into a room that was beautifully decorated and yet looked lived-in. Sherri hadn't realized that she'd literally been holding her breath until her chest hurt. She hurriedly exhaled.

Katrina and Max claimed matching recliners and she and Greg sat on the sofa across from them. There was a huge plasma television hanging on one of the walls. A basket of knitting sat beside Katrina's chair. She reached into the basket and pulled out her knitting. Her hands stayed busy as Max said, "Don't mean to sound rude, but why, after all these years, did you decide to come back here? Oh. Wait. Katrina called you, didn't she?"

"Yes, Mother called me but we were already planning to come. We just moved the trip up."

"All right. You're here. Now tell me why."

Sherri waited with the other three to hear Greg's answer.

Greg leaned forward, propping his elbows on his knees. "I've been doing a lot of thinking since you were in Austin. I took a hard look at myself and discovered that everything I've done to live my own life hasn't worked because I'm just like you. So wherever I am and whatever I do, you're there. I figured since that was the case, I might want to get to know you better."

Max stared at him in surprise. He looked at Katrina. "I'm not certain, but I think I've just been insulted."

Katrina rolled her eyes. "He's your son, Max. Of course he's just like you. He always has been. I have no doubt that he's a workaholic who bottles up his thoughts and emotions just like you, that he's got to control everything around him and that he keeps himself aloof from the world."

Max looked from Katrina to Greg. "Did you two plan this?"

Greg shook his head. He smiled. "Like it or not, we're very much alike. To dislike you means I dislike myself. I set out to be the exact opposite of you. Instead, I became you." He grinned at Max.

"Well, hell. I don't know what to think. You'd think if we were alike, we'd get along."

"We did. Until I became an adult and decided I didn't want the life you'd planned for me."

"Kyle didn't mind taking your place."

"Then you should be happy."

Max shrugged. "I'm always happy." He sat there wearing his perpetual scowl.

Greg laughed and before long Katrina joined him. As amused as Sherri was, she didn't want him to think she was laughing at him.

"Have you looked into a mirror recently?" Greg asked.

The corners of Max's mouth lifted. "Not if I can avoid it."

"Take my word for it. You look far from happy. I'm here because I need to know you better without wearing filters from the past."

"Humph."

"So…Sherri and I plan to spend the day and night with you and fly back to Austin tomorrow afternoon."

Max raised his eyebrows. "Well, well. I dare say it will be an interesting weekend."

"So what's the deal with your health?"

"There's not a blasted thing wrong with me."

"Actually," Katrina said calmly, "that isn't true, but we'll leave that alone for now. Just enjoy your time together."

Nineteen

Sherri was asleep when Greg slipped into bed with her late that night. His cold hands and feet immediately woke her.

"Hey! Your hands are freezing."

"I know. I thought you'd take pity on me and get me warm."

She turned to face him. "Was this your room growing up?"

She couldn't see his expression in the dark. "Probably."

"You mean you don't know?"

"I wasn't paying any attention. Do you have any idea how many bedrooms there are in the place?"

"At least eight."

"At least." He pulled her closer and nibbled on her ear.

Sherri had known before they left Austin that they would probably be sharing a room this weekend. She had tried not to think about it, but it was obvious that Greg had making love to her very much on his mind.

Her thoughts scattered when he kissed her. When he

paused for a moment, he said, "I feel wicked having sex in my parents' home with someone I'm not married to." He kissed her again. "Deliciously wicked."

"I'm sure you've had sex many times when you weren't married."

"Not here and not since we broke up."

She stilled. "Are you saying you haven't made love to anyone since the divorce?"

"I didn't say I was proud of it. It's just a fact. How about you? Or am I being much too personal?"

"I haven't been on a *date* since our divorce, much less hopped into bed with anyone."

He kissed her again, a long, drugging kiss. "I'm glad," he whispered when they finally paused for air. "I want this to work between us this time. I'll do whatever I have to do to make it work."

He cupped her breast and groaned. "You always have too many clothes on when we're in bed," he grumbled. One of his familiar complaints when they'd been married. He'd wanted her to sleep in the nude, but it was hard to break a habit of a lifetime.

She sat up and pulled her gown over her head before stretching out beside him.

"Mmm. Much better." He tugged on one of her nipples with his mouth. "Much, much better. You taste so sweet."

She couldn't lie still. She moved against him, brushing against his erection. With a deft move he slid her beneath him and entered her in one long surge. She groaned with pleasure.

"Did I hurt you? Am I rushing things?"

"No and no." She held on to him as he set a slow, steady rhythm, taking his time and driving her crazy. She met each thrust, wanting him so badly she thought she'd die from it.

Toward the end he stepped up the pace and they reached a

climax at the same time. Clutching each other, they rode the pleasurable sensations until their hearts stopped racing.

Sherri thought Greg had fallen to sleep when he said, "I'm glad we made the trip."

"How did things go with your father?"

"Better than I expected. I'm sorry I didn't spend more time with you today."

"Now that would have been silly, since you specifically made the trip to talk with him."

"Did Mother entertain you?"

Sherri was grateful for the dark. She didn't want Greg to see her grinning. "Why, yes, she was the perfect hostess. She showed me around the house and gave me the history of it. We did a tour of the gardens and she told me how old they were and…" Wasn't that enough?

"And what?"

"Oh, she told me all about her plans for you to marry one of the debutantes in her circle and made it subtly clear that I didn't deserve you."

He groaned. "Do you want me to say something to her?"

She laughed. She couldn't help it. "Greg. Your mother made it clear how she felt about me in your life when she first met me."

"I don't want her being rude to you."

"She wasn't. She was the personification of the great lady dealing with a member of the lower class. It was all I could do not to laugh."

"You weren't offended?"

"How could I be? She's an absolute stereotype of a person born into privilege and wealth. Almost a caricature, come to think of it. I can't imagine you having a mother like that."

"I saw very little of her when I was a child. Maribeth raised me, doing her best to turn me into something resembling a gentleman. I barely knew my mother. She was the lady who flitted in and out of my life, absently patting me on the head whenever she happened to run across me."

"Greg! That's awful."

"It was normal to me."

"So her opinion of me doesn't make a difference to you?"

"Are you kidding? Now, Maribeth not liking you would have given me pause. Fortunately for any future we might have together, Maribeth thought I'd made an excellent choice. She said she was so pleased that I'd ignored the overbred young ladies Mother tried so hard to foist on me. Her word— *foist*. I thought it rather apt."

Sherri settled her head on his shoulder. "Then the trip has been a success for you," she said, yawning. "Good."

"Having you with me was the best part."

The following Monday was a typical day at the office. Sherri considered it more on the level of controlled chaos. She ignored it and focused on her writing.

One of the women who worked there stopped by her desk that afternoon. "You're certainly cheerful today, considering it's a Monday. You must have had a great weekend."

"I did."

"What did you do?"

"Flew to Connecticut with my ex-husband to see his parents."

The woman's jaw dropped. "That's your idea of fun? My idea of a fun time with my ex would be watching him being washed away by a tidal wave." She looked at Sherri more closely. "I didn't know you were divorced."

"I am."

"And you're spending time with your ex? Doesn't that sort of defeat the purpose of getting the divorce?"

"Probably, but I always believe in second chances...for every-body."

"Better you than me, honey. I'm thrilled at the idea that I will never have to see my ex again." She gave Sherri a little wave and left.

The thing was, Greg was no longer the man she'd been married to. If nothing else, the weekend had changed him in some indefinable way. His father didn't seem any different to her. Whatever he and Greg talked about would be between them, but Greg acted as though a weight had been lifted from his shoulders.

He'd been in a teasing mood all the way back to Austin and she'd laughed more than she had in years. He'd taken her back to her apartment, given her a smacking kiss and told her he'd call her sometime today.

He'd been happier than she'd ever seen him. She was pleased for him.

When Sherri left the building a week later she saw Greg waiting for her in the parking lot. He was leaning against his car in a familiar pose and wearing his leather jacket with the fur collar turned up. As soon as he saw her he started toward her.

Some woman behind her said, "Boy oh boy, would I like some hunk to be looking at *me* that way!"

As soon as he reached her side, he gave her a bear hug and said, "I thought I'd give you a ride home. Save you standing out in the wind and cold waiting for a bus."

She smiled up at him, feeling a surge of love for him that she'd once thought would never return. "Thank you."

"I also have Hannah making dinner for two tonight. How does that sound?"

"I like it. No cooking for me tonight."

He hustled her to the car and carefully closed the door behind her before getting inside.

"Mmm. The car is warm."

He looked over at her and smiled. "I planned it that way."

"If I didn't know better, I'd think you were planning to seduce me later."

"My intentions are much more honorable."

"That's good to know."

He leaned over and lifted her chin slightly and kissed her…a slow, sweet, heartwarming gesture that made no demands.

She sighed when he pulled away. "And hello to you, too."

He laughed. "Do you need to go by your apartment first?"

She thought for a minute. "Well, I need to feed Lucifer. Otherwise, he'll give me nothing but trouble when I get home later."

"It's the darnedest thing, but I actually miss that cat," he said, pulling into the street.

"No way."

"I know. Surprises me. I don't seem to be allergic to him. He's got a distinct personality all his own."

"Without a doubt."

"So we'll go by and feed him and then go to my place."

They were greeted at the door with a litany of complaints about the weather, the dog in the next apartment and the fact that Lucifer's food bowl was empty.

Greg leaned against the counter with his feet crossed and arms folded, watching her routine with her furry feline friend. Once she'd fed him, she said, "As you can see, I'm no longer important in his life. He probably won't notice I've left."

At Greg's home, Hannah greeted her with pleasure, commenting on how well she'd healed since the summer.

Greg asked Sherri, "Care for a glass of wine before dinner?"

"Sounds good." They took their drinks into the den, which

had a cozy fire going. "Everything looks so different here in the winter."

"I like coming home to it, winter or summer."

"I can certainly understand that."

They sat in the two high-backed chairs in front of the fireplace. Greg knew her favorite wine. Let's face it, he knew more about her than any other living human being. She found that almost comforting.

"How are things at work?" she asked after they'd sat staring into the fire for a while. If they didn't start talking, she was going to fall asleep right there.

He smiled. "My boss got transferred today so all is right with my little world."

"You didn't like him very much, did you?"

"Actually, it was the other way around. He thinks his suspicions have been confirmed—I'm really after his job."

"Are you?"

"Absolutely not. I like my job."

"So who will be your next boss?"

He shrugged. "Who knows? I don't really care. I do what I do and I'm good at it. Most people would be pleased to have someone like that working for them."

Hannah appeared in the doorway. "Dinner is ready."

Greg stood and offered his hand to Sherri. "Shall we?"

He led her into the dining room and the alcove where they usually ate. Candles sparkled and were reflected in the windows. "Everything looks so nice, Hannah," Sherri said.

"Thank you."

She served soup and later salad before bringing out their main course.

"I hadn't realized how hungry I was until I smelled the succulent roast beef," she said to Greg. "The woman is amazing."

"That she is." He picked up the bottle of wine and refilled their glasses. Handing Sherri her glass, he said, "I propose a toast."

"Sounds good." She touched the rim of her glass to his.

"To your continued good health and to us," he said.

She looked into his gorgeous eyes that reflected the candle-light and said, "Thank you," and took a sip of her wine.

By the time they finished dinner Sherri was full and relaxed. Hannah cleared the table and brought them each a small cup of crème brûlée and coffee.

"I'm not sure I can eat another bite."

"There's not much there. Eat whatever you want."

She ate the dessert and groaned with pleasure. When she finished, she reached for her cup of coffee.

"Sherri, do you remember leaving your wedding rings on the kitchen counter the day you left?"

She dropped her hand to the table. "I remember everything about that day."

"You'd put them in the box they came in and I almost tossed it away, thinking it was empty."

She could think of nothing to say.

"I wanted to start over completely with you." He pulled out a small box. "I hope you like it."

Sherri took the box, her hand trembling. She opened it and tears filled her eyes.

The ring was a vividly green emerald surrounded by diamonds. "I wanted to match your eyes," he said quietly.

She looked at him, the tears running down her cheeks, and reached for his hand. "I don't know how to thank you."

"I do. Will you marry me?"

"Oh, Greg, this is so beautiful."

"I want you to have it. I hope that you'll consider it an en-gagement ring, but if not, I still want you to have it."

"Of course—" her voice broke "—of course I'll marry you. I can't imagine my life without you in it."

He came around the table and took her hands, pulling her up and into him. The kiss he gave her spoke to her on a deep and emotional level. When it ended, he said, "This time, we'll do it any way you want. Anywhere you want. Any month or year you want. I came close to losing you completely after the accident and I know I don't want to live on the planet without your being here, even if I never see you again." Greg's eyes were moist, as well.

She smiled. "Thank you for that. I've had an idea about how I wanted our next wedding to go, since we were married by the justice of the peace the first time."

"Whatever you want, sweetheart. Whatever you want."

Epilogue

Spring still hadn't reached New England the following April. Mother Nature had saved her most severe weather for early spring. Not that Sherri minded. The church was well-heated. Greg's sister-in-law, Marsha, had helped her dress. She would be Sherri's only attendant this morning. Kyle, Marsha's husband and Greg's brother, was his best man.

"You look like a fairy-tale princess," Marsha said. "You just glow."

"I'm happy."

"I'm glad. I didn't want Katrina's attitude toward the wedding to be upsetting to you."

"Not in the least. She's being honest and I like that in anyone."

"Do you think she'll be here?"

"I have no idea."

There was a tap on the door. "Ready?" a muffled male voice asked.

Marsha opened the door for Sherri and followed her out of the room, carefully holding her train.

Sherri looked up at Max. "This time around, I'm completely ready."

Katrina had been horrified to discover that Sherri and Greg had been divorced when she'd met Sherri. She couldn't believe their deception. So when Greg called to tell her that they would like to have their wedding in the church he'd attended growing up, she'd been incensed with him. She'd declared she would have nothing to do with any of it and she had kept her word.

"Thank you for walking me down the aisle," Sherri said, taking Max's hand.

"Thank you for asking me. I know I can never replace your father, but I have a hunch he's right here with us today."

She hugged him. "I hope so."

When it was time for her to enter, the organ music that had been playing softly in the background changed into a processional and everyone in the church stood. Sherri was amazed to see that the place was packed.

"Who are all these people?" she whispered to Max.

"Family and friends, business associates, the curious."

She nodded, even though she didn't understand. Who had contacted them about the wedding? She had thought it would be a private wedding.

She and Max walked slowly down the aisle toward Greg and Kyle. Sherri couldn't decide who had a bigger grin on his face. Both looked like Max. She couldn't help grinning back at them.

They reached the pastor and stopped. After his opening remarks and a prayer, the pastor asked who gave Sherri to Greg to be married. Max, in a stentorian voice said, "Every member of the Hogan clan, myself included."

Everyone in the congregation laughed.

The rest of the wedding went according to plan. She and Greg had written vows that were deeply personal to them, but Sherri no longer cared if others heard them. Their vows had come out of their pain and loneliness for each other after their first marriage had ended. The vows were filled with hope and new promises that they fully intended to honor and when the pastor told them that they were now legally husband and wife, and told Greg he could kiss his bride, Greg wrapped his arms around her and kissed her as though no one else was in the room.

Once again the congregation stood, laughed and applauded.

Greg turned her and faced those who were there. It was then that Sherri saw Katrina standing next to Max—who was beaming as though he'd just acquired several more companies—daintily wiping her eyes with an embroidered handkerchief.

Sherri and Greg walked back up the aisle until they reached the narthex of the church, where they were surrounded by well-wishers. Greg leaned over and whispered in her ear, "You and Mother have something in common besides marrying a Hogan. You were both pregnant brides." He gave her a wicked smile.

"Somehow I doubt that she'll be thrilled by that piece of information."

"Who cares?" He picked her up and twirled her around. "Dad's going to be happy to add another grandchild to the family."

"Dad?" she whispered.

He grinned. "He said he was tired of being called Father."

It was then that Max and Katrina walked up to greet them. Greg put Sherri back on her feet and grabbed his father's hand with both of his. "Way to go, Dad. I was proud of you."

Max's eyes danced. He nodded toward Sherri and said to Greg. "You got yourself a good one, son. Try not to screw it up again," and hugged first Greg and then Sherri. When he stepped back from her, he said, "Welcome to the family, sweetheart. If he gives you any grief, let me know and I'll straighten him out for you."

"Oh, Max," Katrina said irritably. "You're holding up the line. We'll see them at the reception."

Greg leaned over and kissed Katrina's cheek. "Be thinking up some good names for your next grandchild, Mother. We'll need them by October."

Her eyes widened. She looked at both Greg and Sherri and then at Max. "Did you know about this?" she whispered.

Max shook his head. "Not a word. Guess there was no help for it, then. Greg knew I'd horsewhip him if he didn't do right by this little lady."

Katrina suddenly looked very vulnerable. "Just like my father threatened to do to you."

Max threw his arm around her and kissed her. "What he never knew was that I would have married you whether he approved or not. Greg being on the way was the greatest thing that could have happened to us. It meant that you would marry me when I didn't have two dimes to rub together. You always said it didn't matter to you, which was another reason I was so crazy about you!"

"You were?" she repeated, sounding shaken.

Max sobered. "You mean you didn't know?"

Katrina shook her head.

Max took her hand and said to Greg, "I'll meet you two newlyweds at the reception. Don't wait for us. We may be running a little late." He turned to Katrina and said, "Come with me. I can see I need to give you some convincing of my love for you." He started walking toward the entrance of the church while Katrina, a rosy red, followed him.

Greg looked at Sherri and chuckled. "Looks like there'll be more than one couple having a second honeymoon tonight. Let's go to the reception and get something to eat. I'm starving. And I'll need all my strength for later."

As others stopped by to wish the couple well they spoke to a beaming groom and a very blushing bride.

* * * * *

IAN'S ULTIMATE GAMBLE

by
Brenda Jackson

Dear Reader,

It is with great pleasure that I bring you another Westmorelands love story. After officially introducing Ian to you in *Riding the Storm* – Storm Westmoreland's story – Ian has constantly been on my mind. I think that it is time for him to turn in his player's card.

I love writing stories of former lovers reuniting, and for Ian I thought this would be the perfect way to mend his wounded heart. He thinks he broke off his affair with Brooke Chamberlain for all the right reasons. But when their paths cross again four years later, he is forced to deal with sexually charged memories and the lingering emotions that he can't put to rest. The question of the hour is, does he really want to? Ian is left wondering if he acted too hastily in ending things with Brooke.

And just like the Westmoreland men before him, Ian has to learn a hard lesson about love – some things are just meant to be.

I hope you enjoy Ian and Brooke's journey back to never-ending love.

Enjoy,

Brenda Jackson

BRENDA JACKSON

is a die "heart" romantic who married her
childhood sweetheart and still proudly wears
the "going steady" ring he gave her when she
was fifteen. Because she's always believed in
the power of love, Brenda's stories always have
happy endings. In her real-life love story, Brenda
and her husband live in Jacksonville, Florida,
and have two sons.

A *USA TODAY* bestselling author, Brenda
divides her time between family, writing and
working in management at a major insurance
company. You may write to Brenda at PO Box
28267, Jacksonville, Florida 32226, USA, by
e-mail at WriterBJackson@aol.com or visit her
website at www.brendajackson.net.

To Gerald Jackson, Sr, my husband and hero.

To all my readers who love the Westmorelands.

To my Heavenly Father who gave me
the gift to write.

Happy is the man that findeth wisdom,
and the man that getteth understanding.
—*Proverbs 3:13*

Prologue

"I won't do it, Malcolm!" Brooke Chamberlain said sharply as she absently pushed a dark-brown dread that had fallen in her face back behind her ear. If she'd had any kind of warning of the reason she'd been summoned to her boss's office, she would have found an excuse not to come.

As far as she was concerned what he was asking her to do was totally unacceptable. First, she had just come off one assignment, where a successful vineyard had been caught producing more than vintage wine, and second, he wanted her to go back out west and literally spy on the one man who hated her guts—Ian Westmoreland.

Malcolm Price rubbed a frustrated hand down his face before saying, "Sit down, Brooke, and let me explain why I decided to give the assignment to you."

Brooke gave an unladylike snort. As far as she was concerned there was nothing he could explain. Malcolm was more than just her boss. He was a good friend and had been since their early days with the Bureau when he'd been a fellow agent. Because they had been good friends, he was one of the few people who knew of her past relationship with Ian as well as the reason they had parted ways.

"How can you of all people ask me to do that to Ian, Malcolm?" she said, pacing the room as she spoke, refusing to do as he'd asked and sit down.

"Because if you don't, Walter Thurgood will be assigned to do it."

She stopped moving. "Thurgood?"

"Yes, and once he is, it will be out of my hands."

Brooke sat down in the chair Malcolm had offered her earlier. Walter Thurgood, a hotshot upstart, had been with the Bureau for a couple of years. The man had big goals, and one was to be the top man at the FBI. After several assignments he'd earned the reputation of being one of those agents who got the job done, although there were times when how he'd gone about it had been questionable.

"And even if Ian Westmoreland is clean, by the time Thurgood finishes with him, he'll make him seem like the dirtiest man on this planet if it makes Thurgood look good," Malcolm said with disgust in his voice.

Brooke knew Malcolm was right. And she also knew what Malcolm wasn't saying—that when you were the son of someone already at the top, the people around you were less likely to spank your hand when you behaved improperly.

"But if you think Ian is running a clean operation and you don't suspect him of anything, why the investigation?" she asked.

"Only because the prior owner of the casino, Bruce Aiken, was found guilty of running an illegal betting operation there, and we don't want any of his old friends to come out from whatever rock they hid under during Aiken's trial and start things up again without Westmorland's knowledge. So in a way you'll be doing him a big favor."

Brooke's gaze dropped from Malcolm's to study her hands, clenched in her lap. Ian would not see things that way, and both of them knew it. It would only widen the gap of mistrust between them. But still, she knew there was no way she could allow Thurgood to go in and handle things. It would be downright disastrous for Ian.

She lifted her head and met Malcolm's gaze once again. "And this is not an official investigation?"

"No. You'll be there for a much-needed vacation, while keeping your eyes and ears open."

She leaned forward as anger flared in her eyes. "Ian is one of the most honest men I know."

"In that case you don't have anything to worry about."

She stared at Malcolm thoughtfully for a moment and then said. "Okay."

Malcolm lifted a dark brow. "That means you're going to do it?"

She narrowed her eyes. She was caught between a rock and a hard place and they both knew it. "You knew I would."

He nodded and she saw another certainty in the depths of his dark blue eyes. The knowledge that four years after their breakup she was still in love with Ian Westmoreland.

One

Ian Westmoreland sat at his desk, knee-deep in paper-work, when for no apparent reason he felt a quick tightening in his gut. He was a man who by thirty-three had learned to trust his intuition as well as his deductive reasoning. He lifted his head to glance at the wood-paneled wall in front of him.

He reached out, pressed a button and watched as the paneling slid back to reveal a huge glass wall. The people on the other side who were busy wandering through the casino, taking their chances at the slot machines, gambling tables and arcades, had no idea they were being watched. In certain areas of the casino they were being listened to, as well. More than once the security monitors had picked up conversations best left unheard. But when you operated a casino as large as the Rolling Cascade, the monitors and one-sided mirror

were in place for security reasons. Not everyone who
came to a casino was there to play. There were those
who came to prey on the weaknesses of others, and
those were the ones his casino could do without. His
huge surveillance room on the third floor, manned by
top-notch security experts viewing over a hundred
monitors twenty-four hours a day, made sure of it.

Since the grand opening, a lot of people had made
reservations merely to check out the newly remodeled
casino and resort and to verify the rumors that what
had once been a dying casino had been brought back to
life in unprecedented style. People Magazine had announced in a special edition that the Rolling Cascade
had brought an ambience of Las Vegas to Lake Tahoe
and had done it with class, integrity and decorum.

Ian stood and moved around to sit on the corner of
his desk, his eyes sharp and assessing as he scanned the
crowd. There had to have been a reason he was feeling
uptight. The grand opening had been a success and he
was glad he'd made the move from riverboat captain to
casino owner with ease.

A few minutes later he was about to give up, consider
his intuition as having an off day and get back to work,
when he saw her.

Brooke Chamberlain.

He stood as his entire body got tense. What the hell
was she doing here? Deciding he wasn't going to waste
time trying to figure that out, he reached back to the
phone on his desk. His call was quickly answered by the
casino's security manager.

"Yes, Ian?"

"There's a woman standing at the east-west blackjack table wearing a powder-blue pantsuit. Please escort her to my office immediately."

There was a pause when his security manager asked a question. And in a tight voice Ian responded, "Yes, I know her name. It's Brooke Chamberlain."

After hanging up the phone, his full attention went back to the woman he'd once come pretty damn close to asking to be his wife…before her betrayal. The last time he'd seen her had been three years ago in Atlanta at his cousin Dare's wedding. Since she'd once worked for Sheriff Dare Westmoreland as one of his deputies, she'd been invited, and Ian had deliberately ignored her.

But not this time. She was on his turf and he intended to let her know it.

Ian was watching her.

Brooke wasn't sure from where but the federal agent in her knew how. Video monitors. The place was full of them, positioned so discreetly she doubted the crowd of people who were eager to play the odds knew they were on camera.

"Excuse me, Ms. Chamberlain?"

Brooke turned to stare into the face of a tall, husky-looking man in his late forties with blond hair and dark blue eyes. "Yes?"

"I'm Vance Parker, head of security for the casino. The owner of this establishment, Ian Westmoreland, would like a few words with you in his office."

Brooke's lips curved into a smile. She seriously doubted that Ian had just a "few words" to say to her. "All right, Mr. Parker, lead the way."

And as Vance Parker escorted her to the nearest elevator she prayed that she would be able to survive the next two weeks.

With his gaze glued to the glass, Ian had watched the exchange; had known the exact moment Vance had mentioned his name. Upon hearing it, Brooke's reaction hadn't been one of surprise, which shot to hell the possibility that she hadn't known he owned the place. She had knowingly entered the lion's den, and he was determined to find out why.

He stood and moved around his desk, suddenly feeling that knot in his gut tighten even more. And when he heard the ding, a signal that someone was on their way up in his private elevator, the feeling got worse. Although he didn't want to admit it, he was about to come face-to-face with the one woman he'd never been able to get out of his system. Whether deliberately or otherwise, during the two years they were together, Brooke had raised the bar on his expectations about women. Deputy by day and total woman at night, she had made any female that had followed in her wake seem tremendously lacking. He'd had to finally face the fact that whether he liked it or not, Brooke Chamberlain had been the ultimate woman. The one female who had robbed his appetite for other women. The one woman who'd been able to tame his wild heart.

Not only tame it, but capture it.

The memory brought a bitter smile his lips. But today he was older and wiser, and the heart she once controlled had since turned to stone. Still, that didn't stop his breath from catching in his throat when he turned at the sound of the elevator door opening.

Their gazes connected, and he acknowledged that the chemistry they'd always shared was still there. Hot. Intense. Soul stirring. He felt it, clear across the room, and when he felt the floor shake, he placed his hand on his desk to keep his balance.

This was the closest they'd been to each other since that morning when he'd found out the truth and had walked out of her apartment after their heated argument. At Dare and Shelly's wedding, Ian had kept his distance, refusing to come within ten feet of her, but those gut-wrenching vibes had been strong then, nonetheless.

Over the years it had been hard to let go of the memory of the day they'd met in Dare's office, when she'd been twenty-two. Even in her deputy uniform she had taken his breath away, just as she was doing now at twenty-eight.

Despite their separation and the circumstances that had driven him to end what he'd thought was the perfect love affair, he had to admit that in his opinion she was the most beautiful woman he'd ever set eyes on. She had skin the color of sweet almond; expressive eyes that turned various shades of brown depending on her mood; lips that could curve in a way to make every cell in his body vibrate; and the mass of dreds that came to her shoulders, which he loved holding on to each and every time he entered her body.

His hand balled into a fist at his side. The thought that Brooke could make him dredge up unwanted memories spiked his anger, and he forced his gaze away from her to Vance. "Thanks, Mr. Parker. That will be all."

Ian watched his good friend lift a curious brow and shrug big wide shoulders before turning to get back on the elevator. As soon as the elevator door closed, Ian's attention returned to Brooke. She had moved across the room and was standing with her back to him, staring at a framed photo of him and Tiger Woods and another of him and Dennis Rodman.

She surprised him when she broke the silence by saying, "I heard Tiger and Dennis have homes in this area."

Ian arched a brow. So she wanted to make small talk, did she? He shouldn't have been surprised. Brooke had a tendency to start babbling whenever she was placed in what she considered a nervous situation. He'd actually found it endearing the night of their first date. But now it was annoying as hell.

He didn't want her to make small talk. He didn't want her there, period, which brought him back to the reason she was here in his office. He wanted answers and he wanted them now.

"I didn't have Vance bring you up here to discuss the residences of Woods and Rodman. I want to know what the hell you're doing here, Brooke."

The moment of reckoning had finally arrived. Brooke had grabbed the chance to take her eyes off Ian when he'd all but ordered Vance Parker to leave them alone. Although she had prepared for this moment from the day she'd left Malcolm's office, she still wasn't totally ready for the encounter. Yet there was nothing she could do but turn around and hope that one day, if he ever found out the truth, he would forgive the lie she was about to tell.

On a sigh, she slowly turned, and the moment she did
so their eyes locked with more intensity than they had
earlier when Vance had been present. Her internal temperature suddenly shot sky high, and every cell in her
body felt fried from the sweltering heat that suddenly
consumed her.

Words momentarily failed her since Ian had literally
taken her breath away. He had always been a good-
looking man, and today, three years since she'd seen
him last, he was doubly so; especially with the neatly
trimmed beard he was sporting. He'd always had that
drop-dead-gorgeous and let-me-bed-you-before-I-die
look. He'd been a man who'd always been able to grab
the attention of women. And now this older Ian was a
man who exuded raw, masculine sexuality.

When she had returned to Atlanta to take the job as
one of Dare Westmoreland's deputies, she had heard
about the two Westmoreland cousins who were the same
age and ran together in what women had called a wolf
pack. Ian and his cousin Storm had reputations around
Atlanta of being ultimate players, the epitome of leg-
endary lovers. Storm had been dubbed the Perfect Storm
and Ian, the Perfect End.

It was rumored that any woman who went out with Ian
got the perfect ending to their evening, after sharing a bed
with him. But all that had changed when he'd begun
showing interest in her. He'd called her a hard nut to crack;
she'd been one of the few women to rebuff his charm.

Instead of willingly falling under his spell like other
women, she'd placed it on him to earn his way into her
bed. The result had been two years of being the exclusive recipient of his special brand of sexual expertise.

The rumors hadn't been wrong, but neither had they been completely right. She had discovered that not only was Ian the Perfect End but he was the Perfect Beginning as well. No one could wake a woman up each morning the way he could. The memories of their love-making sessions could still curl her toes and wet her panties. He had been her first lover and, she thought further, her only lover.

"Are you going to stand there and say nothing or are you going to answer my question, Brooke?"

Ian's question reclaimed Brooke's attention and reminded her why she was there. And with the angry tone of his voice all the memories they'd ever shared were suddenly crushed. Placing her hands on her hips she answered with the same curt tone he'd used on her. "I'll gladly answer your question, Ian."

Ian folded his arms across his chest. How could he have forgotten how quick fire could leap into her eyes whenever she got angry, or how her full and inviting lips could form one perturbed pout? Over the years he had missed that all-in-your-face, hot-tempered attitude that would flare up whenever she got really mad about something.

The women he'd dated after her had been too meek and mild for his taste. They'd lacked spunk, and if he'd said jump, they would have asked how high. But not the woman standing in front of him. She could dish it out like nobody's business and he had admired her for it. That was probably one of the reasons he had fallen so hard for her.

"The reason I'm here is like everyone else. I needed

time away from my job and decided to check in here for two weeks," she said, intruding into his thoughts.

Ian sighed. As far as he was concerned her reason sounded too pat. "Why here? There are other places you could have gone."

"Yes, and at the time I booked the two weeks I didn't know you were the owner. I thought you were still a riverboat captain."

For a few seconds he said nothing. "Hurricane Katrina brought a temporary end to that. But I'd decided to purchase this place months before then. It was just a matter of time before I came off the river to settle on land."

He studied her for a moment, then asked, "And when did you find out this place was mine?"

Brooke gave a small shrug. "A few days ago, but I figured what the hell, my money spends just as well as anyone else's, and I can't go through life worrying about bumping into you at the next corner."

She released a disgusted sigh and raked her hands through her dreads, making them tumble around her shoulders. "Oh, for heaven's sake, Ian, we have a past, and we should chalk it up as a happy or unhappy time in our lives, depending on how you chose to remember it, and move on. I heard this was a nice place and decided it was just what I needed. And to be quite honest with you I really don't appreciate being summoned up here like I'm some kind of criminal. If you're still stuck on the past and don't think we can share the same air for two weeks let me know and I can take my money elsewhere."

Anger made Ian's jaw twitch. She was right, of course—he should be able to let go and move on;

however, what really griped his insides more than anything was not the fact that they had broken up but why they had. They'd been exclusive lovers. She was the one woman he had considered marrying. But in the end she had been the woman that had broken his heart.

Even when she had moved away to D.C. to take that job with the Bureau, and he had moved to Memphis to operate the *Delta Princess,* they'd been able to maintain a long-distance romance without any problems and had decided within another year to marry.

But the one time she should have trusted him enough to confide in him about something, she hadn't. Instead she had destroyed any trust between them by not letting him know that a case she'd been assigned to investigate had involved one of his business partners. By the time he'd found out the truth, a man had lost his life and a family had been destroyed.

As far as her being here at the Rolling Cascade, he much preferred that she leave. Seeing her again and feeling his reaction to her proved one thing: even after four years she was not quite out of his system and it was time to get her out. Perhaps the first step would be proving they *could* breathe the same air.

"Fine, stay if you want, it's your decision," he finally said.

Brooke lifted her chin. Yes, it would be her decision. There was no doubt in her mind if it was left up to him, he would toss her out on her butt, possibly right smack into Lake Tahoe. "Then I'm staying. Now if you'll excuse me I want to begin enjoying my vacation."

She went to the elevator and without glancing back

at him pushed a button, and when the doors opened she stepped inside. When she turned, their gazes met again, and it was during that brief moment of eye contact before the doors swooshed closed that he thought he saw something flicker in the depths of her dark eyes. Cockiness? Regret? Lust?

Ian drew his brows together sharply. How could he move on and put things behind him when the anger he felt whenever he thought of what she'd done was still as intense as it had always been?

Moving around his desk he pushed a button. Within seconds Vance's deep voice came on the line. "Yes, Ian?"

"Ms. Chamberlain is on her way back down."

"All right. Do you want me to keep an eye on her while she's here?"

"No," Ian said quickly. For some reason the thought of someone else—especially another man—keeping an eye on Brooke didn't sit well with him. Deciding he owed his friend some sort of explanation he said, "Brooke and I have a history we need to bury."

"Figured as much."

"And another thing, Vance. She's a federal agent for the FBI."

Ian heard his friend mutter a curse word under his breath before asking, "She's here for business or pleasure?"

"She claims it's pleasure, but I'm going to keep an eye on her to be sure. For all I know, some case or another might have brought her to these parts, and depending on what, it could mean bad publicity for the Cascade."

"Wouldn't she tell you if she were here on business?"

Ian's chuckle was hard and cold. "No, she wouldn't tell me a damn thing. Loyalty isn't one of Brooke Chamberlain's strong points."

Knowing video monitors were probably watching her every move, Brooke kept her cool as she strolled through the casino to catch the elevator that connected to the suite of villas located in the resort section. All around her crowds were still flowing in, heading toward the bar, the lounge or the area lined with slot machines.

It was only moments later, after opening the door to her villa and going inside, that she gave way to her tears. The look in Ian's dark eyes was quite readable, and knowing he hated her guts was almost too much to bear. If he ever found out the real reason she was there…

She inhaled deeply and wiped her cheeks, knowing she had to check in with Malcolm. Taking the cell phone from her purse, she pressed a couple of buttons. He picked up on the second ring.

"I'm at the Rolling Cascade, Malcolm."

He evidently heard the strain in her voice and said, "I take it that you've seen Ian Westmoreland."

"Yes."

After a brief pause he said, "You know this isn't an official investigation, Brooke. Your job is to enjoy your vacation, but if you happen to see anything of interest to let us know."

"That's still spying."

"Yes, but it's beneficial to Westmoreland. You're there to help him, not hurt him."

"He won't see it that way." Her reply was faint as more

tears filled her eyes. "Look, Malcolm, I'll get back to you if there's anything. Otherwise, I'll see you in two weeks."

"Okay, and take care of yourself."

Brooke clicked off the phone and returned it to her purse. She walked through the living room and glanced around, trying to think about anything other than Ian. The resort was connected to the casino by way of elevators, and the way the villas had been built took advantage of paths for bicyclers and joggers, who thronged the wide wooden boardwalk that ran along the lake's edge. Since this was mid-April and the harsh winter was slowly being left behind, she could imagine many people would be taking advantage of those activities. The view of the mountains was fabulous, and considering all the on-site amenities, this was a very beautiful place.

After taking a tour of her quarters, she felt a combined mixture of pleasure and excitement rush through her veins. Her villa was simply beautiful, and she was certain she had found a small slice of paradise. This was definitely a place to get your groove on.

The view of Lake Tahoe through both her living room and bedroom windows was breathtaking, perfect to capture the striking colors of the sunset. Brooke was convinced the way her villa was situated among several nature trails was the loveliest spot she had ever found. This was a place where someone could come and leave their troubles behind. But for her it was a place that could actually intensify those troubles.

Pushing that thought from her mind, she once again entered her bathroom, still overwhelmed. It was just as large as the living room and resembled a private, tropical spa. This was definitely a romantic retreat, she thought, crossing the room to the Jacuzzi tub, large enough to accommodate four people comfortably. Then there was the trademark that she'd heard was in every bathroom in the villa—a waterfall that cascaded down into a beautiful fountain.

She breathed in deeply, proud of Ian and his accomplishments, and recalled the many nights they would snuggle in bed while he shared his dream of owning such a place with her. When the opportunity came for him to purchase the *Delta Princess,* a riverboat that departed from Memphis on a ten-day excursion along the Mississippi with stops in New Orleans, Baton Rouge, Vicksburg and Natchez, she had been there on his arm at the celebration party his brothers and cousins had thrown. And when his cousin Delaney had married a desert sheikh, she had been the one to attend the weddings with him in both the States and the Middle East.

She sighed, knowing she had to let go of the past the way she'd suggest that he do. But the two years they were together had been good times for her, the best she could have ever shared with anyone, and she had looked forward to the day they would join their lives together as one.

She frowned. Four years ago Ian had refused to hear anything she had to say; had even refused to acknowledge that if the FBI hadn't discovered Boris Knowles's connection to organized crime when they had, all of the man's business dealings would have come under scrutiny, including his partnership with Ian.

Common sense dictated that she tread carefully where Ian was concerned. He was smart and observant.

And he didn't trust her one iota. There was no doubt in her mind that he would be watching her.

Brooke's breathing quickened at the thought of his eyes on her for any amount of time, and moments later a smile curved the corners of her lips. Then she laughed, a low, sultry sound that vibrated through the room. Let him watch her, and while he was doing so maybe it was time to let him know exactly what he'd lost four years ago when he'd walked out of her life.

Ian glanced at the clock on his office wall and decided to give up his pretense of working, since he wasn't concentrating on the reports, anyway. He had too many other things on his mind.

He resisted the urge, as he'd done several times within the past couple of hours, to push the button and see what was going on in the casino, in hopes he would get a glimpse of Brooke. His hand tightened around the paper he held in his hand. He thought he was downright pathetic. And just to think, she was booked for two weeks.

It took him a minute to notice his private line was blinking, and he quickly picked up his phone. "Yes?"

"Ian, how are you?"

He smiled as he recognized Tara's voice. A pediatrician, she was married to his cousin, Thorn, a nationally known motorcycle builder and racer. "Tara, I'm doing fine. And what do I owe the pleasure of this call?"

"Delaney's surprise birthday party. Shelly and I are finalizing the guest list and we wanted to check with you about someone who's on it."

Ian leaned back in his chair. It was hard to believe

that his cousin Delaney would be thirty. Her husband, Prince Jamal Ari Yasir, wanted to give his wife the celebration of a lifetime and he wanted it held at the Rolling Cascade. It seemed only yesterday when he, his brothers and cousins had taken turns keeping an eye on the woman they'd thought at the time was the only female in the Westmoreland family in their generation.

Delaney hadn't made the job easy, and most of the time she'd deliberately been a pain in the ass, but now she was princess of a country called Tahran and mother of the future king. And to top things off, she and Jamal were expecting their second child.

"Who do you want to check with me about?"

"Brooke Chamberlain."

Ian rubbed a hand down his face. Talk about coincidences. Hearing Brooke's name brought a flash of anger. "What about Brooke?"

"I know Delaney would love to see her again, but we thought we'd better check with you. We don't want to make you uncomfortable in any way. I know how things were at Dare and Shelly's wedding."

Ian leaned back in his chair. He doubted anyone knew how difficult things had been for him at that wedding. "Hey, don't worry about it. I can handle it."

There was a slight pause. "You sure?"

"Yes, I'm sure." He decided not to bother mentioning that Brooke was presently in the casino and they were sharing the same air, as she'd put it. "I got over Brooke years ago. She means nothing to me now."

Ian sighed deeply and hoped with all his heart that the words he'd just said were true.

Two

Sitting at a table in the back that afforded him a good view of everything that was going on, Ian saw Brooke the moment she walked into the Blue Lagoon Lounge. Under ordinary circumstances he would have given any other beautiful woman no more than a cursory glance. But unfortunately, not in this case. Brooke was, and always had been, a woman who warranted more than one glance, and her entrance into any room could elicit looks of envy in most women's eyes and a frisson of desire down many men's spines.

Taking a deep breath, he frowned in irritation when he saw the look of heated interest in several masculine gazes as she wove her way through the crowded room with confidence, sophistication and style. And what bothered him more than anything was the fact that the same heated interest in other men's eyes was reflected in his, as well. And her outfit wasn't helping matters. Talk about sexy….

She was wearing her hair up in a knot on her head but had allowed a few strands to fall downward to capitalize on the gracefulness of her neck and the dark lashes that fanned her eyes. And her luscious lips were painted a wicked, flaming-hot red.

But it was that sensuous black number draping her body that had practically every male in the room drooling. Emphasizing every curve as well as those long, beautiful legs, the short dress had splits on both sides, and Ian actually heard the tightening of several male throats when she slid onto a bar stool and exposed a generous amount of thigh. Before she could settle in the seat, he watched as several men stood, eager to hit on her.

Ian took a leisurely sip of his drink. Unless she had changed a lot over the past four years, the poor fools that were all but knocking over chairs to get to her were in for a rude awakening. Although she probably appreciated a hot stare as much as the next female, Brooke was not a woman to fawn over male attention. He had learned that particular lesson the hard way the day they'd met. From that day forward he had never underestimated her as a woman again.

And after being deeply involved with her, he also had a more intimate view of the woman who was the center of every male's attention in the lounge tonight. Without a doubt he was probably the only man in the room who knew about the insecurities that had plagued her through most of her young life. Her father and two older brothers had been known as the Chamberlain Gang, robbing banks as they zigzagged across state lines before the FBI brought an end to their six-month crime spree.

As a teenager, Brooke and her mother had moved to Atlanta to start a new life and find peace from the taunts, ridicule and insensitivity of those less inclined to put the matter to rest. It was then, while in high school, that Brooke decided to bring honor and dignity back to the Chamberlain name by working on the right side of the law.

The activities in the room reclaimed Ian's attention, and he chuckled as one man after another was treated to Brooke's most dazzling smile, followed by her more than courteous refusal. He lifted his drink, and before taking another sip he muttered quietly, "Cheers."

There must be a full moon in the sky, Brooke thought, idly sipping her drink. The wolves were definitely out on the prowl and had erroneously assumed she was an easy prey.

What woman didn't enjoy knowing a man thought she was attractive? But there were some men who thought beauty went hand in hand with stupidity. One man had even offered her the chance to be his second wife, although he claimed he was still happily married to the first.

"I see you haven't lost your touch."

Brooke glanced over at the man who slid into the seat beside her. The smile in his eyes threw her for a second, but that was only after a flutter of awareness inched up her spine. "Thanks. I'll take that as a compliment," she said, sipping her drink when her throat suddenly felt dry.

She fought to keep her body from trembling and, in an attempt at control, studied her reflection in the glass she held instead of placing her full attention on Ian, the way she wanted to do.

"I really thought I wouldn't see you anymore tonight," he said, taking a sip of his own drink.

With that Brooke cocked a brow and turned to him, first taking in how he was dressed. He had changed out of the business suit he was wearing earlier and was wearing another, just as tailormade and just as appealing. And, like the other one, it represented his status as a successful businessman. Whether he wanted to or not, he stood out as the impeccably dressed owner of this casino and was doing so in style.

"Why?" she asked, her concentration moving back to his comment. "Why did you think you wouldn't see me anymore tonight? Did you assume I'd hide out in my villa, Ian, after our meeting earlier? Like I told you, I can't go through life worrying about running into you at every corner like I did something wrong."

Ian's eyes narrowed. "A man's life was lost," he said in a tight voice.

"Yes," she said coolly. "But Boris Knowles should have considered the consequences. He didn't get involved with a group of amateur criminals, Ian. He was involved in organized crime. Don't try and make me feel guilty for the choices he made."

"But had I known, I—"

"Had you known, there wouldn't have been anything you could have done. He was in too deep. Why is it so hard for you to believe that? Telling you would not have changed a thing, other than involve you in a situation you didn't need to be in."

Brooke didn't know what else she could say to get

through that thick skull of his. He refused to believe he wouldn't have made a difference, and that not knowing about Boris had been a blessing.

She heard his muttered curse and knew it was a mistake to have come to the lounge, a place where she figured he would be. "Look, Ian, evidently you and I will always have a difference of opinion about what happened and why I kept things from you. And I'm tired of you thinking I'm the bad guy."

She stood and threw a couple of bills on the counter. "See you around. But then, maybe it would be better if I didn't."

Ian muttered another curse as he watched Brooke disappear through the door, leaving her sensuous scent trailing behind. He felt that familiar stab of pain he encountered whenever he thought of her betrayal. But Brooke's words reminded him of the same thing Dare, a former FBI agent himself, had told him. Organized crime wasn't anything to play with, and regardless of the outcome, Boris had made his choices.

Dare had also tried to make Ian understand that when Brooke had taken the job as a federal agent, she had also made an oath to uphold the law and to maintain a rigid vow of confidentiality. Had she told him about the case, and security had been breached, it would have risked not only Brooke's life but the lives of other federal agents.

Ian had understood all of that, but still, he believed that when two people were committed to each other, there weren't supposed to be any secrets between them. So in his mind she had made a choice between her job and him. That, in a nutshell, was what grated him the most. Yet at some point he had to let go and move on or the bitterness would do him in. He couldn't continue to make her feel like a "bad" guy, especially when he of all people knew how much becoming an agent had meant to her. Twice her application had been turned down when background checks had revealed her family history—namely her father and brothers. It had taken Dare, who'd still maintained close contacts within the Bureau, to write a sterling letter of recommendation to get her in.

Ian pulled in a deep breath. It was time for him and Brooke to finally make peace. He knew that because of all that had happened between them, the love they once shared could never be recovered, but it was time he put his animosity to rest and make an attempt at being friends.

Brooke angrily stripped out of her dress. Ian West-moreland was as stubborn as any mule could get. He refused to consider that she had been doing her job four years ago and if she had told him anything about the case, her own life could have been in jeopardy. No, all he thought about was what had happened to a man who'd been living a lie to his family, friends and business associates.

Fine, if that was the position Ian wanted to take, even after four years, let him. She refused to allow him to get on her nerves, and somehow and in some way she would wipe away the memories she found almost impossible to part with. More than anything she had to somehow eradicate him from her heart. But in the meantime she planned to enjoy herself for the next two weeks and wouldn't let him stand in the way of her doing just that.

She slipped into the two-piece bathing suit, thinking a late-night swim might make her feel better. Swimming had always relaxed her, and she was seriously considering adding a pool to her home in D.C. The question was whether or not she would have the time to enjoy it. In a few months she would have made her five-year mark with the Bureau and it was time to decide if she wanted to remain out in the field or start performing administrative duties. Her good friend and mentor, Dare Westmoreland, had cautioned her regarding Bureau burnout, which was what had happened to him after seven years as an agent.

Brooke had just grabbed her wrap when she heard the knock at her door. Evidently room service had made a mistake and was at the wrong villa. Making her way across the room, she leaned against the door and glanced through the peephole, and suddenly felt a sensation deep in the pit of her stomach. Her late-night caller was Ian.

She tensed and shook her head. If he thought he would get in the last word he had another thought coming. After removing the security lock she angrily snatched open the door. "Look, Ian, I—"

Before she could finish, he placed a single white rose in her hand. "I come in peace, Brooke. And you're right. It's time to put the past behind us and move on."

Ian's heart slammed against his chest. He had been prepared for a lot of things, but he hadn't been prepared for Brooke to open the door in a two-piece bathing suit with a crocheted shawl wrapped around her waist that didn't hide much of anything.

There were her full, firm breasts that almost poured

out of her bikini top and a tiny waist that flared to shapely hips attached to the most gorgeous pair of legs any woman could possess. And her feet—how could he possibly forget her sexy feet? They were bare, with brightly painted toenails, encased in a pair of cute flat leather sandals.

Her unique scent was feminine and provocative and the same one he had followed out of the lounge. It was the same scent that was filling her doorway, saturating the air surrounding him, getting into his skin. She was and had always been a woman of whom fantasies were made. And seeing her standing there was overwhelming his sense of self-control.

He sighed deeply, inwardly wishing he could focus on something other than her body and her scent. He wanted to concentrate on something like the rose he had given her, but instead his gaze lowered to her navel, which used to be one of his favorite spots on her body. He could recall all the attention he used to give it before moving lower to…

"Ian?"

He snatched his attention back to her face and cleared his throat. Damn, he had come to make peace, not make love. They would never share that type of relationship again. "Yes?"

"Thanks for the rose, and I'm glad we can move forward in our lives, and I hope that one day we can be friends again," she said.

Brooke was watching his eyes, probably noting the caution within their dark depths when he said, "I hope so, too."

She nodded. "Good."

He leaned in the doorway. "You're going out?"

"Yes, I thought I'd go for a swim at one of the pools. The one with the huge waterfall looks inviting."

Ian nodded. It was. He had passed the area on his way here, and another thing he noted was that it was crowded with more men than women. He then remembered that the Rolling Cascade was hosting a convention of the International Association of Electricians. There were over eight hundred attendees, eighty percent of them men who probably thought they were capable of finding a woman's hot spot and wiring her up in a minute flat. He drew his dark brows together sharply. Not with this woman.

"That pool is nice, but I know of one that's a hundred times better," he said, when an idea suddenly popped into his head.

"Really, where?"

"My penthouse."

She met his eyes then, and he could imagine what thoughts were going through her mind. Hell, he was wondering about it himself. He had no right to feel possessive, as if she was still his. But just because she wasn't didn't mean he shouldn't have a protective instinct where she was concerned, did it?

Feeling better about the reason he was inviting her to his suite, he reached out and took her hand in his. "Look, it was just an invitation for you to use my private pool. Besides, I'd like to catch up on how things have been going for you. But if you prefer we don't go any further than the rose, that's fine."

Brooke took a second to absorb Ian's words. He wanted them to become friends again and nothing more. He had given her a peace offering and now he wanted them to catch up on what had been going on in their lives. She doubted that he knew she asked about him often, whenever she and Dare spoke on the phone. She knew Ian was back at the top of his game, had reinstated his role of the Perfect End and now claimed he would never, ever settle down and marry. With his cousin Storm happily married, Ian much preferred being the remaining lone wolf of the Westmoreland clan.

"I'd love to go swimming in your private pool and visit," she said, and hoped and prayed she could get through an evening alone with him in his private quarters.

The smile that touched his lips sent heat spreading through her. "Good. Are you ready to leave now?"

"Yes. I just need to grab a towel."

"Don't bother. I have plenty."

"Okay, let me get my door key."

Moments later she stepped out and closed the door behind her. As they walked together, side by side, toward a bank of elevators, she was fully aware that Ian was looking at her, but she refused to look back. If for one instant she saw heated desire in his eyes, she would probably do something really stupid like give in to the urgency of the sexual chemistry that always surrounded them and ask him to kiss her. But knowing what ironclad control Ian could have, he would probably turn her down.

"Welcome to my lair, Brooke Chamberlain."

Ian stepped aside to let her enter, and Brooke's breath caught the moment she stepped into the room. His personal living quarters was a floor above his office, and both were connected by a private elevator, an arrangement he found convenient.

The moment Brooke crossed over the threshold it was if she had walked into paradise. She had figured that, as the owner of the Rolling Cascade, Ian would have a nice place, but she hadn't counted on anything this magnificent, this breathtaking.

His appreciation of nature was reflected in the numerous plants strategically arranged in the penthouse, which encompassed two floors connected by a spiral staircase.

The first things she noticed were the large windows and high ceilings, as well as the penthouse's eclectic color scheme—a vibrant mix of red, yellow, orange, green and blue. She was surprised at how well the colors worked together. For symmetry, the two fireplaces in the room were painted white, and then topped with drapery of a hand-painted design.

It appeared the furniture had been designed with comfort in mind, and several tropical-looking plants and trees gave sections of the room a garden effect.

"Come on, let me show you around," he said, taking her hand in his.

The warmth of the strong hand encompassing hers sent a sea of sensation rippling through her. She tried not to think about what expert hands they were and how he used to take his thumb and trail it over her flesh, starting at her breasts and working his way downward, sometimes alternating his thumb with his tongue.

His silky touch could make her purr, squirm, and elicited all kind of sounds from her. And when he would work his way to her navel—heaven help her—total awareness for him would consume her entire body, making her breathe out his name in an uncontrolled response to his intimate ministrations.

"You okay?"

His words snatched her back from memory lane, and she glanced up at him. "Yes, why do you ask?"

"No reason," he murmured, and the tone sent a shiver all through her.

Brooke raised a brow. Had she given something away? Had she made a sound? One he recognized? One he remembered?

They walked together while he gave her a tour. French doors provided a gracious entry from room to room, and the kitchen, with its state-of-the-art cabinets and generously sized island, showed a comfortable use of space. The skill of an interior designer touched every inch of Ian's home, and Brooke thought this was definitely the largest penthouse she'd ever seen. It encompassed more square footage than her house back in D.C.

Ian told her that Prince Jamal Ari Yasir was his primary investor and that Ian's brothers, Spencer and Jared, and his cousin Thorn had also invested in the Rolling Cascade. The one thing Brooke had always admired about the Westmoreland family was their closeness and the way they supported each other.

When he showed her his bedroom a spurt of envy ran through Brooke at the thought of the other women who'd shared the king-size bed with him. But then she quickly reminded herself that Ian's love life was no business of hers.

"So, what do you think?" he asked casually.

His question momentarily froze her, and she shifted

her eyes from the bed and met his gaze. "I'm really proud of you, Ian, of all your accomplishments. And you are blessed to belong to a family that fully supports what you do. They are really super."

Ian smiled. "Yes, they are."

"And how are your parents?"

"They're doing fine. You do know that Storm got married?" he asked, leading her out of the bedroom, down the spiral stairs, to an area that led toward an enclosed pool.

She smiled up at him. "Yes. I can't imagine marriage for the Perfect Storm."

The corners of Ian lips curled in a smile. "Now he's the Perfect Dad. His wife Jayla and their twin daughters are the best things that ever happened to him. He loves them very much."

When there was a lull in the conversation, Brooke said, "And I heard about your uncle Corey's triplets."

He chuckled. "Yeah, can you believe it? He found out an old girlfriend had given birth to triplets around the same time he was united with a woman who'd always been his true love. He's married now and is a very happy man on his mountain."

Brooke nodded. She had visited Corey's Mountain in Montana with Ian and knew how beautiful it was. "I also heard that Chase got married and so did Durango."

He nodded, grinning. "Yes, both were shockers. Chase and Durango married two sisters, Jessica and Savannah Claiborne. Durango and Savannah eloped and held their wedding here."

He then looked over at her. "I see Dare's been pretty much keeping you informed."

She shrugged. She detected a smile in his voice, although she didn't see one in his face. "Yes. Do you resent knowing Dare and I keep in touch?"

"No, not at all," he said, his tone making it seem as if such a notion was ridiculous. "Dare knew you for a lot longer than I did. You used to be his deputy and the two of you were close. I didn't expect you to end your relationship with him just because things didn't work out between us, Brooke. The Westmorelands don't operate that way."

Moments later he added, "And I also know that you've kept in touch with other family members." He shook his head, grinning. "Or should I say they kept up with you. Delaney let me know in no uncertain terms that our breakup had no bearing on your friendship."

"Did she?" Brooke asked, attempting to conjure an air of nonchalance she was far from feeling. She and Delaney had remained friends, and a few years ago when Delaney had accompanied her husband to an important international summit in Washington, the two of them had spent the day shopping, going to a movie and sharing dinner.

"Here we are."

They stopped walking, and Brooke's breath caught. Now this was paradise. Ian's enclosed pool was huge, including a cascading waterfall and several tropical plants, and connecting to his own personal fitness center and games room.

"You like it?"

"Oh, Ian, it's wonderful, and you're right—it's better than the one by the villas."

He reached behind her and handed her a couple of towels off a stack. "Here you are, and I meant to ask earlier, how's your mom?"

Brooke smiled. "Mom's doing fine. Marriage agrees with her. While Dad was living—even though he was incarcerated—she refused to get involved with anyone. She was intent on honoring her wedding vows to him although she'd always deserved better. She refused to divorce him."

Ian nodded. "I heard about your father. I'm sorry."

Brooke shrugged. "He was a couple of years from being up for parole and what does he do?" she asked angrily. "He causes a prison riot that not only cost him his own life but the lives of four other inmates, as well."

"And how are your brothers?"

"Bud and Sam are okay. Mom stays in contact with them more than their biological mother," she said of her father's first wife. When her mother had married Nelson Chamberlain, her brothers were already in their teens.

"I write them all the time and have taken Mom to see them on occasion. I think they've finally learned their lessons and will be ready for parole when the time comes," she said.

Brooke appreciated Ian asking about her family. She had loved her dad and her brothers even though they had chosen lives of crime. And she simply adored her mother for having had the strength to leave her husband to provide her daughter with a better environment.

She was about to remove her wrap when she nervously glanced over at Ian. "Will you be taking a swim, too?"

He smiled, shaking his head. "No, not tonight. The pool will be all yours. There are a couple of calls I need to make, so I'm going to leave you alone for a while. Do you mind?"

"No, and I appreciate you letting me use your pool."

"Don't mention it."

"And I enjoyed our chat, Ian."

"So did I." He glanced at his watch. "I'll be back in around an hour to walk you to your villa."

"All right."

After Ian left, Brooke licked her suddenly dry lips, remembering how quickly he had exited the room. Was she imagining things? Had the thought of her undressing in front of him—doing something of as little significance as removing the wrap of her bathing suit—sent Ian running? Um. Maybe that ironclad control he used to have wasn't as strong as she'd thought.

The possibility that the attraction they'd once shared was just as deep as before sent a warm feeling flowing through her. And suddenly feeling giddy, she removed her wrap, walked over to the deep end of the pool and dived in.

Ian's hand trembled as he poured wine into his glass. Talk about needing a drink. It had taken everything within him not to pull Brooke into his arms at several points during their conversation. And even worse, he had picked up on that vibe, the same one she always emitted whenever she wanted him to make love to her.

It had been awkward to stand beside her and know what her body wanted and not oblige her the way he would have done in the past. Angrily he slammed down the glass on his coffee table. *This is not the past, this is the present and don't even think about going back there, Westmoreland. The only thing you and Brooke can ever be is friends, and even that is really pushing it.*

He muttered a curse, and at the same time the phone rang. It was his private line. "Yes?"

"Hey, you're okay?"

Hearing his cousin Storm's voice, Ian shook his head and smiled. It had always been the weirdest thing. His brother Quade was his fraternal twin like Chase was Storm's. But when it came to that special bond he'd heard that twins shared, it had always been he and Storm and Quade and Chase.

Quade worked for the Secret Service, and half the time none of the family knew what he doing or where he was. But they could depend on Chase to know if Quade was ever in trouble with that special link they shared. Likewise, Ian knew that only Storm could detect when something was bothering him, even thousands of miles away.

"And what makes you think something is wrong?" Ian asked, sitting down on a leather sofa. This spot gave him a view of Brooke whenever she swam in the shallow end of his pool.

Storm chuckled. "Hey, I feel you, man. The one night I should be getting a good night's sleep, now that the girls are sleeping through the night, I'm worried about you."

Ian lifted a brow. "Worried about me?"

"Yes. What's going on, Ian? What has you so uptight that I can sense it?"

Ian's attention was momentarily pulled away from his phone conversation when Brooke swam to the shallow end of the pool. He shifted slightly on the sofa to get a better view and knew from where he sat that he could see her but she couldn't see him.

He watched as she stood up, emerging from the water like a sex goddess as she tossed her wet hair back from her face. But it wasn't her hair that was holding his attention. *Have mercy!* She had a body that made men drool, curves in all the right places—and he was familiar with those curves, every delectable inch. And that bikini, wet and clinging to her, looked good on her. Too good. He could only imagine the reaction she would have gotten from other men. But just the thought that he had once touched her all over, licked her all over, made love to that body in more ways than he could count, sent blood surging through his veins. "Damn."

"Hey, man. Talk to me. What's going on?"

Storm's words reminded Ian he was still holding the phone in his hand, and it was taking every ounce of strength he had to continue to do so. He suddenly felt weak, physically drained.

"Brooke," he finally said, whispering her name softly, drawing out the sound deep from within his throat on a husky sigh. "She's here."

"What do you mean she's there?"

Ian rolled his eyes upward. "Just what I said, Storm. She checked into the Rolling Cascade for two weeks for some R and R. But at this moment she happens to be in my penthouse, using my pool. We're trying to put the past behind us."

"Brilliant. That's just brilliant, Ian," Storm chuckled. "Don't tell me, let me guess. You and Brooke are trying to put the past behind you and become friends. Come on, Ian. Think about it. Do you actually believe you can be just friends with the only woman who's ever had your heart?"

Ian frowned. "Yes, since the key word here is *had*. I stopped loving Brooke years ago."

"So you say."

"So I mean. Good night, Storm."

Three

Ian stood and walked across the room to the wall-to-wall, floor-to-ceiling window that gave a breathtaking view of Lake Tahoe.

When he had reopened the casino after extensive remodeling, he'd given it more than just a new name and a new face. He had given the place a new attitude. He had painstakingly combined the charm of the Nevada landscape with the grandeur of a world-class casino, then added an upscale nightlife whose unique ambiance appealed to a sophisticated clientele.

His penthouse had the best view of the lake. Strategically set on the west side of the casino and covering portions of both the eighth and ninth floors, his domain was away from the villas, the various shops and restaurants, the golf courses with cascading waterfalls and the tennis courts. He considered his personal quarters as his very own private hot spot, although between the hours he'd spent making sure things were perfect for the grand opening nine months ago, his time had been too consumed in business matters to pursue any intimate pleasures, and he had not yet invited a woman up to his lair, other than members of his family and now Brooke.

Brooke.

He cocked his head, and a smile touched his lips when he heard the sound of her splashing around in the pool. For some reason, he liked knowing she was there, and regardless of what Storm thought, he and Brooke held no emotional ties. The most they could ever be again was friends.

Brooke swam back and forth through the calming water as she did another lap around Ian's pool. After several more laps she pulled herself up on the ledge thinking that she'd had a wonderful workout. She felt rejuvenated in one sense and exhausted in another. Beside the pool was a long padded bench that looked absolutely inviting, and she decided to rest a while.

She lay flat on her back and stared up at the ceiling. All she could think about was Ian's dark eyes and the way they had looked at her moments before he'd left her alone. Swim or no swim, she'd been fantasizing about him ever since. She was trying to keep a part of herself distanced; especially knowing how quickly she could be consumed by desire for him. Though she hadn't been completely honest with him about the real reason she was there, she couldn't control her attraction to him. Basic urges were exactly what they were. Basic. And she knew firsthand how skilled Ian was in taking care of anything that ailed her.

She flipped onto her stomach and studied a nearby plant. Anything to get Ian off her mind. But it wasn't working. As her eyes closed, her mind shifted back to a time when he had moved his mouth all over her breasts, sucking and lapping at her nipples while his fingers skimmed just beneath her panties....

Ian wasn't sure how long he stood at the window looking out, idly sipping his wine while seeing various yachts, sailboats and schooners cruising the lake, resembling fireflies below as they went by. Tomorrow was another busy day. He had meetings with Nolen McIntosh, his casino manager, Vance on security matters and Danielle on PR. Then of course there was that discussion with his event planner regarding the final details for Delaney's surprise birthday party.

It took Ian only a minute to notice something was different. There was no sound coming from the pool. He set his wineglass on a nearby table, moved away from the window and headed toward the room where he'd left Brooke almost an hour earlier.

The pool was empty, so he glanced around the room and then saw her. She lay flat on her stomach on the padded leather bench, asleep. The intensity of the emotions he felt at that moment hit him from every angle. When was the last time Brooke had slept at his place? It had been years. Their angry parting words—mostly from him—still burned fervently in his veins. She had tried to explain; tried presenting her side of things. But he hadn't wanted to listen. He hadn't wanted to ever see or talk to her again.

So what was happening here? Why was he talking to

her, seeing her again? Why had he allowed her to invade his space, the only place free of his memories of her?

She moaned in her sleep, and hearing the sound he stepped closer, allowing his gaze to rake over her shapely body, feeling a rush of adrenaline. A deep swallow made its way down his throat as his gaze moved to the tie that held the top part of her bikini in place, the smooth curve of her back, the flare of her hips beneath the thin scrap of material that was supposed to be a bikini bottom. Her skin looked soft, inviting and warm to the touch. He wanted his hands all over her thighs, and he would do anything to cup her delicious bottom. And he didn't want to think about how he wanted to use his mouth on her breasts.

He sighed deeply. Considering their history, it was only natural that he would feel this heated lust, this mind-searing desire. There was a time when, if he'd found her like this, he could have awakened her by making love to her, gently flipping her on her back and using his hands and his mouth to show her what real moans were all about. His stomach begin trembling at the memories, and hot liquid fire filled his body at the very thought. But he knew things were different. They no longer had that kind of relationship, and he doubted they ever would again. She was no longer his to touch at will.

That realization dictated his next move. Reaching to a table behind him he grabbed a huge towel and gently covered her. He would not wake her. He would let her rest. But neither would he leave her. He wanted to be there when she awoke. Call it pure torture, but he wanted to look into the depth of those eyes, catch her drowsy, sleepy, tousled look, the sexy one she got whenever she

was rousing from sleep. That look used to stir up everything male within him and arouse him to no end. And
that look would drive him to take her with a passion that
could never be duplicated with any other woman.

Removing his jacket, he folded it neatly and placed
it across the back of a wicker sofa before settling down
in a wicker chair and stretching his legs out in front of
him. From this position he could to watch her while she
slept and see her when she woke up.

And as he sat there, his mind went back to that day
six years ago when they had met. He had walked into
Dare's office, and from that day on his life had never
been the same.

Slowly released from the throes of a deep sleep,
Brooke kept her eyes closed as she drowsily inhaled
gently and then yawned. There was nothing like a swim
to work the aches and pains out of her muscles, and that
thought made her recall where she was and why the
familiar scent of one particular man was surrounding her.

She slowly opened her eyes and they immediately
connected to the dark penetrating ones of Ian Westmoreland. Sitting in a chair across the room, he looked
slightly disheveled, as if he'd been sitting there for a
while, but nothing could erase that sexy look he wore
so well. What had been a crisp white shirt now had a
few buttons undone, and the sleeves were rolled up.
With his legs stretched out in front of him, his trousers
were pulled tight against muscular, well-defined thighs.

A sensual shiver ran down her body and she felt the
huge towel covering her and knew he had placed it
there. The thought of him being that close to her, placing

a covering over her body, stoked her insides, creating a heavy warmth.

A part of her wanted to sit up, stretch her legs, apologize for falling asleep, but she couldn't do any of those things. She couldn't move; could barely breathe. His gaze was holding her in place and making her remember happier times, passionate times, and she wondered if he was doing the same.

She watched his eyes darken even more, and in response a rush of hormones that had lain dormant for four years rushed through her system. Liquid awareness churned in her stomach, and her entire body suddenly felt sensitive, acutely aware of him as a man. However, not just as any man.

He was the man who had first introduced her to the pleasures that a couple could share; the man who used to wake her up each morning by using his hands and lips on every part of her body; a man who, besides being the best lover any woman could possibly have, had become her confidant and her best friend.

Brooke blinked, was caught momentarily off guard when he stood and began walking toward her, showing telltale proof of how much he wanted her. The bulge in his pants couldn't lie. Her body instantly responded, recognizing the sexual chemistry that emanated from him and quickly overpowered her.

She raised her body to a sitting position, stretched out her legs and braced her hands on both sides of her. She couldn't help wondering what he was thinking. She definitely knew her thoughts. The heated look in his eyes, the hot familiarity, gave her an idea. There was still a lot unsettled between them. There were some things that could never be as they used to be. But there would always be a level where they would be in accord. And this was it.

Deep down a part of her wished otherwise; wished she could expunge him from her heart as she knew he had done her. He might still want her, desire her, but he no longer loved her. But right now, at this moment, heaven help her, it didn't matter. She needed to feel his body pressed close to hers, she needed to once again feel his arms holding her, his mouth tasting hers.

He came to a stop in front of her and the light that poured down from overhead highlighted the darkness of his skin in contrast to his white shirt. She stared up at him, as blood throbbed through her veins, and she took in his broad chest and strong lean body.

She slowly stood, wondering if her legs could hold her weight, but that concern quickly vanished from her mind when she heard a sensual moan escape through his clenched teeth, and she knew he was trying to resist her, fight what they were both feeling.

But when he began to lean closer, she knew he had given up the battle and was giving in to temptation. Common sense was being overwhelmed by lust. And when their mouths connected and their tongues mingled, flames sparked inside of her and she completely lost whatever control she'd had. This is Ian, her mind and body taunted. And she did what seemed so natural, which was to kiss him back in all the ways he had taught her to.

Ian made love to Brooke's mouth with as much skill as he possessed. *Mercy.* He wanted this. He needed this.

Four years hadn't eliminated the yearning, the urgency or the hunger. She wasn't out of his system, and maybe this would be the first step in ridding her from it. But the more their tongues consorted, fused and intertwined, the harder it was to regain control. And when he brought her body closer to his, let his hands slide over her backside with a possessiveness he had no right to feel, he wanted to do more than taste her. He wanted to place her back on the bench, further stroke the heat between them, remove his clothes, straddle her body, remove her bikini bottom and make her his again.

His again.

That thought made him lift his head sharply, knowing that was the last thing he wanted. Things could never go back to being the way they were. He refused to let them. There were some things you could never recover from, and one was a broken heart. He'd loved and he'd loved hard. And whether she had intended to or not, she had destroyed that love.

He looked down and his gaze swept over her features. His eyes touched each and every part of the face he would always cherish. But that was as far as things would ever go. He would want her, lust after her, but he would never love her again.

"Come on and let me walk you back to your villa," he said in a husky voice tinged with regret.

As if he had kissed any and every word from her mouth, Brooke merely nodded, gathered the towel around her and followed him as he led her to his private elevator.

"I didn't mean to overstay my welcome," she finally was able to say when the elevator doors opened.

He looked down at her, his features tight. "You didn't."

For some reason she didn't believe him. One thing she knew about Ian was that he was a man who didn't forgive easily, nor was he quick to forget. He claimed he wanted them to move on and be friends, but she wondered if that's what he really wanted, or if that was something he would ever be willing to tolerate. Brooke opened her mouth to say something and then closed it. Chances were he would be keeping his distance for the remainder of her stay.

When they reached her door he stepped aside to let her unlock it. She thought this was where he would tell her good-night, and he surprised her when he took her hand and followed her inside, closing the door behind him.

"Hidden video cameras in the halls," he whispered in a throaty voice before gently pulling her into his arms. He then leaned down and kissed her again, the connection slow and lingering, but just as thorough as before. The kiss sent shudders all through her.

Moments later his mouth left hers to trail heated kisses along her neck and jaw. The feel of his beard rubbing against her skin was eliciting sensations deep in the pit of her stomach. A man like Ian was deadly in more ways than one.

"Will you go sailing with me tomorrow, Brooke?"

She raised her chin, still shuddering, surprised at his request. "Are you sure that's what you want?" she asked.

He was silent for a moment and stared deep into her eyes. It was all Brooke could do not to melt right there on the spot from the heat generating in his gaze. "Yes, I'm sure." He stepped back. "I'm beginning to realize something, Brooke."

"What?" she asked, having a difficult time swallowing.

"Moving beyond what we once shared isn't going to be as easy as I thought."

She lifted her brow and fought back the thick lump of emotion that clogged her throat, almost kept her from breathing. "What do you mean?"

"Mere friendship between us won't ever work."

"You don't think so?"

"No." His voice was clipped, cool and confident. "And since things can never be like they were, we need finality. Closure. A permanent end."

She knew that what he was saying was true, considering the kisses they had shared, but still, hearing him say it hurt deeply. "So, how do you suggest we go about it? Do you want me to leave?" she asked, knowing that wasn't an option even if he wanted her to.

He stared at her for a long moment, then answered by saying, "No. I don't want you to leave. What I want, what I need, is to have you out of my system, and I know of only one way that can be accomplished."

Brooke sighed deeply. She knew of only one way that could be accomplished, as well, and she wasn't going for it. It might get her out of his system, but it would only embed him deeper into hers.

She shook her head vehemently. "It won't work."

"Trust me, it will."

She lifted her chin and glared at him, trying to ignore the way her inner muscles clenched in response to the huskiness of his voice. "It might work for you, but not for me."

Ian leaned in closer to her, his voice low and deep, his lips just a hair away from touching hers. "I'd love to prove you wrong, Brooke. Even now you feel it, the heat, the urge, the cravings. You remember how things used to be between us as much as I do. You remember our out-of-control hormones, wild nights when we couldn't wait to make love, going so far as to start stripping naked as soon as the door closed behind us."

"Ian."

"And how I would take you right then and there, wherever—on the wall, the floor, the sofa, giving you everything you wanted, whatever you needed. And how you would practically—"

"Stop it, Ian," she said sharply, stepping back away from him to halt the trembling that had begun in her stomach. "I won't let what you're suggesting happen."

She read his expression, saw the challenge in his eyes, the deep-rooted stubbornness. "Okay," he said with a smile that said he didn't believe her any more than she believed herself. "I'll be by to pick you up to go sailing at noon. See you later, Brooke."

Brooke tilted her head, watched him cross the room, open the door and walk out without looking back. She pulled the towel tighter around her body when a chill touched it. After spending so much time in the pool tonight she should be smelling of chlorine. But she smelled of Ian. His manly scent seemed to be all over her.

She dropped the towel and quickly moved toward her bathroom, needing a shower. She would send him a message, letting him know she had changed her mind about going sailing with him.

He might like the idea of playing with fire, but she did not.

Four

"We have reason to believe one of our guests is smoking in his room," Joanne Sutherlin, resort manager, said to the employees around the conference table during the resort's regular status meeting.

"We haven't been able to find any proof, but a housekeeper reports she's smelled smoke. It seems the guest has been trying to disguise his smoking by spraying heavy cologne in the air," she said.

"If we can prove he's breaking a hotel policy, then we can end his stay with us."

Everyone at the table nodded. They knew Ian had very low tolerance when it came to anyone not abiding by the Rolling Cascade's smoke-free policy.

The next item up for discussion by the management team was entertainment. The activities director confirmed that he had booked deals with top performers for the next eighteen months. Highlights of the upcoming schedule included a two-week billing for Mariah Carey in June, Michael MacDonald in September and Phil Collins in December. Smokey Robinson opened tonight in a two-week engagement that was already sold out for every night of the event.

Nolen, the casino manager, indicated security had alerted him that a couple of prostitutes had tried peddling their wares in the casino. Although Nevada had legalized prostitution, it was only allowable within a licensed brothel. Unfortunately, casinos were a prime target for call girls looking for potential "dates." Ian was committed to keeping the Rolling Cascade prostitute free.

"We have the matter taken care of," Nolan assured him.

Ian nodded. That's what he wanted to hear. He glanced at his watch. He had ordered a picnic basket from one of the restaurants for his lunch date with Brooke. He had left a message for her that he would be picking her up at noon and couldn't wait to get her on his boat.

He remembered their conversation last night. He had deliberately walked out the door without looking back. To say he had ruffled a few of her feathers would be an understatement. But then, he had merely been up-front with her. It was too late to start playing games. He knew what they needed and she did as well. In order to bring closure, they needed to expunge each other from their systems, and until that was done there would always be this emotional tug-of-war between them.

He suddenly felt goose bumps cover his body at the thought of seeing her again and of the afternoon he had planned. A hint of a smile tugged at his lips. She might be one resistant female now, but once he got her on his sailboat and made her remember all the stimulating things she was trying to forget, their day would end the way they both wanted it to.

His pulse began beating wildly an hour later as the status meeting ended. He quickly headed toward his penthouse to change into more comfortable clothes.

"Mr. Westmoreland?"

He turned before stepping into his private elevator. "Yes?" he asked Cassie, a young woman who worked in the resort's business center.

"This message was left for you this morning."

He took the sealed envelope she handed him. "Thank you." He tore it open and read the note.

I've changed my mind about going sailing with you, Brooke.

Ian frowned. If Brooke thought she could dismiss him just like that, she had another thought coming.

"Is there anything you need me to do, sir?"

It was then that Ian realized Cassie was still standing there. He lifted his head and met her gaze. This wasn't the first time he'd seen the heated look of lust in the depths of her dark eyes, and he could recognize a flirtatious comment when he heard one. He recalled what he knew about her. She was a recent college graduate with a degree in hotel management. He had decided long ago, after operating his riverboat, that he would never become sexually involved with his employees. And even though, due to his busy schedule, it had been almost a year since he'd slept with anyone, the only woman his body craved had just canceled their lunch date.

* * *

Brooke propped a hand on her hip and stared at the outfits she had placed on the bed. Both were suitable for an afternoon of shopping, but which one should she wear?

The capri pant set was what she would have worn had she gone sailing with Ian. It had a bit more style than the cotton shorts set, and was a designer outfit she'd purchased while in San Francisco last month. The shorts set would provide better comfort of movement as she walked from store to store making purchases. She was about to hang the capri set back in her closet when she heard a knock on her door.

Leaving her bedroom, she wondered if it was housekeeping. The lady had come earlier, but since Brooke had ordered room service for breakfast she had asked the woman to come back later.

Brooke didn't want to think of herself as a coward, but she had dined in her room this morning because she hadn't wanted to run into Ian. They needed at least a couple of days of distance for him to rethink that preposterous suggestion he'd made. In the meantime she would avoid him by taking advantage of all the amenities the resort had to offer. He needed time to cool off, and the interlude would give her the opportunity to asses his operation.

She glanced out the peephole and her heart slammed against her ribs the moment she did so. It was Ian. Did he not get her message canceling their date to go sailing?

When she opened the door, she wasn't quite ready for the fluttering sensation she felt in her chest. He stood in the doorway casually dressed in a pair of khakis and a blue polo shirt and holding a picnic basket. She'd forgotten how good he looked in everyday clothes. He looked sexy in a suit, but in casual wear he was drop-dead gorgeous.

"You ready?" he asked, cutting into her thoughts.

She raised a brow and pulled her robe tighter around her. "Didn't you get my message?"

He smiled as he walked around her, entering the room without an invitation. "Yes, I got it, but I assumed there must have been a mistake."

She glared at him, wondering why he would think that. "Well, you assumed wrong. There is no mistake. I'm not going sailing with you."

He set the basket on the table, crossed his arms over his chest and asked, "Why? Are you afraid to be alone with me?"

"I'm not afraid, Ian, just cautious," she said as she struggled to maintain her composure.

"And why do you feel the need to put your guard up, Brooke?"

Ha! He had the nerve to ask her that!

Irritation settled in her spine. "I'm not new to this game of yours, Ian."

He cast her an innocent look. "What game?"

She didn't hesitate in answering. "Your game of seduction."

His lips quirked. "Since you think you know me so well, why are you so uptight about spending time with me? You used to know how to handle me. At least you thought you did."

A soft chuckle escaped Brooke's lips. "I didn't think anything. I did handle you. I proved that I wasn't like those half-brain tarts you used to mess around with," she said, crossing the room to him and lifting her chin.

"And furthermore, Ian Westmoreland," she added, reaching out and tapping him on the chest with her finger, "your brand of seduction won't work with me."

"And why won't it?" he asked, grabbing her finger before she jabbed a hole in his chest. "It's always worked before."

"Always worked before? Oh really, well we'll just see about that," she said over her shoulder after turning toward the bedroom. "I'll be ready in five minutes."

"Need any help getting dressed?"

"No, thank you. And if I remember correctly your expertise was in getting me undressed."

When she slammed the bedroom door shut, Ian couldn't help but smile. He remembered that fact, as well. It appeared that he would have to change his strategy a bit today, but eventually he'd have her right where he wanted her.

It was a beautiful day for sailing. The last time she had been on a boat was a couple of years ago when Malcolm had tried fixing her up with an old college pal of his. They had double dated on a deep-sea fishing trip. Unfortunately, she and the guy didn't hit it off, had nothing in common and she'd spent the entire two hours comparing him to Ian. Luckily for her, but unluckily for Malcolm, his date got seasick, and they had to return to shore earlier than planned.

"So what do you think?"

Ian's words intruded into her thoughts, and she glanced over at him and then wished she hadn't. He stood tall next to the railing, silhouetted against the noonday sun and looking every bit a sexy ship's captain. She dismissed that image from her mind and tried concentrating on the sailboat instead. According to Ian, the boat was owned by the casino, which in essence meant it was his. "This boat is a beauty, Ian."

He had surprised her by how expertly he handled the boat and all the sleek maneuvers as it glided across the waters of Lake Tahoe with ease. Whether Brooke wanted to admit it or not, it was the perfect day for an afternoon sail, and so far Ian had been the most gracious host in addition to being a well-behaved gentleman. The latter really surprised her.

The food had been delicious yet simple: ham and cheese sandwiches, chips, wine and cheesecake. Nothing fancy, nothing meant to impress. And because it shouldn't have, it did anyway. Sharing lunch with him had been wonderful. He had told her how Stone and his wife had met when they'd been on a plane together bound for Montana. He also told her of his uncle's three children. The cousins had forged a family bond with their newfound Westmoreland cousins from Texas, Uncle Corey's triplets—Clint, Cole and Casey.

"You'll like Casey if you ever get the chance to meet her," he said, taking a sip of his wine. He smiled when he added, "Her brothers had just as much trouble keeping the guys away from her as we did Delaney when she was growing up."

Brooke lifted her eyes toward the sky and breathed in the fresh April air. It was a beautiful day and being out on the lake was exactly what she needed. Had she remained at the resort she would have probably spent way to much money shopping. "I bet it was hard on the three of them, already adults before finding out their father was alive and not dead as they'd thought."

Ian nodded. "Yes, Clint and Cole are handling things okay. It's harder for Casey to come around. She was close to her mother and when Casey found out her mother had lied to them all those years, it hurt."

Ian surprised Brooke by sliding closer to where she sat. "We've talked enough about my new cousins. Now it's time to play," he said, leaning toward her with a hint of mischief in his eyes. It was then she thought that maybe she'd given him credit for being well behaved and a gentleman too soon.

"What sort of game?" she asked, suddenly feeling off balance by his closeness.

"I watched you the other night."

She had an idea where this was going and decided to see if she was right. "And?"

"You were sitting at the blackjack table."

"Go on," she encouraged.

"And I noticed something about you."

"Which was?"

"You can't play worth a damn."

Brooke's eyes widened just seconds before she burst out laughing. This definitely wasn't where she'd thought the conversation was going. And he'd said it so seriously that she quickly inwardly agreed he was telling the truth. She couldn't play worth a damn, but playing blackjack wasn't anything she did on a regular basis. "You plan on giving me a few pointers?"

He surprised her by saying yes and pulling out a deck of cards. "It's the only fair thing to do," he said grinning. "I can't have you losing all your money in the casino. It might be bad for business. So pay attention, Ms. Chamberlain."

And he spent the next hour trying to make a proficient gambler out of her.

"I really had a nice time, Ian," Brooke said later that afternoon when they had returned to the casino and he walked her to her villa.

"Prove it by going to a show with me later tonight," he said, taking her hand in his as they continued to walk toward her door.

"A show?"

"Yes, Smokey Robinson opens tonight."

Brooke's eyes widened. "*The* Smokey Robinson?"

At Ian's nod, she smiled and said. "I think he was the only other man my mother loved besides my father."

"In that case, the least you can do is go and swoon in her honor?" Ian said with a grin. He knew his mother felt the same way.

"That would be the daughterly thing to do, wouldn't it?" she asked with a teasing glint in her eyes.

He chuckled. "Of course."

"All right. Then I'll go."

They stopped in front of her door. He studied her for a long moment before saying, "I'll be by to get you for the second show at ten."

"Wouldn't it be easier for me to meet you downstairs somewhere?"

He gave her a smooth grin. Not hardly, he wanted to say. If she looked anything tonight like she had the other night when she'd shown up at the lounge, the last thing he wanted was other men hitting on her. "It's no problem. I need the exercise, anyway," he said smiling.

"Okay."

When they just stood there a minute, she gave in and asked. "Would you like to come in for a minute?"

He continued to look at her, knowing if he were to go into that room with her, it wouldn't be for just a minute. Patience, he'd discovered, was the key. He hadn't stirred up any stimulating memories like he'd originally planned to do today, but he had enjoyed the time they had spent together. And there would be other times, other opportunities. He would make sure of it.

"No, there're a couple of things I need to do before tonight," he said, stepping back. "But I dare you to ask me that same question after the show," he said, his expression suddenly turning seductive.

She grinned up at him and he knew she was taunting him when she said, "Um, I'll think about it."

He chuckled. "Yeah, you do that." And then he turned and walked away.

When Smokey sings...

The room was packed. People were even crowded around the wraparound bar in the back. But everyone's attention was on the man who'd taken center stage and was belting out "The Tracks of My Tears." His high tenor was his calling card, and the lyrics had meaning. They filled the room with love and romance.

He then did a medley of his Motown tunes and when he began singing "Oh Baby Baby," Brooke's gaze shifted to Ian. She found him staring back at her. Was he thinking the same thing she was? That in the relationship they'd once shared they had both made mistakes, or did he still blame her for everything?

She was so deep in thought that she was startled when everyone stood, began clapping and gave Smokey Robinson the standing ovation he deserved. Moments later he went into his final number, "Going to a Go-Go," and the place came alive. Older couples, who remembered the song and the dances of that day and time, got on the floor and began gyrating their bodies in all kinds of ways. Brooke couldn't help remembering her mom doing those same dances around the house when Brooke was a little girl.

"You want to go out there and try it?" Ian asked, leaning over to her. When he evidently saw the hesitancy in her eyes, he chuckled and asked, "Hey, what do we have to lose?"

She glanced at the crowd dancing and then back at him. "Parts of our face if we got in the way. They're doing a dance called 'the jerk' and I'd hate to be the recipient of one of their elbows."

Ian laughed, and although it could barely be heard above the loud music, Brooke felt the richness in the sound and was suddenly hit with a bit of nostalgia, of other times they had gone out on the town together, dancing, partying, having fun. If anyone had told her a couple of days ago that the two of them would be able to put their anger, hurt and resentment on hold for an evening, she would not have believed them. The pain had been too deep on both sides.

He leaned forward again and took her hand in his. "Come on. Let's show these old folks how to really get down."

The next thing Brooke knew they were out on the dance floor, shaking their bodies like everyone else. Ian had complimented her earlier on her choice of attire, a short, chocolate-brown silk chiffon dress with a swirling, handkerchief hemline. It gave her all the ease she needed as she moved to the music.

She couldn't recall the last time she'd gone dancing, let herself go, allowed herself a moment to feel free. Only with Ian could she be this way. Only with him.

When the music came to an end, he pulled her closer to him, lowered his head, keeping their mouths separated by a mere inch and said, "Come with me for a moment. I want to show you something."

She knew she should ask what he wanted to show her, and just where he was taking her when he led her out of the lounge. But she didn't. She couldn't. The only thing she could do was walk by his side as they held hands and pray wherever they were going, that she would still be in control when they got there.

Brooke tried not to feel nervous as they rode up in Ian's private elevator. He was leaning on the opposite wall and looking positively delicious in one of his designer suits. He stared at her and sent a torrent of sensations all through her body. The man could make everything inside of her flutter with those dark eyes of his, and she was doing everything within her might not to succumb.

"So where are you taking me?" she asked after they passed the floors to his penthouse.

He smiled before pushing off the wall. "Be patient. We'll get there soon enough."

That's what had her worried. "And just where is

'there'?" The elevator was still moving up and although she knew they were on his private side of the casino, she had no idea of where they were going. Already they had gone beyond the eighteenth floor.

Before he could open his mouth to respond—not that he would have anyway—the elevator came to a stop. She hated admitting it but he had aroused her curiosity. He had also aroused something else. Being confined in an elevator with Ian wasn't a good idea and it was taking a supreme effort on her part to downplay his sexiness. His charisma was touching her in all kinds of places, causing her body to feel hot. What she needed was a splash of cold water. The elevator door opened and she turned to follow him when he stepped out.

Her breath caught. Ian had brought her to his private conservatory. From up here, she could see everything. It was a beautiful April night, and when she glanced up she saw the sky was a beautiful shade of navy-blue. The stars sparkled like glistening diamonds above and the half moon provided a warm glow and a feeling of opulence.

Ian's conservatory was the ideal place to create a snug and relaxing haven while surrounded by the beauty of God's universe. The lighting inside the conservatory created pools of soft illumination. It was an intimate atmosphere that used the moon and stars to the best advantage. The room was furnished with several pieces of rattan furniture. Each piece was richly detailed, intricately designed out of woven banana leaf with a natural wash finish. The puffy cushions on the sofa and chair looked too comfortable for words, and the other accessories—the coffee table, side table and foot stool, added a dramatic finishing touch to the decor. Everything in the room seemed to fit. Even the tall, handsome man standing beside her.

"So what do you think?" he asked, breaking into her thoughts.

To say she was impressed was an understatement. He never ceased to amaze or surprise her. But then, she really should not have been surprised. She'd known that Ian was a very smart man who'd graduated from Yale University, magnum cum laude, at twenty-two with a degree in physics. But he definitely wasn't your ordinary geek. After working for a year at NASA's Goddard Space Flight Center, he had returned home when his grandfather died. Wanting to be close to his family he began working for a research firm in Atlanta and it was there that the gambling bug hit him. The way Ian saw it, beating the odds was based on scientific probability. To him it was a matter of science rather than a game of chance. Fortunately, he was very good at science.

"I think this place is beautiful, Ian. And the furniture and live plants enhance everything. There's nothing like having a comfortable environment with the outside all around and the sky up above."

Ian nodded. That's exactly the way he felt. He'd always loved watching the sky at night, and when he got older it had seemed the most natural thing to choose a career studying it. Although he no longer worked in that profession, he hadn't given up his love of astronomy.

"Come look through this," he said, taking her hand and leading her over to a huge, mounted telescope.

Brooke peered through the telescope at the moon, the stars and the other cool celestial objects that were now visible in the sky. She smiled when she saw a shooting star. According to myth, shooting stars fell to the earth creating a flower with each impact.

She straightened, suddenly feeling Ian's heat, and knew he had come to stand directly behind her, so close she could feel the warmth of his breath on her neck. A long, tense moment passed before she could draw in enough air to ask, "You come here often?"

"Whenever I need to get away or just to think."

Ian knew he would never tell her that although this was the first time she had been in his conservatory, he thought of her often when he was up here. It was the only place he allowed himself to let the memories of the love they'd once shared slip through the tough exterior he had built around his heart.

At one time she had been his own special star. She had shone brightly even when the skies had been gray for him and menacing dark clouds had appeared on his horizon. Brooke had been his sun after every storm.

His career change from scientist to casino owner hadn't been easy, but she, along with his family, had motivated and encouraged him to pursue his dream. Brooke had been there by his side when he had celebrated the purchase of the *Delta Princess*.

He sighed deeply, knowing two things for sure. Brooke was still deeply embedded in his system, and no matter what it took he was going to get her out of it. Just the thought of having her in his bed one last time sent a wave of heat coursing through him. But it wouldn't be fair to rush her into a night of hot, wild passion, even though that might be what they both needed.

He had to be patient.

* * *

Brooke pointed up toward the sky, trying to deflect the sensations she felt flowing through her body as a result of Ian's closeness. "Look at that star," she said.

Ian grinned and wrapped his arms around her waist, pulling her body closer to his, and whispered, "I hate to disappoint you, but that's a satellite."

"Oh." Her heart jumped, and heat suddenly flooded her spine where his chest was pressing against it. Then there was the feel of her backside pressed against the zipper of his pants. She felt the firmness of his arousal, getting thicker by the minute, and wished there was some way to defuse the tension steadily growing between them. Of course she knew that Ian would have his own ideas of how they should go about rectifying the problem.

Deciding she couldn't take much more of what she realized was his sly attempt to seduce her, Brooke turned around to suggest they go back to the lounge. Her move was a huge mistake. Turning around placed her face-to-face and body-to-body with him. When she gazed up into his eyes, she suddenly had a memory lapse, and every coherent thought froze in her brain. At that moment nothing mattered but the man staring down at her.

He reached out and traced the pad of his thumb across her jaw, and when he did, currents of electricity shot to every part of her. He leaned down and brought his face closer to hers. Up this close, underneath the beauty of a moonlit, star-glazed sky, her gaze swept over his features and her heart reaffirmed her love for him.

"Do you know what it means when a couple kisses beneath a shooting star?" he asked, his voice low and husky.

"No, what does it mean?" she asked.

"According to Greek mythology, Zeus bestows upon the couple the gift of uncontrollable passion."

Uncontrollable passion? Brooke swallowed deeply, thinking they must have kissed beneath a shooting star once before because whenever it came to passion it seemed they'd cornered the market. Back in the old days, he had been able to draw her to him with a magnetic force. Her hormones would go haywire each and every time. She felt her bones melting just thinking about those times.

"In that case I suggest we don't kiss under a shooting star," she said, trying to get a grip on her senses.

"I disagree." He moved his thumb from her jaw to her neck. "Nothing's wrong with a hefty amount of passion every once in a while," he said, leaning closer to her.

Not if you haven't had any in four years, she wanted to say, but the only thing she could do was stand and watch his mouth get closer and closer and…

Her eyes drifted shut when his lips touched hers, and when he deepened the kiss she thought there was nothing like being kissed under the beauty of a night sky, especially when the person doing the honors was the man you loved.

Brooke's insides sizzled as Ian's tongue gently, unhurriedly mated with hers. Kissing was something she'd always enjoyed doing with him and she couldn't help but recall how they had even gone so far as to develop their own technique of French kissing. And the way Ian was using his tongue on her now jarred her senses, melting her insides. She felt heat spread up her thighs, settle between her legs, and she felt the first sign of that special brand of titillation only he could stir within her. When it came to passion, they didn't need a shooting star. Their fiery chemistry came naturally.

The room felt like it was beginning to spin when he intensified the kiss, delved deeper into her mouth, making the taste of him explode against her palate. She grabbed ahold of his shoulders, felt the material of his jacket beneath her fingers, holding on tight lest she be swept away.

When Ian finally released her mouth she could barely breathe, and a moan slipped from between her lips although she fought to hold it back. She felt the solid length of him cradled against her middle and knew what his body wanted. She tilted her head and looked at him, gazed into those dark eyes that could make a woman swoon. She was getting in deeper by the minute.

He continued to stroke the fire within her as he slid his hand up her arms, over her shoulders and leaned closer to place butterfly kisses around her nose and mouth. "I need to leave town for a few days," he said softly against her lips.

She felt her jaw go slack. "What?"

He pulled back just a little, enough for her to see the darkness of his eyes. "I need to leave in the morning for Memphis to finalize the sale of the riverboat. I'll be gone for two days."

"Oh." She tried hiding her disappointment and couldn't. Her pouty expression must have given her away.

He looked somewhat amused when he asked, "Are you going to miss me?"

She gave him a weak smile. Oh, yes, she would miss

him, but then the separation would give her a chance to screw her head back on straight. "Not at all," she said teasingly.

"Um, then maybe I should give you a reason to miss me…and to look forward to my return."

Before Brooke could draw her next breath she was swept off her feet into Ian's strong arms.

Five

Ian didn't have to go far to the sofa, which was a good thing because he was so terribly aroused his zipper was about to burst. Only Brooke could do this to him this quick and fast, with an urgency that made him want to tear the clothes off her body and do it then and there.

But he knew with Brooke he could never just do *it*. Oh, yeah, in the past they would mate like rabbits several times over, and he would take her in every position known to man—even some he'd conjured up that actually defied the laws of gravity—but still, in his mind they had never just done it. Each time they'd come together, intimately connected, it had meant something emotionally, too. They had always made love and never just had sex. Even now when he wanted to work her out of his system, he knew it would mean something.

And that was the gist of his dilemma.

Although he wanted to believe otherwise, making love to Brooke would be more than a means to an end. His best-laid intentions could backfire, and she could get even deeper under his skin. That thought was unnerving.

And yet that possibility hadn't lessened his desire for her, hadn't stopped his testosterone from kicking into overdrive or from giving him the most intense arousal he'd had in four years. In other words, he needed to "do it," like, yesterday, but only with this woman.

He leaned back on the sofa with her in his arms, and before she could open her mouth to utter a single word, his tongue was there, lapping her next breath from her parted lips. He kissed her deeply. His heart throbbed, his pulse was going haywire and his hands seemed to be everywhere, but mostly working their way under her dress.

When he realized that in less than five seconds flat he had his fingers right smack between her legs, he snapped his head up and stared at her. This was madness. This was crazy. This was typical Ian and Brooke.

He drew in an unsteady breath when these thoughts rang through his mind. They had always been hot for each other, and nothing had changed. Together they were spontaneous as hell. Whenever their bodies joined as one all they had to do was think orgasm and it happened.

He saw the darkening of her eyes, a signal that she wanted him as much as he wanted her. But he needed to hear her say it. He had to know before he went any further that whatever they did tonight, she would be with him all the way and there would be no regrets.

"Brooke?"

* * *

She heard her name whispered from his lips in a tone so raspy and sensual it made her breath hitch in her throat. She knew what he wanted. She also knew what he was asking, and at the moment she couldn't deny Ian Westmoreland a single thing. It had been four years for her, and the abstinence had taken its toll. She felt out of her league, something she'd never felt with Ian before. She didn't know how to react. The only thing she did know was that she wanted him.

She reached out and clutched the lapels of his jacket. "I don't understand the intensity of this, Ian," she whispered truthfully, pulling his mouth down closer to hers.

"Then let me explain it to you without words," he said silkily against her lips.

And then he was kissing her again, and with their mouths still connected he slid to the edge of the sofa. Shifting her in his arms he changed her position in his lap and brought her legs around his waist. With her dress bunched up around her waist, she felt the thickness of his arousal pressed against the juncture of her legs. There was no way she could regain her senses now even if she wanted to. She was a goner.

Heat flared through her when she felt the straps of her dress fall from her shoulders, and then he was no longer kissing her. He had turned his attention to her breasts. Being braless left her bare and exposed for his pleasure, and when his mouth latched on to a nipple she knew this was just the beginning. When it came to breast stimulation he was as skilled as they came.

"Ian."

Ian pulled away, deciding he would take more time

with her breasts later. He knew exactly what they both wanted and needed now. He stood with her in his arms when the ring of his cell phone intruded.

"Damn," he muttered as he placed her on her feet while working the phone out of his jacket. "What?" he barked after answering the call.

"Domestic dispute," Vance said, the security manager's words washing over Ian like a pail of cold water. "One of those electricians got a surprise visit from his wife."

"And?"

"She caught him in bed with…" After a brief pause Vance added, "…another electrician. Male."

"What?"

"You heard me right. And now the woman is hysterical."

Ian rubbed his hand down his face. He couldn't very much blame her for that. Because of the satellite floating overhead, the reception was clear, and standing close in front of him he knew that Brooke had heard Vance's words. Ian met her gaze and, regardless of the situation, he was tempted to sweep his mouth down for another tongue-tingling kiss. Instead he said to Vance, "Go on, I'm sure there's more."

"Yes. She's threatened to sue everyone—the electricians' union, the airline that flew him here, the guy he was caught with, as well as this casino for allowing such behavior and conduct."

Ian didn't like hearing the word *sue*. "Where are you?"

"On the fourteenth floor."

"I'm on my way." He flipped the phone shut and gazed into Brooke's face thinking how damn sexy she looked with her hair mussed and her lips swollen from his kisses.

"I need to go," he said regretfully, straightening his jacket.

"I understand how it is when duty calls."

A small smile tugged at his lips. "I appreciate that." Straightening out the situation might take a while, and since it was almost two in the morning, Ian knew it would be two days before he saw Brooke again.

He took her hand in his as he led her toward the elevator. "Enjoy yourself while I'm in Memphis."

She smiled over at him. "I will."

He frowned. "But not too much."

She chuckled. "Okay, I won't."

When the elevator closed behind them, he pulled her into his arms. He thought of asking her to come to Memphis with him but quickly pushed the idea from his mind. Instead he said, "Have dinner with me in my penthouse when I get back."

He thought it was better to ask now. He had a feeling the two-day separation would have her thinking that tonight had been a mistake, and he didn't intend to let that happen.

"Ian, I—"

He kissed the words off her lips. "No, Brooke. We owe it to ourselves to finish what we started."

She stared up at him. "Do we?"

"Yes." And then he kissed her again, liking the feel of her in his arms, her warmth, her closeness and definitely her taste.

When he released her mouth she sighed deeply and said, "All right."

Tension that had been building inside of him slowly left his body. "I'll see you to your suite."

She shook her head. "That's not necessary, Ian. You have a matter that needs your immediate attention. Besides," she said, smiling, "I think I'll stop at one of the blackjack tables and try out some of those skills you taught me today."

He chuckled. "Okay."

"Have a safe trip, Ian."

"Thank you."

As the elevator arrived on the lobby floor, he released her. When she stepped away he suddenly felt a rush of loss through every part of his body. And when she began walking off he called out to her before she was swallowed by the crowd. "Don't forget about dinner Friday night."

She turned around and smiled. "I won't."

"My place. Seven sharp."

She nodded and continued to stare at him until the elevator door closed.

Brooke sat idly at a table in one of the cafés sipping her coffee and thinking of her telephone conversation with Tara Westmoreland that morning. Tara was Delaney's best friend and was married to Delaney's brother Thorn Westmoreland. Tara had invited Brooke to the surprise thirtieth birthday party being planned for Delaney next weekend at the Rolling Cascade.

Brooke was surprised Ian hadn't mentioned anything about the party to her. Perhaps he didn't want her there. She could remember how tense things had been at Dare and Shelly's wedding. But at that time the relationship between her and Ian had been very strained. Now, although they weren't back together or anything like that, at least they were talking…and kissing, she thought, smiling to herself. However, he might not want to give his family the wrong impression, and if they were seen together she could certainly see that happening.

"Enjoying your stay, Ms. Chamberlain?"

Brooke glanced up and met Vance's less-than-friendly eyes. On more than one occasion she had caught the man staring at her as if he was deliberately keeping her within his scope, and more than once she had wondered if Ian had asked him to keep an eye on her while he was gone. If he had, that meant he suspected her of something. It also meant he still didn't trust her.

Her heart quickened and she inwardly scolded herself for jumping to conclusions. This man was head of security at the casino and he was probably programmed to be suspicious of everything and everyone.

"Yes, I'm enjoying myself. This is a beautiful casino."

"I think so, too."

"And please, call me Brooke."

"Okay, and I'm Vance."

Brooke nodded. She was very much aware of who he was. He was the man who had taken her to Ian's office that first day. She had a feeling that had she refused he would have found a way to get her up there anyway with minimum fuss. He had that air about him, a no-nonsense, get-the-job-done sort of guy, and she wondered if he'd had a history at some point with the Bureau.

"Would you like to join me for coffee, Vance?" she asked, nodding to the huge coffeepot sitting in the middle of the table.

He surprised her when he said, "Don't mind if I do." And then he took the seat across from her. She leaned back in her chair. He had asked his question and now it was time to ask hers. He was former military; that was a given from his demeanor. But she needed to know something else about him.

"What Special Forces or federal agency were you affiliated with, Vance?"

His blue eyes, sharp and clear, riveted to hers as he poured a cup of coffee. "What makes you think I was part of the military or an agency?"

She shrugged. "Your mannerisms."

He chuckled. "I guess it takes one to know one."

She raised her brow, and before she could say anything, he said, "Don't bother denying it. Ian told me. Only because he knew he could trust me. So your secret's safe."

She took a sip of her own coffee and then said, "It's not a secret. It's just that my profession isn't anybody's business."

He moved his massive shoulders in a shrug. "Like I said, Ian mentioned it. As head of security here he felt I should know."

She nodded and wondered what else Ian might have told him. "You still haven't answered my question," she decided to remind him.

"I didn't, did I," he said, smiling coyly. "I was in the Corp and then I worked for the Bureau awhile before taking a position in the Secret Service."

The executive branch, Brooke mused. "I take it you know Quade," she said of Ian's twin brother.

Vance grinned fondly. "Yes, I know Quade. In fact I'm the one who trained him for his first assignment. Quade and I worked together for years and that's how I met Ian. When I decided to retire after twenty-five years in the service, Quade knew I wasn't one to sit idle and twiddle my thumbs. He mentioned Ian had a position here that I might be interested in. The rest, as they say, is history."

Brooke smiled. "And from what I can see, the way you run things indicates you're the right man for the job," she said honestly.

"Thanks."

She seriously meant the compliment. Her eyes and ears had been open and she'd seen how he had expertly and professionally, with the authority that could only come from someone with his years of experience, handled several potentially troublesome incidents.

"If I didn't know better I'd think you were a member of my staff, Brooke."

Brooke met his gaze over the rim of her cup after catching his meaning. He was no rookie and although she had tried to be discreet in her inquiries, he had been alert and had picked up on her interests. "Part of the job."

"Yes, but you're not working, are you? At least, that's what Ian told me. He said you were here for rest and relaxation."

She placed her cup down and straightened in her seat, deciding this wily old fox missed nothing. "Ian was right. What I meant when I said part of the job was that after a while, once you've been an agent, certain things become second nature."

"Oh, like being observant and noticing every little thing?"

"Yes, like being observant and noticing every little thing." She couldn't help but wonder if he believed her. She watched as he leaned forward and then he said,

"I guess a second pair of eyes never hurt. But I think we need to clear the air about something. Ian is a good man. Although he's a lot younger than most casino owners, he has a good sense for business. Somehow with that scientific mind of his he has the ability to play the odds and come up a winner. This place is a testimony to that. Investors trust him with their money because he has a proven track record of running a clean, profitable operation. My job is to be his eyes and ears as well as to protect his back. And, more important, Ian is not just my boss, I consider him a good friend."

Brooke picked up her coffee cup and stared down into the dark liquid a moment before meeting Vance's gaze and asking, "Is there a reason you're telling me this?"

He chuckled softly. "Only you can answer that, Brooke."

She held Vance's gaze. "No matter what you or anyone else might think, I trust Ian implicitly."

"But…"

"But I think we should end this conversation," Brooke said frowning, thinking she might have said too much already. Vance was no fool. He was as sharp as they came, and with his history he probably knew she had lied through her teeth when she claimed she was at the casino for rest and relaxation.

Vance laughed, breaking into her thoughts. "You're good, Brooke, and because I like you, I'm going to show you just how good an operation Ian runs," he said as he stood. "How about coming with me."

Two hours later Brooke had returned to her room to rest up a bit before changing for dinner. Vance had given her a tour of the casino's security surveillance center upstairs, and she'd had to agree with him that not too much went on in the casino that he wasn't aware of, including the lovers tryst between those electricians. Although there weren't any video cameras in individual rooms, they were installed in the elevators, hallways, lobby and every other inch of the casino. Security had noticed the excessive amount of time the two men had been visiting each other's rooms during the late-night hours.

Vance had also told her that being the born diplomat Ian was, he had brought a semblance of order to the situation last night, although there was only so much one could do after a woman discovered her husband had been unfaithful, and with someone of the same sex.

Brooke was just about to walk into the bathroom to run her shower when the phone rang. She quickly crossed the room to pick it up. "Hello."

"Miss me yet?"

Although Ian's voice sounded cool and in control, Brooke felt shivers tingle up her spine, anyway. His call had definitely caught her off guard. He had to have been thinking about her to have called. The mere fact that he had brought a smile to her lips. "No, I've been too busy to miss you," she said teasingly.

"Oh, and what have you been doing?"

Brooke glanced out of the window. The view of the mountains was breathtaking, but the mountains weren't the main thing on her mind now. The man she was talking to was.

She thought back to his question, doubting he would appreciate knowing Vance had given her a tour of his security setup. "I've been doing a lot of things but mostly perfecting my blackjack skills."

His laugh sent a warm feeling all through her stomach. "I hope you won't be breaking the casino before I return."

"I'll try not to, but I have been lucky a few times."

"Luck has nothing to do with it. Like I've told you, it's merely a matter of science."

"If you say so. Will you still be returning tomorrow night?"

"Those are my plans and so far things are running on schedule. I should be able to wrap up in the morning and arrive there by late afternoon."

Brooke nodded. She didn't want to admit it but she *had* missed him. The mere fact that until this week she hadn't seen him in four years meant nothing. Once she'd seen him her heart had remembered; unfortunately, so had her body.

"What are your plans for the rest of the day?"

His question pulled in her thoughts. "To shop until I drop." She then decided to mention something that had been bothering her all day. "I got a call from Tara this morning inviting me to Delaney's surprise birthday party. Why didn't you mention it?"

"I really didn't think about it much. Besides, I figured sooner or later you would hear from some member of my family."

"And how do you feel about me being there?" she questioned.

"Why are you asking me that? Is there a certain way I should feel, Brooke?"

"I don't know," she replied quietly. "I know how tense I made you feel being at Dare's wedding."

"At the time, considering everything, I think a certain degree of discomfort for both of us was understandable."

"And now?"

"Now I think we're a lot more at ease with each other, don't you?"

Considering how they'd been spending a lot of their time while they'd been together she would definitely say yes. "I just don't want you to get bent all out of shape if your family starts assuming things about us."

"I'm used to my family, Brooke. Maybe the real question is whether or not you'll get bent out of shape. My mom refuses to believe that you and I won't ever work out our problems and get back together, no matter what I've told her to the contrary. She likes you. Always has."

Brooke smiled. She'd always liked his mom, as well.

"So are you thinking about going?"

"Probably," she replied, hoping that making an appearance wouldn't cause a big commotion. Unfortunately, there didn't seem to be any way to avoid it. Everyone had known how serious her and Ian's relationship was at one time, and she was sure some of them didn't know the reason for their breakup. Although he was close to his family, Ian was a private person when it came to his personal life.

"And you're sure you won't have a problem if I decide to go?" she asked again.

"Yes, I'm sure I won't have a problem with it." He chuckled. "Besides, it's about time I give the family something to talk about. Things have been pretty quiet since Durango got married a few months ago, and I'll be the first to admit that we Westmorelands need a little craziness every once in a while."

* * *

A half hour later Ian sat and reflected on his conversation with Brooke. He'd asked her if she'd missed him and before they'd hung up he'd gotten her to admit she had. That meant he was making progress. But the truth was that he wasn't faring much better. He missed her, too.

He should never have let her back into his life, but now that she was, he was in a bad way. It was crazy what mere kisses could do to a man.

It had been more than just the kisses, though. It had been her presence and the heated attraction that enveloped them each and every time they were together.

"Would you like anything else to drink, sir?"

Ian glanced up at the waiter. He had dined alone at a restaurant known for its sizzling and delicious steaks. The food had been excellent, but the only sizzling and delicious thing on his mind during the entire meal had been Brooke.

"No, that will be all for now."

What Ian wanted was a quiet moment to just sit, sip his wine and pine for the woman he desired more than anything else. He longed to see her again, take her into his arms, make love to her on his bed or hers—which technically was also his because he owned the casino—and take her to a place he hadn't been since they'd separated. A place that had his insides coiling just thinking about it. It had been a place they'd discovered years ago; it had been their own universe, their own solar system, a personal space only the two of them occupied.

The hand holding his wineglass tightened as he felt that same squeeze in his groin. How could one woman stir up his passion, his desire and his lust to such unprecedented proportions?

"Ian?"

Snatched from his heated musings, Ian glanced up at the very attractive woman standing beside his table. He smiled at her. "Casey, what are you doing here in Memphis?" he asked his cousin as he came to his feet. The last time he'd seen her was at his brother Durango's wedding reception in Atlanta.

"I'm on a buying trip for my store," she said smiling back at him. "I'll be here for a couple of days. What about you?"

"I'm here on business and I'll flying out in the morning." Ian knew she owned a fashion boutique back in Beaumont, Texas. "Come join me," he invited, pulling out a chair for her. "Would you like to order something?" he asked, not sure if she'd eaten yet.

"Thanks," she said as she sat down. "But, no. I've just finished eating and was about to leave. I thought it was you from across the room, but I wasn't sure, and for a moment I was hesitant about coming over to ask. You seemed deeply absorbed in thought."

He sat back down and chuckled. "I was," he said without any further explanation. It was best she didn't know what he'd been thinking about. "So are you coming to Delaney's surprise party next week at the casino?"

He saw her grimace slightly and knew she hadn't yet made up her mind. Whereas her brothers Clint and Cole had quickly meshed into the Westmoreland family fold, Casey was still a little reserved. Evidently after thinking for years that her family consisted of only her and her two brothers, the multitude of Westmorelands overwhelmed her.

"Do you know if my father is coming?" she asked.

"Yes, as far as I know Uncle Corey's coming," Ian said, taking another sip of his drink. "I can't see him missing it."

He knew Casey was still struggling to develop a relationship with the father she hadn't known she had. All those years she'd thought he was dead.

"I'm thinking about taking him up on his offer and spending a month in Montana," Casey said.

Ian raised a brow. He'd heard his uncle making the invitation, but Ian hadn't been sure Casey would accept it. For her to be considering the visit was a huge step in building a relationship with her father.

"I think that's a wonderful idea, Casey," Ian said. "And I'm sure Uncle Corey and Abby would love having you spend some time with them."

While kicking back and enjoying the taste of his wine, Ian listened as Casey brought him up to date on her brothers, who were both Texas Rangers. She knew for certain they would be at Delaney's party, but Ian noticed she still hadn't answered his question as to whether or not she would make an appearance.

An hour or so later, Ian opened the door to his hotel room. He glanced across the room. His bags were all packed and he was ready to go. Hell, he would leave tonight if he could get a flight out. To say he was eager to return to Lake Tahoe was an understatement.

Even now he wanted to pick up the phone and call Brooke but he kept reminding himself he had spoken to her earlier. He shook his head as he began undressing, wondering what in the hell was happening to him. Brooke walks back into his life and his mind goes bonkers. Okay, she was the sexiest thing he'd ever laid eyes on, both then and now, but still, that wasn't a good enough reason to get carried away.

But he *was* getting carried away. He was beginning to feel emotions that he hadn't felt in years. He raked his hand over his head thinking that wasn't a good thing, but for now there wasn't anything he could do about it.

Not a damn thing.

Six

Brooke had spent the past two days shopping and enjoying a lot of the amenities the resort had to offer and, of course, keeping her eyes and ears open while doing so. Now the day Ian was scheduled to return had arrived, and as she lowered her body into the warm water of the Jacuzzi tub in her bathroom, excitement filled her to a degree she hadn't known in a long time. She submerged her body deep into the tub and let the jets provide a deep massage for the muscles she had overworked during her two-day shopping spree.

She laid her head back and closed her eyes as the jets and the bubbles whisked her away to another place, tantalizing as well as soothing her state of mind, sharpening her focus and her outlook.

Another moan escaped her lips when she shifted her body and doing so shot a jet of water to the area between her legs. She smiled thinking that was some kind of massage therapy. But she was realistic enough to know that the only way the deep-rooted tension and urgency that had settled in that part of her body could be removed was by the skill of one man.

Ian Westmoreland.

As her eyes remained closed she contemplated how their dinner that evening would go. She could remember sharing meals with him at other times and how things ended. The memories sent shivers all through her body. He hadn't earned the nickname the Perfect End for nothing.

A couple of hours later, after her bath and a short nap, Brooke began getting dressed. Although she didn't agree that one more time between the sheets would get them out of each other's systems, she did agree that they needed one last time together to put an ending chapter to what once had been a beautiful relationship.

The thought of finality tightened the muscles surrounding her heart but she knew it had to be. She had to finally move forward in her life. She was young and believed that sooner or later she would get over Ian, no matter how hard such a thing would be. When she returned to D.C. she would ask Malcolm for a couple of weeks off.

She needed time alone to sort things out and to put her life in order. She also needed to make some decisions regarding her future. If she decided to leave fieldwork, she needed to know what other opportunities the Bureau had to offer. When she had mentioned such a possibility to Vance, he had suggested a job at the White House. Apparently, there were always places for capable women on the first lady's security detail.

A smile touched her lips when she thought of the time she'd spent with Vance. In the end, she'd decided that she liked him because he had Ian's best interest at heart and he was loyal to those he cared about. Ian was like that, too. Ian's sense of loyalty was the main reason he couldn't get past the Boris Knowles case.

She glanced at the underthings she had placed on her bed, items she had purchased that day. Ian always loved black lace on her, and she was going to make sure that tonight he saw a lot of it.

She squared her shoulders after dabbing perfume on her pulse points and between her breasts. The outfit she had bought to wear was an attention getter. It was meant to tease, tantalize, to impress and undress all in one sweep. She intended to make their last time together special.

Tonight she would be the one to give them the perfect end.

It felt good being back, Ian thought, as he walked into the penthouse a little later than he'd wanted. His connecting flight had been hell, with enough turbulence to make even a grown man weep.

The first thing he'd wanted to do when he had arrived at the casino was to find Brooke, but Vance had mentioned he had seen her leave the resort earlier. She had been headed for the shops in town. It had looked as if she intended to do some serious shopping. Ian had ended up going to his penthouse a disenchanted man. He unpacked with the thought that he was preparing for a night he intended Brooke would remember for a long time.

Ian checked his watch a few hours later. It was ten to seven. Where was she? He distinctively remembered

Brooke always showed up at any destination a few minutes earlier than scheduled. Of all the nights for her to change her routine and—

His breath caught when he heard the ringing of his elevator alerting him he was about to have a visitor. Deciding this would be a special night, he had changed into a pair of black trousers and a white button-up shirt. But to give his outfit a casual spin he had left his shoes off. He wanted to look totally at home, totally relaxed and completely in control.

He walked over to the elevator and was standing there when it opened. As soon as it did, his throat suddenly felt tight and he could only stare, almost tongue-tied as he feasted his eyes on Brooke. She was wearing a short, lacy black concoction that seemed to scream, strip me. His fingertips began to itch, wanting to do that very thing.

"I know I'm early, but aren't you going to invite me in?"

Hell, he planned to do better than that, he thought, edging backward so she could take a step forward. When she did, the elevator door swooshed close. "Welcome back, Ian."

God, he'd missed her. In just a couple of days she had gotten back under his skin. Deep. He opened his mouth to reply but no sound came out. His mind couldn't get beyond the fact that she was standing there wearing black lace. She of all people knew how he felt about black lace; especially on her. She could wear it like no other woman. He was aroused to the nth degree from just seeing her in it.

The itching in his fingers intensified and a need he tried to ignore gripped him, made his blood sizzle and his heart pound in his chest. He took a step forward. It was then that he studied her face; a face that had invaded his dreams so many times over the past four years; a face he couldn't forget no matter how he tried.

Ian quickly accepted the fact that it wasn't about the dress Brooke was wearing or how sexy she looked in it that made him so attracted to her. Brooke, the unique individual she'd always been, had captured his interest from the first and still held it tight.

But still…he had to give kudos to the dress. It made a provocative statement, and seeing her in it did the things to him she'd known it would.

"Ian?"

His gaze returned to her face. He watched her mouth quiver and decided to kiss that quiver right off her lips. He intended to give her a proper hello, Ian Westmoreland style. Leaning over, he ran his fingertips along her jaw and then, leaning closer still, he began gently nibbling on her lips, savoring the moment and relishing the sweet taste of her and the feel of her full lips beneath his.

He had wanted to linger, but the need hammering inside of him wouldn't let him. It drove an urgency he couldn't control, and when her moan filled his mouth he indulged her by taking the kiss deeper. All the long-denied needs he'd pretended weren't there were hitting him full force, begging for the kind of release only she could give.

He tightened his hold on her as his mouth mated with hers, slowly yet torridly, taking his breath away with every return stroke of her tongue while it moved sensuously in his mouth, hitting those spots she knew from the past could drive him mad with desire.

One thing he and Brooke had enjoyed doing as a

couple was exploring new things in the bedroom, and on one occasion they'd had a kiss-a-thon. By the time it was over, they had explored every kissing tip known to man and had gone further by inventing some of their own.

And she remembered, he thought, as his hands on her hips tightened and he pulled her closer to him. Not only had she remembered but she was putting some of those techniques into action, making blood pulse through his veins and sending heat spreading all through him; especially his loins. With a mastery and skill that almost made him weak in the knees, she was taking over the kiss, making him groan into her mouth and reminding him why he had fallen so hard for her years ago. Brooke had a way of taking him by surprise.

And she was doing it now.

He definitely hadn't expected this, a kiss that went far and beyond any fantasy he'd ever had. He had figured she would be reluctant, would fight the intensity of the chemistry they were feeling. But she wasn't. In her own way she was letting him know that she needed to move on with her life just as he needed to move on with his. She accepted that there could never be a reconciliation. They needed closure, and this was the only way they would get it. She was kissing him with a passion that sent shivers vibrating through his body and he was greedily lapping it up.

"Brooke," he whispered when she finally released his mouth. But before she could take a step back, he swept her into his arms and once again covered her lips with his.

She could go on kissing him forever, Brooke thought, as Ian kissed her and she greedily kissed him back with equal fervor. And moments later when he released her mouth and began walking with her in his arms, her breath caught in her chest as he moved up the stairs to his bedroom.

She glanced up, saw the smoldering look of desire in his eyes, and the pressure mounting inside her escalated.

When he came to a stop, she glanced around and he slowly placed her on her feet, sliding her body against his in the process, letting her feel the bulge in his pants, evidence of his intense desire for her.

He tipped her chin up and met her gaze. "I want you."

His words made her draw in a shaky breath. It had been four years since she had been with a man, and her body was attuned to Ian in a profound way. He was the one and only man she'd ever been intimate with. Something deep within her began to prepare her for the pleasure she knew only he could give with those wonderful hands, that skillful tongue and that big strong body. Just thinking about what was to come had sensations erupting all the way inside her womb.

"And I want you, too, Ian," she said breathlessly as she felt her center began to quake with a longing she hadn't felt in a long time. "Tonight, I need you," she added.

"Not as much as I need you," he replied, reaching out to remove her dress.

A hiss escaped between Ian's teeth when he pulled the dress over her head and tossed it aside only to reveal more black lace—a sexy bra and silky high-cut panties. Unable to help himself, he dropped to his knees right there in the middle of the room and buried his face in her belly, needing the scent of her in his nostrils and the taste of her on his tongue.

He leaned forward and began licking the hollow of her navel while easing her panties down her legs. He paused only long enough for her to step out of them before nipping at her belly and moving lower.

He pulled back for a moment and looked up at her. He continued to hold her gaze as he reached out and slipped one hand between her legs, letting his fingers go to work in her damp flesh. And when she grabbed hold of his shoulders and began moaning and grinding against his hand he knew she was on the brink of an orgasm so explosive she would have it right there if he didn't do something.

And so he did.

He broke eye contact with her and dipped his head and glided his tongue over her, into her, exploring, probing and loving her in a way he hadn't wanted to do with any other woman. His hands held tight to her thighs as his tongue continued its assault with hard, steady strokes, needing the taste of her in each and every part of his mouth.

He tasted her shivers, felt a shudder shake her body and heard her moan his name as she automatically bucked against his mouth, but he refused to pull back. Instead his tongue seemed to go into a frenzy, and it took her with a greediness that sent tremors through him.

A strangled growl escaped his lips when her spasms ended. He stood and quieted her aftershocks with his mouth on hers, needing to kiss her again. And then he was sweeping her into his arms and taking her to his bed and placing her on his satin bedspread.

He slid a hand to her chest and undid the front clasp of her bra and eased her out of it, tossing it aside. He'd always thought that her breasts were the most beautiful in the world and automatically he leaned forward and rubbed his face against them, licking the area between her breasts before latching his lips onto a hardened nipple and drawing it into his mouth.

Ignoring her moans, he suckled hard, deep, relentlessly, one then the other, once again mesmerized by her taste, and when he couldn't hold back any longer, he stood and hurriedly stripped off his clothes, needing to be joined with her with such an intense need that his entire body was throbbing. And when he came back to the bed, she reached out and her hands captured his engorged flesh as if she needed to touch it, become reacquainted with the feel of it. When she began stroking him, he almost lost it.

"Easy, baby," he murmured as his knee pressed into the mattress. "Too much of that and I'm a goner." He moved to position his body over hers and nudged her legs apart with his knee.

His gaze locked on hers. He knew she'd been taking the Pill for years to regulate her periods, but for both of their protection, he reached into a small table and retrieved a foil square.

Before he could open the small packet, Brooke took it, opened it and carefully placed the sheath on his erection.

He reached out and brushed his hand against her cheek. "I want you so much, Brooke," he murmured softly, and then with a primal growl he entered her, throwing his head back as something wild, primitive and obsessive took control inside him.

She was tight, nearly as tight as she'd been the first time they'd made love and she'd been a virgin. It wasn't his imagination, and he met her gaze, ignoring the hunger that propelled him to start moving. She was so tight that it felt like she was squeezing him, locking her feminine muscles securely around him, claiming him, making sure he couldn't pull out even if he wanted to.

She didn't have that to worry about. He wasn't going anywhere other than deeper inside her once he fully understood just what the tightness of her body meant. He met her gaze, and the look she gave him all but said, You figure it out.

So he did.

"This is the first time for you since…?" He couldn't finish the question, since the very thought shocked the hell out of him. Four years was a long time and her devotion to him was the most touching thing he could ever imagine. The very idea that even now he had been her first and only lover tore a soundless howl of possessiveness from his throat. Her body knew him and only him.

At that precise moment he wanted her with a passion he'd never felt before. Grasping her hips he began moving, stroking back and forth inside of her, going deeper. Her muscles clenched with each and every thrust he made, forcing his strokes to become more frantic.

He had to look at her, had to remember this moment for the rest of his life, and he brought his head forward, met her gaze and saw the heat in her eyes and knew neither of them could last much longer although they were fighting to do so. This would be the last time they came together this way, and they intended to make a memory to last a lifetime.

The thought, the very idea of not making love to her ever again, had him leaning forward, nipping at her shoulders, branding her while he felt her fingertips dig into his back as if to brand him, as well.

"Ian, I—"

He kissed the words off her lips. There was nothing to be said and when an explosion sent a million shudders ramming through his body, a loud growl tore from his throat through clenched teeth. He felt her come apart in his arms which caused another orgasm to rip through him. He thought he was going to die and quickly decided if he was about to take his last breath then this was definitely the way to go about it.

And he knew, as he buried himself inside of her to the hilt again as a third orgasm quickly hit him and triggered a similar explosion inside her body and he began rocking back and forth inside of her with a hunger that wouldn't let up, that he had miscalculated his emotions.

He'd erroneously figured he could sleep with her this one last time and be done with it, effectively getting her out of his system. Instead, as he cupped her buttocks tighter in his hands and felt her thighs quake beneath his at the same time his release shot deep into her womb, he knew that she had burrowed deeper into it.

"Stay here and rest. I'll let you know when dinner is ready," Ian's warm breath whispered against Brooke's ear before he slipped out of bed.

He glanced back over his shoulder long enough to see her eyes slowly drift open at the same time an adorable smile touched her lips as she snuggled under the covers. "Um, okay."

His lips twitched into a smile. He'd totally worn the woman out. She needed rest, and the only way to guarantee that she got it was for him to leave for a while. So after putting his pants back on he quietly eased open the door and slipped out of the room.

Talk about him being obsessed with making love to her. They hadn't made it past the foyer. She'd had no idea he'd set the stage for seduction with romantic lit candles. Their pure vanilla fragrance was sending a sweet scent through the rooms. He knew Brooke was partial to Thai food and so he'd had one of the resort restaurants prepare a special meal for them. He hoped the meal he had selected would please her. Making his way across the room, he picked up the phone and within minutes had instructed room service to deliver their dinner to his penthouse.

Knowing there was nothing for him to do but wait, he walked over to the window and looked out. It was dark outside, but the shape of the mountains could be seen across the lake. He would love to share this beautiful view with Brooke.

If he were to go back to his bedroom now and wake her he would do more than just show her the view. It was bad enough that he had to get her up when their meal came. He wouldn't take any chances. Brooke was too much of a temptation, and now that he had made love to her he wanted her more and more.

The memory of their bodies tangled together in his bed was so vivid in his mind that his blood was racing through his veins a little too fast to suit him. Although they had turned the heat up a notch, in fact had kicked it into a full blaze in his bed, a part of him refused to remain anything but cautious where she was concerned. She had hurt him once and could possibly do it again and he wasn't a glutton for punishment.

"Ian?"

At the sound of her soft voice he felt his entire body go tense. Squaring his shoulders and taking a deep breath, he turned around. Immediately he wished he hadn't. She was wearing the shirt he'd worn earlier, but she hadn't bothered to button it up, giving him a good frontal view.

He heard himself groan as his mind savored what he was seeing. There was nothing more beautiful than a naked or half-naked Brooke. A Brooke who'd recently been made love to or a Brooke who was wearing a let's-do-it-again look on her face.

The memories of what they had shared in his bedroom were tossing his mind every which way but loose. He fought for composure. He fought for control. He fought the urge to cross the room and take her again. If she was trying to get him all hot and bothered again, it was a complete waste of time because he was already there. He hadn't cooled down from the last time.

"Yes, Brooke?" he answered in a low, barely audible voice. "What is it that you want?"

He met her gaze. Heaven help him if she even hinted that she wanted him to make love to her again. There was no way he would be able to resist. Even now his arousal was thickening beneath his zipper. "Just tell me what you want, sweetheart. Your every wish is my command."

Brooke's breath caught as Ian's gaze held hers. She tried to remember the last time he had called her sweetheart and couldn't, it had seemed so long ago. But the endearment had flowed off his lips just as easily as it used to. And then there was the way he was looking at her with dark eyes filled with more than just heat and desire. Hope escalated within her at the thought that maybe, possibly...

She quickly pushed the far-fetched thought from her mind. Ian might desire her but he no longer loved her. She tried to think but decided she couldn't think very well with him looking at her like that. He'd said her every wish was his command. Well, she decided to put him to the test.

"How soon will the food arrive?" she asked, sliding into one of the high-back chairs at the casino-style blackjack table in the room.

"How soon do you want it?"

She smiled, wondering if they were still talking about the food. "If the chef decided to cook slowly tonight it won't bother me," she said silkily.

No sooner had the words left her lips than the zing of the elevator let them know that, unfortunately, the chef hadn't been slow and their food was on the way up. Ian glanced across the room and saw the disappointed pout on her lips. Lips he couldn't wait to devour again.

"There's no law that says we have to eat it as soon as the food gets here. It will keep for a while," he assured her.

Her response was a slow, sensuous smile, and a deliberate shifting of her body in the chair exposed a lot more than a bare leg. He bit back the growl that threatened to roar from deep within his throat.

"Don't you dare move," he said when the elevator arrived on his floor. He quickly left and went to the elevator.

Brooke smiled as a shiver slithered through her, and she found she couldn't sit still as he'd instructed. When she had walked into the room and had seen the flickering candles and inhaled the scent of vanilla, as well as seeing Ian standing at the window shirtless, displaying his muscular shoulders and wearing pants that showed what a great butt he had, she had fought back the need to cross the room and touch him all over, ease down on her knees in front of him and unzip his pants and ultimately savor him the same way he'd done her earlier.

With a long sigh she stood and tried to remain calm. Walking around the blackjack table she concentrated on the huge glass window in front of her and the wonderful view of the mountains.

Moments later when she saw Ian's reflection in the glass, she knew he had come back into the room and was standing not far behind her. Their gazes met, reflected in the glass, and she was tempted to turn around.

Her gaze remained fixed on the windowpane as he walked up behind her and wrapped his arms around her. She leaned back into him, letting her head fall back against the breadth of his chest. She felt the need to share herself with him again, not just her body but her heart, whether he wanted it or not. She loved him and nothing could or would ever change that.

"Brooke."

He said her name in that sexy voice of his while nuzzling a certain spot on her neck that could always turn her on. And then she felt his tongue lick the side of her face, moving to the area just below her ear.

"Feel me," he whispered, and she did when she leaned back against him. She felt the hardness of him pressing deep into her backside at the same time she felt him use his hands to part the front of the shirt she wore. And when one of his hands went to her center to claim the area between her legs, a tantalizing sensation shot all through her.

"Are you sure you aren't ready to eat?" he asked huskily.

"I'm sure," she whispered, barely able to get the words out in a coherent voice. His beard was rubbing sensuously against the side of her neck causing an erotic friction that was sending shivers all through her body.

"Then tell me what you're ready for, Brooke."

He turned her around, evidently needing to look into her eyes when she answered. "You, Ian. I'm ready for you."

Her words made something within him shatter and he lifted her to sit on the edge of the blackjack table and then stepped back to remove his pants. He kicked them aside before going back to her and tugging his shirt from her shoulders and tossing it to join his pants on the floor.

He reached out and lifted her bottom and wrapped her legs around him. "I'm ready for you, too, Brooke. Let me show you just how much."

And before she could take another breath he swiftly entered her, going deep and locking tight. And then he began moving with a furor that bordered on obsession. At this very moment they were beating the odds. If anyone had told him that she would be here in his private sanctuary, he would not have believed them. There was no scientific justification for it. But he didn't want to dwell on logical reasoning now. He just wanted to think about making love to her while she teetered on the edge of his private blackjack table.

Tonight he needed this. He needed her.

The only thing he wanted to concentrate on was the

sensations that coursed through him with each and every stroke into her body. His hands at her waist tightened even more and he lifted her almost clear off the green felt tabletop, straining to achieve a more penetrated connection. He leaned forward and kissed her, long and deep, liking the sound of her moan in his mouth. He'd never made love to a woman on a blackjack table before and now in his mind, played the role of a master dealer. But it wasn't his hand he was playing. It was his body over and over into hers, and the last thought on his mind was getting busted. He was on a lucky streak and was determined to come out the winner.

When he broke off the kiss, Brooke looked up at him with eyes glazed with heated desire. And as if their minds had been running along the same thoughts she whispered, "I got a three and a five." She tightened her hold on his shoulders. "Hit me."

A smile touched Ian's lips. He would hit her all right. He tilted her hips on the table at an angle that gave him greater access and thrust deep inside her, aiming for a spot he knew would drive her wild.

It did.

She screamed his name as an explosion hit. The vibration ricocheted through her directly to him. He threw his head back, loving the feel of her orgasm and knowing it would detonate his body as well. When the climax struck, he shuddered uncontrollably and nothing mattered but the woman he was making love to.

She grabbed hold of his face and brought it back down to her, taking his mouth with a hunger that he still felt. His body was getting hard again. When would they get enough? It was as if they were making up for lost time, but he was okay with that. Tonight they needed each other. Tonight they were both winners.

And they would deal with tomorrow when it came.

Seven

"So what do you think?"

Brooke lifted her head from her meal as a blush tinted her cheeks. If Ian was asking her about the food, her reply could be that it was great. If he was referring to their lovemaking sessions, words couldn't describe how wonderful they had been. No matter what happened after she left the Rolling Cascade to return to D.C., she would always cherish every moment she'd spent with him.

She leaned back in her chair. "You know how much I love Thai food, and your chef did a fantastic job. And if you're asking about something else," she said slowly, provocatively, as she picked up her wineglass to take a sip, looking at him over the rim. "All I can say is that I feel I got treated to dessert before the main course." She then gave him a sultry smile.

Ian chuckled low in his throat. "I'm glad everything was to your satisfaction."

He took a sip of wine and thought about how incredibly sexy she looked sitting across from him wearing only his shirt. At least she had buttoned it up.

The primeval male within him wanted to reach out and pull the shirt open. He wanted to once again see how the flickering light from the candles cast a glow against her dark skin.

"It rated higher than my satisfaction, Ian," she said, reclaiming his attention. "You outdid yourself. I don't think I'll ever be able to look at a blackjack table again without blushing."

He shivered at the memory. Hell, when he saw a blackjack table again he wouldn't blush. He would get aroused. Speaking of aroused, he watched how her fingertips skimmed a trail along her wineglass, remembering how her hands had done that to him. Knowing they were headed for trouble if he didn't get his mind off bedding her again, he asked, "What are your plans for tomorrow?"

She grinned. "I won't be going shopping, that's for sure."

"Would you spend the day with me?"

His question surprised her. She would have thought that after tonight he would avoid her at all cost, if nothing else but to see if she was out of his system. She gazed at him thoughtfully as she leaned forward and rested her chin on her hands. "Um, it depends. What do you have planned?"

He smiled. "After an important meeting with my event planner to make sure all the bases are covered for Delaney's birthday party, I'll be free to do whatever I want. Do you have any suggestions?"

They fell silent as Brooke contemplated his question. "Blackjack is definitely out."

He chuckled. "If you say so."

"Um, what about a game of golf?"

He lifted a brow. "Can you play?"

"No, but I'd like to learn. Would you teach me the basics?"

"Yeah, I can do that."

"And I'd like to go swimming in your pool again if you don't mind."

He studied her for a long moment, remembering her in his pool. "I don't mind, but this time I'll take a dip with you."

She stared at him, thinking that was exactly what she had hoped he'd do. "All right." She glanced at her watch then back across the table at him before standing. "It's late. I'd better get ready to go."

He stood, his gaze intense. "Stay with me tonight, Brooke."

Her heart jumped at the invitation, spoken in a deep, husky voice. Her mind was suddenly bombarded with all the reasons she shouldn't, the main one being that if he ever discovered the truth as to why she was staying at the Rolling Cascade, he would consider her actions deceitful.

"I don't think that's a good idea, Ian. We were supposed to be doing the closure thing, remember?" she said softly.

"I remember," he said, coming around the table to stand in front of her. "But at the moment, the only thing I can think about is doing the opening thing with you."

She lifted a brow. "The opening thing?"

A smiled touched the corners of his lips. "Yes, like this," he said, reaching out and working the buttons free on his shirt she was wearing. When the shirt parted he slid his hands over her waist then upward to her chest, tracing his fingertips over the hardened tips of her breasts.

He met her gaze. "Need I say more?"

The gaze that returned his stare shimmered with passion and desire, and when his hand moved lower and touched her between the legs, her breath caught. "No, you don't have to say anything at all," she said after making a soft whimpering sound.

And then she reached out and wrapped her arms around his neck and pulled his mouth downs to hers, deciding they would work on that closure thing another time.

Ian blinked. "Excuse me, Margaret. What did you say?"

Margaret Fields smiled. It was obvious something else had her boss's attention. He definitely was not his usual alert self this morning. He seemed preoccupied. She couldn't help wondering if the others present for their meeting had detected it. "I said that I spoke with Mrs. Tara Westmoreland yesterday and she faxed me her preference for the menu. I've given it to the restaurant that will be handling the catering services."

Ian nodded. "How many people are we expecting?"

"There are three hundred confirmed reservations."

Ian knew that in addition to family and close friends, because of Jamal's status in international circles, a number of celebrities and dignitaries were included in the mix.

"There's a possibility the secretary of state might make an appearance. We'll know in a few days if her schedule will allow it," Margaret said as if in awe of such an event taking place.

Ian then glanced over at Vance. "I take it security is ready to handle things."

Vance smiled. "Yes, and if the secretary does come, I will work with the Secret Service to make sure her stay here is a pleasant one."

Ian knew that Sheikh Prince Jamal Ari Yasir had also reserved a large portion of the resort to house the guests invited to his wife's surprise birthday bash. Ian glanced at his watch. "Okay, keep me informed of anything that develops. Otherwise, it seems everything is under control."

Ian stood. He was to meet Brooke in half an hour and he clearly had no intention of keeping her waiting. "That will be all, and thanks for all of your hard work. I want for us to do everything in our power to make this a special night for the princess of Tahran."

Brooke sighed as she glanced around. The golf course was a lush green, and the open architecture of the massive clubhouse was breathtaking. The redesigned course had been nominated in Golf Digest as one of the best new resort courses, and she could see why. Measuring over eight thousand yards from the back tees, the fairways that wound through large moss-covered hardwoods, oak and pine trees weren't narrow and didn't appear to be squeezed in by the villas.

Ian had told her last night that the first and last holes played along Lake Tahoe and one of the tee boxes was set on a bluff overlooking the water. Nothing detracted from the ambience of the course. Except for the man she was waiting for.

Ian.

Goose bumps suddenly appeared on her body when she thought of how wonderful it was waking up in his arms that morning. Being the Perfect Beginning that he was, they had made love again and she had fallen asleep, only to awaken an hour or so later to find him dressed and leaning against the bedroom door frame watching her.

They had stared across the room at each other for what seemed like an eternity before he finally moved forward, slowly removing his jacket and tossing it aside. Then he reached for her and pulled her up into his arms and kissed her as if his life depended on it. After a long, deep kiss, he'd left, promising to meet her on the walkway in front of the clubhouse at eleven.

Because Ian had also mentioned that the Rolling Cascade's golf club adhered to a dress code, she had visited one of the golf shops earlier to purchase what would be considered the proper attire. From what the salesmen had told her, golf clothes were often bright and colorful, so she had purchased a black top and a lime-green pair of shorts with belt loops, which the salesman claimed was a must. Shorts with cuffs weren't practical because they had a tendency to trap dirt. The salesman had suggested that she purchase a hat with a visor to keep the sun off her face. And arriving at the clubhouse early, she had gone inside to rent a pair of golf shoes.

Brooke turned and recognized the woman walking down the walkway in her direction. She was the person Brooke had bumped into while out shopping yesterday, knocking the shopping bags out of the woman's hands. Brooke, in one of her rare clumsy moments, hadn't been looking where she was going. She'd been captivated by that black lace dress on a mannequin; the one she'd purchased and worn last night.

"Well, hello again," Brooke greeted, smiling when the woman moved to pass her.

The woman eyed Brooke with surprise and to Brooke's way of thinking acted as if they'd never seen each other before. She decided to jog the woman's memory. "Remember me from yesterday?" Brooke said. "I accidentally bumped into you at one of the shops and knocked your packages out of your hand and—"

"Oh, yeah, that's right. I remember now. Sorry about that. My mind was elsewhere," the attractive thirty-something blonde with a British accent said, grasping for a friendlier tone. "Hello to you, too. Sorry, I didn't recognize you," she quickly added, and plastered what Brooke perceived as a fake smile on her face.

Brooke shrugged. "No problem." She then noticed her outfit and the golf shoes she was wearing and asked, "You're about to play a game of golf?"

"Yes, I'm supposed to be meeting my husband in the lobby, and as usual I'm late."

Brooke nodded. "Well, don't let me keep you. Enjoy your game."

"Thanks." And the woman rushed inside the building.

Brooke frowned as she watched the woman walk away. It was as if the woman had no recollection of their earlier collision.

"Hey, beautiful. What's the frown for? You been waiting long?"

Brooke turned and smiled when she saw that Ian had

driven up beside her in a golf cart. "No, I haven't," she said, sliding into the cart to sit beside him.

"Then why the frown?"

"No reason, I guess, other than a lady who I accidentally bumped into yesterday while shopping didn't remember me today. I'm surprised because I practically knocked all the packages out of her hands and had to help her pick them up. She was pretty chatty then."

"What! You mean there's someone who doesn't remember you? That's not possible," he teased. "You're so unforgettable," he said, and grinned as he pulled the cap over her eyes, just seconds before maneuvering the cart around several trees in their paths.

Brooke shifted toward him. "Hey, let's not be a smart-ass," she said chuckling. She couldn't help wondering if he really thought that. Had he had as hard a time forgetting her as she had forgetting him over the years? But then, she'd never tried to forget him. He had remained an integral part of her nightly dreams.

When Ian continued driving for a while, Brooke asked, "Where are you taking me?"

He smiled over at her as he drove around yet another tree. "To my private golfing spot. If I'm going to teach you the game, I don't want any distractions. Golf is like blackjack. You have to be focused."

"Oh." Just hearing him say the word *blackjack* was eliciting memories of the night before. And with those memories came heated lust. She wondered if it would always be that way with them and quickly remembered there wouldn't be any reason for things to be that way because in a week they would part ways and there was no telling when they would see each other again.

Not wanting to think about that, she turned her attention to her surroundings and the cart path they were taking, keeping clear of the greens and teeing grounds.

Finally Ian eased the cart to a stop and she followed his gaze as he took in the area that sat on a bluff overlooking the lake. Brooke glanced at him. "And what am I supposed to do if I hit a ball over into the water?"

He chuckled. "If you're worried that I'd send you to get it, don't be. This is going to be a practice session, and if we lose a ball we play a new one. I brought plenty of them along."

When he climbed out of the cart, Brooke did likewise and waited by his side while he got the golf bag out of the back. She couldn't help noticing how good he looked in his golf shirt and shorts.

He turned to her after placing the straps of the golf bags on his shoulders and said, "Let's go. Oh, by the way, did I mention that golf involves a lot of walking?"

Over the next half hour he explained about golf etiquette, as well as how to score on a scorecard. "Ready to learn how to swing?" he asked, and handed her a club. He then came to stand behind her.

She was about to tell him no, that she wasn't ready and that the nearness of his body pressed against her back would make it impossible to concentrate. But evidently she was the only one with the problem. The close body contact didn't seem to bother him one bit.

Wrapping his arms around her and placing his hands on top of hers, he showed her the proper way to hold the club and swing it. "Just remember," he whispered right close to her ear, "when you're doing a backswing, make sure your body doesn't move more slowly than the club.

And for a downswing," he said, demonstrating, "you don't want your body to move more quickly than your swing. Your club shouldn't play catch-up with your body."

For the next hour they went through a series of swings, some she decided would work for her and some she knew wouldn't. But her golf swings weren't the only thing she was thinking about with Ian almost glued to her back.

"Okay, when do I get to play with the balls?" she asked him, glancing up at him over her shoulder.

"Only you would ask me something with a double meaning such as that at a time like this," he whispered huskily in her ear before pulling her body back to his, letting her know of his aroused state.

She laughed quietly, knowing what balls he was alluding to and moved away from him. "Sorry." She glanced around, trying not to look at him below the belt. "So what's next?"

"Kissing you isn't such a bad idea," he said.

They stood so close that his bare legs brushed lightly against hers. The contact was enough to send heat sizzling through her body, and the fact that he was aroused wasn't helping matters. And when his scent, which had been playing games with her senses for the past couple of hours, finally took hold she parted her lips on a breathless sigh.

That was just the opening Ian needed and he leaned over, and when his mouth touched hers he literally lost it. Never had he needed a kiss more or his common sense less. Now was not a time he wanted to think rationally, since thinking irrationally suited him just fine.

When he'd been teaching her the various golf swings, the feel of her butt against his groin had nearly driven him crazy, overtaken his mind with lust, and he'd been hard-pressed not to do something about it. Even now, if he'd thought for one minute that they had complete privacy, he would be peeling the clothes off her body this very second. He couldn't take the chance, but he could and would make sure they had some private time together later.

His hands tightened around her waist as he continued to kiss her deeply. He knew he had to slow things down a bit, but still, the taste of her was driving him to get all he could because the getting was definitely good.

The sound of a golf cart coming along the path grabbed both their attention, and Ian broke the kiss and took a step back. He glanced over at her and watched as she nervously nibbled her lower lip. Feeling a tightening in his gut, he groaned softly.

Lacking the ability to resist doing so, he cupped her face in his hands and kissed her again. Moments later, pulling back, he rubbed the tip of his finger across her top lip. "You still up for swimming?" he asked, knowing he needed to find the nearest pool to cool off.

"Yes, what about you?"

He chuckled deeply from within his throat. "Yes, I am definitely up for it."

"Ian," she admonished, watching him take a step back to grab the golf bag and place it on his shoulder. But before she could take him to task, he took her hand in his and pulled her toward the cart.

"What about the rest of my lessons?" she asked.

He smiled as her looked at her. "They're coming." Just like you'll be doing pretty soon, he thought as they continued to walk together.

"Can I ask you something, Ian?"

He glanced over at her as they continued walking. "Sure."

"Am I out of your system yet?"

He stopped walking and stared at her. "No. Now you're so deeply embedded there, it's like you've become an ache."

She smiled as they began walking again. She could imagine how much an admission like that had cost him. "Need an aspirin?" she asked coyly.

He stopped walking again and reached up and lightly brushed the side of her face with the palm of his hand. "Now who's being a smart-ass? No, I don't need an aspirin. I just need you, Brooke. And you know what's so scary about that?"

She held his gaze. "No."

"I swore that if I ever saw you again I would avoid you like the plague. But now I can't seem to bear having you out of my sight."

She smiled slowly. "Sounds like we have a problem."

Ian chuckled, although deep down he really didn't find the situation very amusing. "Yeah, it seems that way. Come on. Let's grab some lunch."

"So what sport do you want to try next while you're here?" Ian asked after taking a sip of his soda. He and Brooke were sitting outside on the verandah at one of the cafés enjoying hot dogs, French fries and their favorite soft drinks.

She lifted her gaze from dipping a fry into a pool of ketchup and looked at him, smiling. "It doesn't matter as long as it's not a contact sport."

He laughed. "Are you saying that my touch bothers you?"

"No, it doesn't bother me exactly."

"Then what does it do to you?"

She leaned closer so others sitting around them wouldn't hear. "Makes me hormonally challenged."

A smiled touched the corners of Ian's lips. "Define."

She rolled her eyes. He *would* ask that. She was sure that having such an analytical mind he could definitely figure it out. But if he wanted her to break it down for him, then she would. "Whenever you touch me, or brush up against me, the only thoughts that occupy my mind are those of a sexual nature."

"In other words you get horny?" he asked, seemingly intrigued by her explanation.

"No, Ian. Men get horny. Women become hormonally challenged."

"Oh, I see."

Brooke figured that he did. She couldn't believe the two of them were sitting here having such a conversation while sharing a meal when just a few days ago there had been more bitterness between them than she cared to think about. And yet just as Ian had admitted on the golf course, they were no closer to concluding what they'd once shared than before.

"So what have you been doing for the past four years?" he asked casually, taking another sip of his drink.

Brooke raised a brow. She wasn't stupid. He was really getting around to asking what she hadn't been doing. A woman's body didn't lie, and Ian knew hers better than any man. He was sure after making love to her the night before he had a good idea what she hadn't been doing. "Mainly working. I've had a couple of tough assignments."

Ian nodded. He'd never liked the fact that she was putting her life on the line with every assignment. But he'd had to accept what she did for a living. After all, she had been a deputy when he'd met her. Besides, he had seen her in action a couple of times. She knew how to kick butt when she had to.

"Do you know how much longer you're going to be an agent?" he asked. When they'd talked about marriage, she'd said she would remain an agent until they decided to start a family.

She shrugged. "I'm not sure. Lately I've been thinking that I'm getting too old for field work. I've made my five-year mark, and the undercover operations are beginning to take their toll. I want to get out before I suffer a case of burnout like Dare did."

Ian was about to open his mouth to say something when his cell phone rang. "Excuse me," he said, standing and pulling it from the snap on his belt. "Yes?"

Moments later, after ending the call, he was looking at her apologetically. "Sorry, that was my casino manager. There's a matter that needs my immediate attention."

"I understand."

"We're still on for a swim later? At my place?"

She smiled. "Yes."

"I'll even feed you again."

She chuckled. "It's hard to resist an invitation like that."

"I was hoping that it would be. Let's say around five. Is that okay?"

She nodded. "That's perfect."

"Good." He then leaned over and whispered in her

ear. "And bring an overnight bag so I can help you with that hormonal thing," he said and quickly walked away.

Brooke continued to watch him until he was no longer in sight. It was only then that she released a deep breath. She doubted he would be able to help her with her wacky hormones. If anything, he would probably make them worse. Ian was and had always been too damn sexually potent for his own good. She smiled at the thought of that, since she of all people should know.

She picked up her drink to take another sip when across the verandah a couple sitting at a table caught her eye. It was the woman she had bumped into yesterday. She frowned. There was something about her, but what it was she couldn't quite put her finger on.

Ian had joked about Brooke being an unforgettable person, which she knew wasn't true. But still, she couldn't understand why the woman had not recognized her. Moments later it dawned on Brooke that today her hair was pinned back and she was wearing a hat. Yesterday her hair had been down. That had to be it, she thought. But still, there was something tugging at her brain, something she should be remembering.

Brooke took another sip of her soda, deciding it must not have been important.

Brooke arrived at Ian's penthouse ten minutes early, wearing a very daring, flesh-tone crocheted dress with a see-through bodice. The scalloped hemline was short and showed off the beauty of her legs. Ian knew he was in trouble the moment the elevator door opened.

He took a step back and eyed her up and down. He then pulled in a deep breath. "Hmm. I'm surprised you made it up here in one piece," he said, imagining how many men's eyes had popped out of their heads when they'd seen her. He figured his housekeeping staff was in the lobby mopping up drool as he spoke.

She chuckled as she stepped closer to him and placed her overnight bag down at her feet. "Have you forgotten that I can handle myself?"

No, he hadn't forgotten and had always admired her ability to do so. When she came to stand directly in front of him, the scent of her perfume began playing a number on his libido. He cleared his throat while scanning her outfit again "I thought we were going swimming."

"We are. This time instead of wearing my bathing suit I decided to bring it with me. But I see you're ready."

In more ways than one, he thought, although he knew she was referring to the fact that the only thing he was wearing was a pair of swimming trunks. "Yes, I thought we'd get our swim out of the way and then enjoy dinner. It will be delivered in a couple of hours. But if you'd rather we eat first, then…"

"No, that's fine. I'll probably be quite hungry by then."

He smiled. He intended to make sure she was totally famished. "I'll take that," he said, leaning down to pick up her overnight bag. He looked surprised because the bag was heavy.

She shrugged and smiled. "When have you known me to travel light?"

"Never."

"Then nothing's changed."

He furrowed his brow. "And what about when you're on assignment and you have to travel light?"

"Then I make an exception."

Ian smiled and nodded quietly. "I'll take this up to the bedroom. You're welcome to change in there if you like or you can use one of the guest rooms," he said.

"I'll change in your bedroom."

He moved aside to let her lead the way, and when they got to the stairs and she began climbing ahead of him, his body became more aroused with every step she took. Every time she lifted her foot to move up a step, her short hemline would inch a little higher and emphasize the sweet curve of her bottom.

He pulled back, deciding to just stand there and watch her, or else he would find himself tumbling backward. When she got to the landing she noticed he wasn't behind her and turned around. She lifted a brow when she saw he was still standing on the fourth stair. "Is something wrong?"

"Nothing other than the fact that we need to do something about that dress."

She leaned against the top banister, and he wondered if she knew that from where she was standing with that particular pose, and with the aim of his vision, he could see under her dress. He might be wrong since her outfit was flesh tone and everything seemed to blend in, but he couldn't help wondering if she was even wearing panties.

"What do you suggest we do with it?"

He blinked and met her gaze. His mind had totally gone blank. "Do with what?"

She chuckled. "My dress. You said we had to do something about it."

"We can burn it."

She grinned. "No we can't. It's an exclusive design."

Ian lifted a brow. "Is it?"

"Yes. Don't you like my outfit?"

"A little too much. I suggest you change into your swimming suit before I decide a swim isn't what we both need."

He then began walking up the stairs toward her. When he reached the landing he handed her the overnight bag. "I think this should be as far as I go considering…"

"Considering what?"

"Considering I wouldn't mind taking you right now on that banister you're leaning against." He'd been fantasizing about her every since he'd left her in the café. He'd barely kept his concentration while waiting for her to show up at the penthouse.

She smiled at him as she straightened and gripped the overnight bag. "This should be one interesting afternoon."

He smiled back at her. "Trust me. It will be."

Ian couldn't wait. He had to dive into the pool to cool off. It was either that or change his mind and go upstairs to Brooke. But he knew once he was in that bedroom with her, chances were that's where they would stay until dinner arrived.

He just couldn't get rid of the memory of the two of them on the golf course. Brooke had always been a quick study, and today had been no different. If she practiced there was no doubt in his mind that she would become one hell of a player.

Then there was that point at lunch when he had been tempted to reach out, snatch her up out of her seat and kiss her. Just watching her drink, the way her mouth had fit perfectly around the plastic straw and the way she'd slowly sucked her soda from the cup had made him hard.

He was taking his fourth lap around the pool when he heard her voice. "So you couldn't wait for me."

He glanced over his shoulder and immediately was grateful he was in the shallow end, otherwise he would have clearly sunk to the bottom. Brooke was standing there beside the pool in the skimpiest bathing suit he had ever seen. The one she'd been wearing the other night had been an eye scorcher but this one, this barely there, see-how-far-your-mind-can-stretch piece was definitely an attention getter and erection maker, not that he needed the latter since he was already there.

He pulled himself up and stood in the water and reached out his hand, and in a thick, throaty voice said, "Come here."

Brooke swallowed. When he'd stood, she couldn't ignore how his dripping-wet swimming trunks gave a pretty substantial visual of just how aroused he was. But that didn't keep her from crossing the room, stepping into the pool and taking his outstretched hand.

"You like playing with fire, don't you, Brooke?" he asked when she was standing directly in front of him, so close that their thighs were touching. So close that she could feel his hardness settle against her midsection.

"Not particularly," was the only response she could come up with, since she was so captivated by the dark heat in his eyes.

"Oh, I think you do. And since you like playing with fire I want to see just how hot you can get."

"You already know how hot I can get, Ian," she said, then sucked in a breath when he reached out and wrapped his arms around her waist, bringing her closer to the fit of him.

Ian smiled. Yes he did know. That was one of the things he always loved about Brooke: her ability to let go when they made love and not hold anything back. And speaking of hot…she was like the blast of an inferno, the scorching of volcanic lava, the hottest temperature at the equator. Hell, a summer solstice had nothing on her. And during the four years they'd been apart she hadn't changed.

She'd said she was hormonally challenged, but that was only because her sex life had stopped after him. It didn't take a rocket scientist to figure that one out. When he'd entered her body and found her so tight, he'd known inactivity was the cause. Whatever the reason she hadn't slept with any other man, he intended to remedy that by helping her make up for lost time.

All the reasons why he should be working her out of his system escaped him, probably because at the moment he couldn't think. All the blood from his brain had suddenly rushed downward to settle in the lower part of his body. The part that desperately wanted her.

"I thought we were going to swim," she whispered as he began lowering his mouth to hers.

"We are. Later." And then his mouth devoured hers with all the want and need he'd been holding inside since he'd last made love to her. Had it been just this morning? The hunger that was driving him made it seem a lot longer than that. She had tempted and teased him since then, bringing out the alpha male inside of him.

As usual, she tasted fiery, seductive and spicy. He hungrily consumed her mouth with wanton lust, but kissing her wasn't enough. He reached out and, without breaking the kiss, with a flick of his wrist he undid the tie of her bikini top at her back. Umm, now all that was left was her bottom.

Moments later he pulled back and, kneeling down, grateful they were still in the shallow end, he began peeling the thong bikini down her hips. His hand ran up the length of her inner thigh and he stroked her slowly, liking the sound of her erratic breathing. He stood back up and lifted her hips.

"Wrap your legs around me, Brooke." And the moment she did he slipped between her thighs to widen them and then he buried himself inside of her to the hilt at the same exact moment he buried his tongue inside her mouth.

She sucked in a breath, and with their bodies connected he moved against the pool wall. Of all the places they had made love, they had never made love in a pool. He'd heard that water was a highly sensual playground and he was about to find out if that was myth or a fact. When her back was braced against the wall, he began moving inside of her, flexing his hips, thrusting in and out.

Brooke closed her eyes, absorbing the intensity of Ian moving between her legs. Her fingers bore down on his shoulders as a scream gathered in her throat. He was amazing and was giving her just what she needed. What she wanted. And just seconds before an orgasm was about to hit, he pulled out of her and spun her around with her back to him.

"Lean over and rest your hands on the ledge, sweetheart," he said, whispering in her ear.

The moment she did so he tilted her hips and parted her slightly and pressed into her, entering her from behind. His body went still and he leaned over and kissed her shoulder and asked in a hoarse tone of voice, "You okay?"

"Yes, but do you know what I want?" she asked, gripping the ledge of the pool, liking the feel of his firm thighs right smack up against her butt.

"No, what do you want?"

"More of you. Now!"

She heard him suck in a deep breath just seconds before he began moving. Each stroke was like an electrical charge that sizzled inside her body. She moaned each and every time his hips rocked against her; each contact was a sexual jolt on her mind and her senses.

A guttural sound tore from her throat the same exact moment he screamed her name and gripped her hips tight, holding her steady for his release. And when it came it shot into her womb like a stream of hot molten lava, stimulating each and every part of her body and bringing her to yet another orgasm.

She moaned in surrender, groaned in pleasure and purred with the satisfaction of a kitten just fed. And she knew that no matter what happened once they parted ways, what they were sharing now, this moment, was hers and hers alone. This memory was one that no one could ever take away from her.

Eight

Instead of cooling down, things were only getting hotter and hotter between her and Ian, Brooke thought, almost a week later as she took an afternoon stroll along the lake's edge. Every morning they woke up in each other's arms and she was spending more time at his penthouse than at her villa.

They did almost everything together. He had taken her sailing again, had played a couple of rounds of golf, had taught her how to play poker, and one night they had even gotten together and whipped up dinner in his kitchen.

And they took long walks and talked about a number of things: how they felt about the state of the economy, war and the storms that seemed to get worse each hurricane season. But what they didn't talk about was what would happen after she checked out of the casino on

Sunday, which was only three days away. And she was smart enough to know that things would never be like they used to be between them. No matter how good things were going now, there was no second chance for them. She felt that he would never fully trust her the way he had before they broke up.

For the past couple of days Ian was busier than usual with Delaney's upcoming party. He had asked her to go as his date, and they pretty much decided they would answer his family questions as honestly as possible by saying, "No, we aren't back together. We've decided to be friends and nothing more."

Friends and nothing more.

That thought pierced a pain through Brooke's heart but there was nothing she could do about it. Things had happened just as she'd predicted. In trying to work her out of his system, Ian had only embedded himself deeper in hers. Although she loved him, he didn't love her.

The shrill ring of her cell phone broke into her thoughts and she quickly pulled it out of the back pocket of her shorts. "Hello."

"So, how are things going, Brooke?"

Brooke drew in a deep breath, surprised that Malcolm had called. Their agreement was that he would hear from her only if she had something to report. Within a few days her two-week stay at the Rolling Cascade would be over, and so far, as she'd known he would, Ian was running a clean operation.

"Things are going fine, Malcolm. Why are you calling?"

"I happened to overhear something today that might interest you."

"What?"

"Prince Jamal Ari Yasir is planning a birthday party for his wife there and he plans to present her with a case of diamonds that's worth over fifteen million dollars."

Brooke folded her arms across her middle. "I'm aware of that."

"And how did you come by that information? Not too many people are supposed to know about the diamonds."

"Ian mentioned it. I'm sure you're aware that the sheikh's wife is his first cousin."

"And Westmoreland trusted you enough to tell you about the diamonds?"

Brooke thought about what Malcolm has just asked her. Yes, he had trusted her enough. "He probably thought it wasn't such a big deal. It's not like I'm going to go out and mention it to anyone. And what do the diamonds have to do with the Bureau?"

"Probably nothing, but one of our informers notified our major theft division of a possible heist at the Rolling Cascade this weekend. And the target is those diamonds."

Brooke shook her head. "That's going to be hard to pull off since Ian's security team is top-notch. I've seen their operation. Besides, the jewels arrived this morning and are in a vault that's being monitored by video cameras twenty-four hours a day."

"That might be the case, but we're dealing with highly trained professionals, Brooke. The informer's claiming it's the Waterloo Gang."

Brooke sucked in deeply. "Are you sure?" The Waterloo Gang was an international ring who specialized in the theft of artwork and jewelry and had a reputation for making successful hits. The group was highly mobile, moving from city to city and country to country, and had been on the FBI's most-wanted list for years. Their last hit, earlier this year, had been a jewelry store in San Francisco where over ten million dollars in jewels were taken. Six months ago they had hit a museum in France where artwork totaling over thirty million was stolen.

"We're not sure if our informer's information is accurate. But the Bureau doesn't want to take any chances because such a theft might have international implications. Although Prince Yasir is married to an American, he's still considered a very important ally to this country and we don't want anything to place a strain on that relationship."

Brooked nodded. "I can see where having his wife's birthday present—especially one of such value—stolen might be a lot to swallow."

"And you're sure you haven't noticed anything unusual?"

"Not really. I'd say strange but not unusual. There are some obsessed gamblers, adulterers and someone with a split personality," she said, thinking about the woman she had bumped into while shopping last week. She'd briefly run into her a few times, and certain days she would be friendlier than others; a regular Dr. Jekyll and Ms. Hyde. "Just the kind of characters you'd expect to find at a casino," she concluded.

"Well, notify me if you notice anything. The reason the Waterloo Gang's hits are so well orchestrated and planned is that they have their people in place well in advance, mainly to study the lay of the land, so to speak."

"Will Ian be advised of any of this?"

"Not until we determine if our information is accurate."

Brooke frowned. "That's not good enough, Malcolm. By then it might be too late. He should be told so that he can take the necessary precautions. Don't ask me not to tell him."

For a long time there was a pause, and Brooke hoped Malcolm wouldn't pull rank and demand that she not mention anything to Ian. She was determined to warn Ian what was going on regardless of what Malcolm dictated. If she was fired because of it, then that's the risk she would take.

"Something else you should know is that Walter Thurgood has been assigned to the Waterloo Case," Malcolm said when he finally spoke moments later.

"Why?"

"Because if our informer is right and Thurgood can be credited with stopping a major jewel heist, especially one with possible international connections, that feat would be a great-looking feather in his cap. Someone upstairs is trying like hell to make him look good."

"Yeah, like we don't know who that is," Brooke said sarcastically. "Personally I don't give a damn about him getting credit for anything. I just don't want Ian left in the dark about what might be going on."

"Call me if you notice anything, Brooke, and remember that this is hearsay from an informer. Nothing has been verified yet."

"Okay, and I understand."

Ian smiled, hanging up the phone. Talking to his mother always made him chuckle. It wasn't good enough for Sarah Westmoreland that she now had two married sons, she was still determined to marry the rest of them off in grand style sooner or later.

And today she was ecstatic because Durango had called and said there was a possibility that Savannah might be having twins. An ultrasound was being scheduled in a couple of weeks to confirm or deny such a possibility.

Ian shook his head. He hadn't gotten used to Durango being a husband, much less a father, but that just went to show that some things were meant to be.

Like him and Brooke.

He sighed deeply and walked over to the window in his office. It seemed that today Lake Tahoe was more beautiful than ever. Or maybe he thought that way because he was in such a good mood. And all because of Brooke.

Spending time with her had made him realize that what had been missing in his life was the same thing he'd turned his back on four years ago. But now, waking up with her beside him, gazing into the darkness of her eyes, enjoying a warm good-morning smile was what he needed in his life. But only with her. The time they'd spent together over the past week and a half had been wonderful. He couldn't remember the last time he'd smiled or enjoyed himself more. And then the memories of nights they'd shared in each other's arms could still take his breath away.

Over the years he'd tried to shove her into the past and replace her with more desirable women. However, he hadn't found anyone he desired more or who could replace her in his heart. Just the thought that in three days she would be walking out of his life was unacceptable. He wanted what happened in the past to stay in the past, and he wanted to move forward and reclaim her as his and his alone.

His smile widened when he decided that he would tell her how he felt tonight. He loved her. God, he loved her and would go on loving her. He sighed when that admission was wrung from deep inside of him. He hadn't counted on falling in love with her all over again, and if he were completely honest with himself, he would admit that he'd never stopped loving her. And just to think he'd actually assumed he could work her out of his system. More than anything, he wanted to make her a permanent part of his life.

He walked back over to his desk and picked up the phone. He planned on making tonight one that she wouldn't forget.

"Brooke?"

Brooke was on her way up to see Ian in his office when she turned, following the sound of her name being called, and glanced around. Smiling, she crossed the casino's lobby to give Tara Westmoreland a hug.

"Tara, when did you get here?"

"A few hours ago. Since Jamal asked that I coordinate everything for Delaney's party, I thought it was best for me to be in place a couple of days early. Ian's taking Thorn around, showing him some of the new additions, and I thought I'd just wander around in here and play a couple of the slot machines."

Tara gazed at Brooke with a lift of her brow. "But my question is what are *you* doing here? Did you decide to come up early, too?"

Brooke shook her head, chuckling. "No, I've been here for a week and a half now. I'm here on vacation."

"Hmm," Tara said grinning.

"It's not what you think." Brooke then rubbed a frustrated hand down her face before adding. "At least not really."

As if she understood completely, Tara smiled and took her hand. "Come on. Let's go someplace and have some girls' chat time."

"A strawberry, virgin daiquiri, please," Tara told the smiling waitress.

"And the same for me," Brooke tagged on. Not wanting to jump into a conversation about her and Ian just yet, Brooke asked, "And how do you plan on surprising Delaney?"

Tara chuckled. "Jamal is flying her here straight from Tahran. She believes that he's coming here for an investors' meeting with Ian, Thorn, Spencer and Jared, so seeing me and Thorn, Jared and Dana won't give anything away. She also thinks that Jamal is flying her to France to celebrate her birthday once she leaves here."

She paused when the waitress returned with their drinks. "Most of the family and other invitees will begin arriving that day or the day before. It's going to be up to Jamal to keep Delaney occupied while everyone checks in."

Tara smiled. "One good thing is that everyone is being housed in a separate part of the resort than where Jamal and Delaney are staying. That should minimize the risk of her running into anyone."

"And when will Delaney arrive?"

"Tomorrow."

Brooke took a sip of her drink then asked, "You don't think her seeing me here will give anything away, do you?"

Tara's smile widened. "No. She'll assume, like the rest of us, that you and Ian have finally made amends and are back together." Tara then lifted an arched brow. "Well, is that true, Brooke?"

More than anything, Brooke wished she could say yes. But she couldn't. "No. The only thing Ian and I have managed to do while I've been here is to bury any hostility we've felt and become friends. I feel for us that is a good thing. I care a lot for Ian."

Tara chuckled. "Of course you do. You still love him."

Brooke's cheeks tinted in a blush. "Am I that obvious?"

"Only because I'm in love with a Westmoreland man myself. They seem to grow on you, and once you fall in love with one, it's hard as the dickens to fall out of love…no matter what."

Brooke had to agree. From the first Ian had grown on her and once she fell in love with him that was that. Four years of separation hadn't been able to cure her of being bitten by the love bug. "So what am I supposed to do?"

"Wish I could answer that." Tara leaned in closer and reached for Brooke's arms, squeezing reassuringly. "We all know how smart Ian is, but unfortunately he has a tendency to analyze things to death. But I'm sure once he sits down and considers things rationally, he'll reach the conclusion that you are the best thing to ever happen to him."

Brooke just hoped Tara was right. But then, there was

a lot Tara didn't know, like the real reason Brooke was at the Rolling Cascade. Even if Ian was able to put behind him what happened four years ago, how would he feel if he ever found out that she was now here under false pretenses?

"Don't look now but here come our Westmoreland men," Tara said, breaking into Brooke's thoughts. "I swear they are like bloodhounds on our scent. I doubt there's anywhere we could hide where they wouldn't find us."

Brooke glanced up, and her gaze collided with Ian's as he and his cousin Thorn moved toward their table. Her pulse began beating so wildly that her hand began shaking and she had to put her drink down.

Surprisingly, it was Thorn who pulled her out of her chair to give her a huge hug. Thorn, who used to be the surliest of the Westmorelands, had definitely changed. It seemed that marriage definitely agreed with him. She remembered that at Dare's wedding Thorn and Tara hadn't been getting along any better than she and Ian. Then a few months later she'd received a call from Delaney saying Thorn and Tara were getting married. She had been invited to the wedding, but in consideration of Ian's feelings, she had declined the invitation.

"Did Tara tell you our good news?" he asked Brooke once he released her.

Brooke glanced over at Tara and raised a brow. "No, what news is that?"

"We're having a baby," he announced, grinning broadly.

Brooke rushed around the table and gave Tara a huge hug. "Congratulations. I didn't know."

"We just found out a few days ago, so we haven't told anyone yet," Tara said, smiling over at her husband. Brooke could see the love they shared shining in their eyes.

"Well, I think it's wonderful, and this calls for a celebration, don't you agree, Ian?" Brooke asked, glancing over at him.

He smiled. "Yes, but not tonight since we have special dinner plans."

"Oh." Special dinner plans? This was certainly a surprise to her.

"Meet me at six o'clock in the conservatory, all right?" he asked.

She nodded. "Sure."

Ian then checked his watch. "I hate to run but I have a four-o'clock conference call." He turned to leave.

Brooke knew she needed to tell him about her conversation with Malcolm. "Ian, can we talk for a minute?"

He turned back around and smiled. "I'm in a hurry now, sweetheart, but we'll have time to talk later. I promise." And then he was gone.

Brooke looked down at herself as she stepped into Ian's private elevator. She had decided to wear a pair of chocolate-colored tailored slacks and a short-sleeved beige stretch shirt. Although he'd said it was a special dinner, he had not hinted at how she should dress. Assuming that it would only be the two of them, she figured casual attire would be okay.

It seemed that today the elevator moved a lot faster than it had that first ride up to Ian's special place. Before she could take a deep breath it had stopped at the conservatory.

The door automatically swooshed open, and there he

was, waiting for her. Heat suddenly filled her and he
took a step back when she took one forward. Over his
shoulder she saw a beautiful, candlelit table set for two.
"I hope I'm not too early."

"And I'm glad that you are," he said, and then he
leaned down and captured her lips, using his mouth, lips
and tongue to churn her brain into mush.

At that moment nothing mattered, not even the
thought that all he probably intended for tonight was a
chance for them to say goodbye before things got too
hectic because of Delaney's birthday party. And if that
was his intent, she was fine. She had no regrets about
the time she had spent with him these few days.

He released her mouth but kept her close to him, in
his arms. "I think we did stand beneath a shooting star
that night," he said in a low voice, tracing the tip of his
thumb over her lips. "There hasn't been anything but
nonstop passion between us since then."

She smiled, thinking of all the times they had spent
together since that night, and inwardly she had to agree.
"There's always been a lot of passion between us, Ian,"
she reminded him.

He leaned down and brushed a kiss on her lips. "Yes,
things were always that way, weren't they. Do you know
that you spoiled me for any other woman?"

"Did I?"

"Yes. I tried to forget you but I couldn't, Brooke."

She sighed. This didn't sound like the goodbye
speech she had been expecting. This was a confession.
She decided to follow his lead. "I didn't even try forgetting you, Ian. It would have been useless. You were
my first lover and a girl never forgets her first."

He grinned. "Sweetheart, the way I see it…or perhaps a better word is the way I *felt* it, I am your one and only. Do you deny it?"

"No. I couldn't stand the thought of another man touching me."

Ian pulled her into his arms. Hearing her admit such a thing touched him deeply.

"Ian?"

He pulled back and looked at her. "Yes?"

"I don't understand why we're talking about these things," she said, confused.

He smiled. "Let's eat and then I'll explain everything."

"Okay, but there's something I need to tell you."

He leaned down and brushed another kiss on her lips. "We'll talk after dinner."

Ian led her over to the beautifully set table and seated her. "Would you like some wine?" he asked, his voice so husky it sent shivers all the way down her spine.

"Yes, please." She watched as he poured the wine in her glass and then in his.

"I had the chef prepare something special for us tonight," he said.

"What?"

He chuckled. "You'll see." And then with the zing sounding on the elevator he said, "Our dinner has arrived."

A half hour later Brooke was convinced there was nothing more romantic than dining beneath the stars; especially when the person you were with was Ian Westmoreland. Dinner was delicious. Melt-in-your-mouth yeast rolls, a steak that had been cooked on an open grill, roasted potatoes, broccoli, the freshest salad to ever touch her lips and her favorite dessert—strawberry cheesecake.

Over dinner he surprised her by sharing with her his dream to open another casino in the Bahamas. He also mentioned the conversation he'd had with his mother earlier and her excitement over the prospect of her first grandchildren being twins.

"I just can't imagine Durango married," Brooke said, shaking her head, thinking about Ian's brother who'd been the biggest flirt she'd ever met. But then, Durango was also a really nice guy and she really liked him.

"Neither could I at first, but after meeting Savannah you'll see why. They may have married because of her pregnancy, but now there's no doubt in my mind that Durango really loves her. So it seems another Westmoreland bachelor has bitten the dust."

"Yes, it seems that way," Brooke said, lowering her head to take another sip of her wine to avoid looking into Ian's eyes. Maybe it was her imagination but she had caught him staring at her a number of times during the course of the evening.

When dinner was over he stood and crossed the room to turn on a stereo system. Immediately, music began playing, a slow instrumental performed by Miles Davis. Ian returned to her chair and stretched out his hand. "Will you dance with me, Brooke?"

Brooke sighed, wondering where all this was leading. The thought that he was going through all this just to tell her goodbye was unsettling, and when he wrapped his arms around her, she placed her head on his chest, fighting back the tears. They'd barely made it through the song when she pulled out of his arms, not able to take it anymore, and took a step back, withdrawing from him.

"Brooke? What's wrong?"

"I'm sorry, Ian, but I can't take it anymore. You didn't have to go through all of this. Why don't you just say the words so I can leave."

Ian lifted a brow. He had planned on saying the words, but for some reason he had a feeling that the words he planned on saying weren't what she was expecting to hear. "And what words do you think I'm going to say, Brooke?" he asked, balling his hands into fists by his side to keep from reaching out to her.

"You know, the usual. Goodbye. *Adios. Sayonara. Arrivederci. Au revoir.* Take your pick. They all mean the same thing in whatever language."

He took a step closer to her. "Um, how about *Je t'aime. Te amo. Kimi o ai shiteru. Nakupenda.* And only because I hear Jamal say it often to Delaney in Arabic, how about, *Ana behibek.*"

He took another step closer as his gaze roamed over her. "But I prefer the plain old English version," he said, reaching out and taking her hand and pulling her close to him. "I love you."

The tears Brooke had fought to hold back earlier flowed down her face. Ian had admitted he loved her. Did he really mean it?

As if reading her mind he tipped her chin up to meet his gaze. "And yes, I mean it. I never stopped loving you, Brooke, although God knows I tried. But I couldn't. Spending time with you this week and a half has been wonderful and it made me realize what you mean to me. I've been living and functioning these past four years, but that's about all. But the moment you walked into my office that day and I breathed in your scent, a part of me knew what had been missing from my life, and this morning when I admitted in my heart what you meant to me, I decided I don't plan to let you ever go again."

Brooke's heart felt like it was going to burst in her chest because she knew if he ever discovered the real reason she'd been here he would feel differently. She knew then that she had to tell him everything. "Ian, there's something I need to tell you. There're things you need to know."

"Sounds serious, but the only serious thing I want to hear is for you to tell me that you love me, too."

"Oh, Ian," she said, reaching up and smoothing a fingertip over his bearded chin. "I do love you. I never stopped loving you, either."

He smiled and pulled her into his arms. "Then as far as I'm concerned, that says it all."

And then he leaned down and gave her a kiss that made everything and every thought flee from her mind.

Brooke awoke the next morning in Ian's bed to find it empty. They had made love under the stars in the conservatory and then they had caught the elevator to his penthouse and made love again in his bed.

She threw the covers off her knowing she had to find him immediately and tell him what was going on. The sooner he knew the better. Half an hour later she ran into Vance, literally, in the lobby.

"Whoa." He grinned, reaching out his arms to steady her. "Where's the fire?"

"Where's Ian, Vance?"

"He's somewhere on the grounds with Jared and Dare. The two of them arrived with their wives this morning." Vance studied her. Saw her anxious look. "Is something wrong, Brooke?"

She sighed deeply. "I hope not, but I think we should take every precaution."

"Okay. Do you want to tell me what it is?"

"Yes, but we have to find Ian first."

Vance nodded. "That's not going to be a problem," he said, taking his mobile phone out of his jacket. He punched in one number and said, "Ian? You're needed. Brooke and I are on our way to your office. Meet us there."

Vance then clicked off the phone, placed it back in his jacket, smiled and gently took hold of Brooke's arm. "Come on. He's on his way."

Ian arrived a few minutes after they did. He walked in with Dare. Dare Westmoreland was tall and extremely handsome just like all the Westmoreland men. At any other time Brooke would have been glad to see her mentor, but at the moment she preferred not having an audience when she told Ian everything; including why she's been there for the past week and a half. She quickly concluded that now would not be the best time to tell him that particular part of it. She would tell him that later. But she needed to tell him about her conversation with Malcolm.

She gladly accepted the huge hug Dare gave her. The Westmorelands were big on hugs, and she always accepted any they gave her with pleasure. As soon as Dare released her, Ian moved in and circled his arms around her. He had a worried look on his face. "Brooke, what's wrong? Are you all right?"

She smiled. "Yes, I'm fine, but I found out something

yesterday that you should know. I tried telling you last night but…" She lowered her head, studying the ceramic tile floor, knowing he knew why she'd stopped talking in midsentence and also felt that Dare and Vance had a strong idea, as well.

"Okay, you want to tell me now? Or is it private between the two of us?" he asked in an incredibly low and sexy voice.

She raised her head and met his gaze. "No, in fact Vance needs to hear it and Dare might be able to lend some of his experience and expertise."

Ian frowned. "This sounds serious."

"It might be," she replied.

"Then how about you tell us what's going on."

For the next twenty minutes she repeated her conversation with Malcolm. Most of it, anyway. It would have taken less time if Dare and Vance hadn't interrupted with questions. Both Dare and Vance had heard of the Waterloo Gang.

Ian turned to Vance. "What do you think?"

Vance's face was serious. "I think we should do as Brooke suggested and take additional precautions."

Ian nodded. "I agree." He then turned to Brooke. "According to what you've said, it's this gang's usual mode of operation to set up shop within their targeted site, right?"

"Yes."

"That means they're probably already here then," he said, and she could hear the anger in his voice.

Brooke nodded. "More than likely. But keep in mind nothing has been confirmed yet. The Bureau is still checking out this informer's claim."

"In that case," Dare said, "who gave you the authority to share this information with Ian?"

Brooke met Dare's gaze. She knew what he was asking her and why. "No one gave me the authority, Dare. I felt Ian should know. Even if it's not true at least he should be prepared."

"And if it is true," Vance said, his voice thickening with anger, "then we'll be ready for them."

Ian sighed. "And let's make sure of it. Come on. We need to get up to the surveillance room."

When Vance and Dare turned toward the elevator, Ian called over his shoulder, "You two go ahead. Brooke and I will be there in a minute."

Once Vance and Dare had left, Ian crossed the room to sit on the edge of his desk. He drew in a deep breath as he continued to look at her. Then giving her a questioning look, he said, "You're extremely nervous about something. There's more isn't there? There's something you aren't telling me."

Brooke sighed. She knew the time of reckoning had arrived. For a moment she didn't say anything and then, "Yes. I didn't want to say anything in front of Vance and Dare."

He nodded. "Okay, what is it?"

She lifted her chin a notch and met his direct gaze. "There's a reason I've been here at the casino this past week and a half, Ian."

He frowned. "So you weren't here for rest and relaxation like you claimed?"

She shook her head. "No."

Silence surrounded them for a moment and then Ian asked, "You tracked the Waterloo Gang here?"

Her expression became somber. "No, it had nothing to do with the Waterloo Gang," she said, walking over to the window and looking out, trying to hold on to her composure.

He raised a brow. "Then what?"

She turned back to him. "You. I was asked to come here to make sure you were running a clean operation. But at no time did I—"

"What!" he said, coming to his feet. "Are you standing there saying that you were sent here to spy on me and that all those times we spent together— days and nights—meant nothing to you other than you doing your job? That I was nothing but an assignment?"

Brooke quickly crossed the room to him. "No! That's not what I'm saying. How could you think that? It really wasn't an official assignment and—"

"I don't want to hear anything else!" Ian said in a voice that shook with anger.

"Ian, please let me explain things to you," Brooke said, reaching out to grab hold of his hand.

He flinched. "No. I don't think you need to say anything more. You've pretty much said it all."

Nine

Both Vance and Dare glanced up when Brooke walked into the security surveillance room. Vance lifted a brow. "Where's Ian?"

Brooked shrugged as she approached the two men. "Not sure. He left a couple of minutes before I did."

They nodded, too polite to probe any further. "I'm having my men run the tapes of the vault to see if there's any particular person or persons who made frequent trips over in that area," Vance said.

He then turned to the man sitting at a monitor. "Show us what you have, Bob."

Before Bob could pull anything up, Ian walked in. Although everyone glanced his way, no one said anything. It was obvious from his expression that he wasn't in the best of moods. Vance explained to Ian what they were doing.

"Okay, Bob, let her roll," Vance said.

They viewed over thirty minutes of footage, and nothing stuck out to arouse their suspicions. At one point, Brooke glanced over her shoulder and found Ian staring at her. The look in his eyes nearly broke her heart. Whatever progress they had made over the past week had been destroyed. The man who had expressed his love for her last night looked as if he resented her in his sight today.

"Hold it there for a moment," Vance said to Bob, breaking into Brooke's thoughts and claiming her attention. "Give me a close-up."

The monitor zeroed in on the red-haired woman's facial features. Vance shrugged and said, "Okay, move on. I thought for a second she reminded me of someone."

Brooke, who had been sitting in an empty chair beside Dare, stood, her mind alert. She stared at the woman they had just brought up on the screen. "Hey, wait a minute."

Dare glanced up her. "What?"

"I've got a funny feeling."

Dare chuckled and said, "If history serves me correctly, that means she might be on to something."

Brooke glanced over at Vance. "Can we do a scan of the casino for a minute?"

Vance nodded to Bob, and the man switched to another monitor that showed the occupants who were milling around in the casino. Dare laughed. "I see my wife is spending money as usual," he said, when the scanner picked up a pregnant Shelly Westmoreland strolling into a gift shop.

"Can you give us a clue as to what we're looking for?" Ian asked in an agitated tone.

Brooke glanced over her shoulder. "Remember that woman I mentioned last week that I bumped into while shopping and who didn't remember me the next day?"

"What about her?" Ian asked.

"I've always found it strange that every time I ran into her in the casino she acted different. I always got bad vibes from her. It seemed as if she had a split personality."

"Could be she was just a moody person," Vance interjected.

"Or you may have run into her on her bad days," Dare added.

Brooke nodded. "Yes, but there were other things, and something in particular that I just can't put my finger on," she said, tapping her fingers on the desk. Then she remembered.

"That first day I bumped into her and accidentally knocked packages out of her hand, she mentioned she was on her way somewhere but not to worry because she was known to always be an early bird and that she would be on time for her appointment. The next day I saw her at the golf course, she mentioned being habitually late everywhere she went."

Brooke turned her attention back to the monitor and watched as it continued to scan all the occupants in the casino. "Okay, Bob," she said, moments later. "There she is. The blonde standing next to the tall guy with shoulder-length black hair. That's supposed to be her husband."

By this time, everyone's curiosity was piqued and they stood staring at the monitor.

"Do a profile check, Bob, to see who they are," Vance instructed when the screen had zeroed in on the couple's faces. Moments later information appeared on the screen. The woman was Kasha Felder and the man, Jeremy Felder. They lived in London. Both had clean records, no prior arrests or violations. Not even a parking ticket.

"Now go back and run a profile check on the woman with the red hair."

Bob quickly switched screens. "Um, that's strange. I'm not coming up with an ID on her. It's like she doesn't exist."

Brooke nodded and glanced up at Vance. He now knew where she was going with this. "Scan both women's facial structures," Vance instructed.

Moments later, it was evident that even with different color hair, the women had the same facial structure. A more detailed breakdown showed the woman with red hair was a natural blonde and she was wearing a wig.

Ian came to stand beside Brooke. "Same woman?" he asked, frowning.

Brooke shook her head. "No, I don't think so."

He glanced over at her, lifting a brow. "Twins then?"

"More than likely, which would explain my split-personality theory. But I have a gut feeling there's more." She glanced over at Vance. "Can we look at the tapes around the vault from last week?"

Vance smiled. "Certainly."

Brooke chuckled. She could almost imagine the adrenaline running in the older man's veins. He probably hadn't experienced this much excitement since leaving the nation's capital.

For the next thirty minutes they scanned the footage. Ian, who was still standing beside her, asked, "Just what are we looking for now?"

She glanced up at him and immediately felt her pulse jump at his closeness. "A third woman."

Dare raised a brow. "Triplets?"

"Possibly," she said. "These two are wearing bracelets on their right wrists. One day I happened to notice that she was wearing a bracelet on her left arm." Moments later she told Bob, "Back it up a second and slow it down." Then, "Okay, hold it right there. The lady with the dark-brown curly hair. Let's zero in on her for a second."

Bob did, and after they viewed the facial structure, it showed conclusive evidence they were viewing three different women with identical facial structures. All with natural blond hair. Triplets.

"Damn," Vance said. "No wonder they can pull those hits off. We're dealing with triplets, and no telling who else is tied in to their operation."

Ian turned to Vance. "Do you think they have an inside accomplice?"

"That's how it works most of the time." He then turned to Bob. "Okay, let's go through the footage for the past week and a half. I want to concentrate on all three women. What I want to know is whether or not they meet up with any of our employees, no matter how casual it appears."

Three hours later they had their answers. The triplet with the brown curly wig had met on two occasions with Cassie, who worked in the casino's business office. In one piece of footage, Cassie was even seen handing the woman an envelope.

"I think we've seen enough, don't you?" Ian said with anger in his voice.

"Yes," Vance said, shaking his head. "For now. Let's

get Cassie in here and ask her a few questions. She's only twenty-three and the thought of jail time, especially in a federal prison, should shake her up. I bet she'll end up spilling her guts to save her skin."

"Then what?" Ian asked, shaking his head as he remembered all the times the young woman had tried to come on to him.

Vance smiled. It was apparent to everyone that his mind was already working, going through numerous possibilities. "And then we set a trap for the Waterloo Gang. One that will put them out of operation permanently."

Vance had been right. Fearful of jail time, Cassie had confessed, explaining that she had met a man in the casino by the name of Mark Saints, a Brit who wanted to have a good time. She had gone to his room one night and ended up getting drugged. While she was unconscious, Mark had taped a damaging video which he used to blackmail her into doing what he needed her to do—provide the information he needed about the jewels and the setup of where the vault was located.

Cassie didn't know much about anything else, specifically how the heist would be carried out. However, she did mention Mark and a woman claiming to be his sister were particularly interested in the security system and the location of the video cameras.

It was late afternoon by the time Brooke had left the security surveillance room, no longer able to handle Ian's contempt. She was walking across the lobby when she heard her name being called and turned and smiled when she saw Tara, Shelly and another woman she didn't know. Introductions were made and she discovered the other woman was Dana. Dana was married to Ian's brother, Jared. She had a beautiful and friendly smile and Brooke liked her immediately.

"Would you like to join us for dinner?" Shelly asked, smiling. "It seems we've been dumped by our husbands. They plan to hit the poker tables and then go up to Ian's penthouse to see what other trouble they can get into."

Brooke smiled. "Sure, I'd loved to." For the past several days she'd eaten dinner with Ian, but she had a strong feeling that he wouldn't want her company this evening or any other evening. She then glanced around. "Has Delaney arrived yet?"

Tara chuckled. "Yes, they got in around noon today."

"And you still aren't worried about her running into anyone?"

A grin touched the corners of Tara's lips. "No. Jamal has been given strict orders to keep his wife occupied for the next couple of days, and I have a feeling he's more than capable of doing that. Delaney won't be leaving her room anytime soon…if you know what I mean."

Brooke shook her head, grinning. Yes, she had a pretty good idea just what Tara meant. "Isn't she pregnant?"

Tara nodded and said seriously, "Yes, but trust me, that has nothing to do with it. Even after five years of marriage, the attraction between Delaney and her desert sheikh is so strong, keeping her behind close doors for forty-eight hours will be a piece of cake for Jamal."

Brooke enjoyed having dinner with the three women. Afterward, they left the restaurant to check out the various shops, especially the lingerie boutique in the lobby. Deciding to call it an early night she departed their company and was in her room before nine o'clock.

She took a leisurely soak in the Jacuzzi and then slipped into a nightgown.

A trap had been set and if everything worked out the way they hoped, they would catch the Waterloo Gang red-handed trying to steal the jewels Jamal was to present to Delaney Saturday night.

Brooke had made a decision that once the gang was apprehended, she would leave and not attend Delaney's birthday bash. She was to go as Ian's date, but she figured she would be the last person he would want to show up with.

As she settled in bed, tears she couldn't hold back rolled down her cheeks. If only Ian would have let her explain. But he hadn't. He had refused to listen to anything she had to say in her defense. Once again he saw her as a very deceitful person. He didn't trust her, and without trust, love was nothing.

"Hey, Ian. You want to play blackjack with us?"

Ian refused to turn around from his stance in front of his penthouse window. Instead he closed his eyes as memories of the night he had made love to Brooke on the same blackjack table at which Jared, Dare and Thorn were seated raced through his mind.

"Ian?"

He recognized the concern in Jared's voice. Being the firstborn, Jared had been bestowed with the dubious responsibility of looking out for his younger siblings. And now, thirty-plus years later, nothing had changed.

Deciding it was best to give him an answer, he turned around and said, "No, you all go ahead and play without me." He couldn't help but smile when he saw the look of relief on their faces. He was a natural ace when it came to blackjack and they all knew it.

"One of you act as dealer while I talk to Ian for a while," Dare said to the others.

Ian raised his eyes to the ceiling. Dare, being the oldest of all the Westmoreland men—although he was only older than Jared by a few months—had always felt responsible for his younger siblings and cousins. He'd always taken being "the oldest" seriously, but at times he could be an outright pain in the rear end. Ian pretty much figured this would be one of those times.

"We need to talk," Dare said when he approached him.

"If it's about Brooke *we* have nothing to say," Ian said before taking a sip of his drink.

"The hell we don't. So let's go somewhere private."

Ian figured he wouldn't be able to get Dare off his case until he complied with his request, and figured the sooner he did so, the better off he'd be. "Fine. We can go into my office."

Dare followed Ian to the room he'd set aside as a small office and closed the door behind them. Ian moved to sit down behind his desk while Dare chose to stand in front of it with his hands on his hips and his expression anything but friendly.

"Say what you have to say, Dare, so we can get this over with," Ian said, setting his glass aside.

Dare leaned over to make sure he could be heard. "For a man who's extremely smart you're not acting very bright."

Ian's lips curled into a smile. Leave it to Dare to speak his mind. "Why? Because I refuse to let the same woman break my heart twice?"

"No, because twice she's looked after your best interest and you're too blind to see it. I know what has you pissed with her, but if you would have given her the chance to explain, she would have told you that if she hadn't agreed to come here to make sure things were running smoothly, they would have sent the federal agent from hell. Although she knew how you felt about her, she came anyway because she trusted you and knew she wouldn't find anything wrong with your operation."

Ian sat back in his chair in a nonchalant posture. "Did she tell you that?"

"No, Vance did."

Ian sat up. "Vance? How the hell does he know anything?"

"Because of his connections within the Bureau. He didn't buy her story of just being here on vacation, so he made a few calls. He approached her while you were out of town and of course she didn't let on to anything. And before you ask, the reason Vance didn't tell you of his suspicions is because he didn't see Brooke as a threat, especially after she told him…and I quote, "No matter what you or anyone else might think, I trust Ian implicitly.""

When Ian didn't say anything, Dare continued. "I don't know of too many men who can boast of such loyalty from a woman. But you can, Ian." Without saying anything else, Dare turned and walked out of the room.

Ian remained where he was, sitting in silence while he thought about everything Dare had said. He stood and began pacing the room, replaying in his mind all the times he'd spent with Brooke since she'd arrived at the Rolling Cascade, and he knew Dare was right. She had come here to look out for his best interest.

He rubbed a hand down his face. Why did love have to be so damn complicated? And why was he so prone to letting his emotions rule his common sense where Brooke was concerned? Mainly because he loved her so much. Deep down a part of him was afraid to place his complete heart on the line. But he would. He knew what he had to do. He had to swallow his pride and surrender all.

He moved to the door with an urgent need to see Brooke, wondering if she was downstairs in the casino. His cell phone rang and he stopped to answer it. "Yes?"

"This is Vance. It seems they're going to make their move earlier than planned."

Ian understood. "Is everything in place?"

"Down to the letter. It's like watching a movie and I've saved you a front-row seat."

"I'm on my way."

He quickly walked out of his office and glanced over at Dare. "It seems the triplets are about to put their show on the road. Come on."

Ten

Ian's gaze lit on Brooke the moment he and Dare walked into the security surveillance room. He wanted to go to her, ask her forgiveness and tell her how much he loved her, but knew it was not the time or the place.

Even so, he couldn't help studying her. It wasn't quite eleven o'clock, however it appeared as if she'd been roused out of bed. She had that drowsy look in her eyes, although he knew that with what was going down, she would be alert as a whip.

Knowing that if he continued to stare at her, he would eventually cross the room and kiss her, he fought the temptation and turned to Vance. "Okay, what do we have?"

Vance chuckled. "They did just as we figured they would. They placed the video monitors in a frozen mode so the images my men are seeing are images from three hours earlier. Unknown to our intruders we installed additional video cameras and are able to see everything they're doing. Take a look."

Ian came to stand before the monitor. He saw two figures dressed in black as they silently moved across the room toward the vault. "Where's the third woman? And the guy?"

"They're in the casino," Brooke answered, and Ian could tell she was deliberately not looking at him. She pointed to another monitor that brought the couple into view. "What they're doing is establishing an alibi," she explained. "For the past hour they have been hopping from table to table, playing blackjack, poker, talking with the casino workers, anything they can do to make sure they're seen. Their alibi would be it's impossible to be in two places at the same time."

"It's possible if you're dealing with identical triplets," Dare said, frowning. "But then, no one was supposed to know that."

Ian shook his head. The foursome could have pulled this off as the perfect jewel heist if Brooke hadn't suspected something with that woman. No longer able to fight the urge any longer, he moved to stand beside Brooke and heard the sharp intake of her breath when he did so.

"Did we ever find out why we couldn't pick up a solid ID on the other two triplets?" he asked Vance.

"Yes. It seems they were separated at birth and raised by different families. They hooked up while in college, and nothing is recorded of them getting into any trouble. In fact, all three are from good homes. One of their adoptive fathers is a research scientist in Brussels."

He shook his head and continued. "It's my guess

they're doing this for kicks to see if they can get away with it. For four years they have eluded the law, which has made them bolder and bolder and almost unstoppable." A smile lit Vance's eyes when he added, "Until they decided to do business in my territory."

Everyone crowded around the monitor and watched as the two figures tried their hands at getting inside the vault. "They have successfully bypassed the alarm, which makes me think that one of them is a pro at that sort of thing," Brooke said.

Ian knew he didn't have to ask if their security men were in place. What the two intruders didn't know was that once they entered the vault, they would trigger a mechanism that would lock them inside.

He decided to move away from Brooke. Her scent was playing havoc with his mind and had aroused him to a high degree. He walked over to stand beside Dare, who was watching the activity on the monitor intently. Just as Ian knew this was not the time and place to kiss Brooke, he also knew it wasn't the time and place to thank his cousin for taking him to task, making him realize what a jewel he had in Brooke.

"See that wristwatch blondie is wearing," Brooke said, indicating the blond woman who was standing with her husband and chatting with one of the casino workers. "It's my guess it relays signals to and from the two who are working the vault. If something goes wrong she'll be the first to know."

"And my men will be ready if they try anything," Vance said. "All eyes are on them. In fact the woman that blondie is being so chatty with is one of my top people. She's pretending to be a casino worker tonight."

Ian shook his head. "Damn, Vance, you thought of everything."

Vance laughed. "That's why you pay me the big bucks."

They watched as the vault door opened. The kicker to the trap was to make sure both women went inside the vault. To make sure they did, Vance's team had put fake jewels in a big box that would require both of the women to lift it to stuff the jewels into the black felt bags they were carrying.

The plan worked. The moment both women were inside, the door slammed shut behind them. Everyone switched their gazes from that monitor to the one of the casino. And just as Brooke predicted, they read the look of panic on blondie's face when she received a signal from her sisters that something was wrong.

They watched as the woman leaned over and whispered into her husband's ear, not knowing her every word was being picked up. "Something went wrong. I got a distress signal from Jodie and Kay." The couple turned, no doubt to make their great escape, and barged right into several security men who were waiting to arrest them.

Vance grinned and said, "Those two are taken care of, so let's go meet and greet the other two."

Two hours later Ian's office was swarming with the local FBI and the news media. Everyone wanted to know how Ian's security team had been able to pull off what no law officials could—finally end the reign of the Waterloo Gang.

"I have to credit an off-duty FBI agent who just

happened to be vacationing at the Rolling Cascade," Ian said into the microphone that was shoved in his face. "This agent was alert enough to notice something about one of the women that raised her suspicions. She brought it to me and my security manager's attention. Had she not, we would have suffered a huge loss here tonight. I'm sure Prince Yasir is most appreciative."

Ian glanced around, but he didn't see Brooke anywhere and figured with all that had gone down, she was probably in one of the lounges getting a much-needed drink. "I also have to thank my cousin, Sheriff Dare Westmoreland, who just happens to be visiting from Atlanta. He helped us figure things out."

Ian then glanced over at Vance and grinned. "And of course I have to credit the Rolling Cascade's security team for making sure we had everything in place to nab the Waterloo Gang and to obtain the evidence we need to make sure they serve time behind bars. The entire thing was captured on film. We have handed the tapes over to the local FBI."

Ian checked his watch. It was almost two in the morning. More than anything he wanted to find Brooke, talk to her, beg her forgiveness, kiss her, make love to her...

"Mr. Westmoreland, were you surprised the Waterloo Gang was triplets?"

"Yes." And that was the last question he was going to answer tonight. He needed to see Brooke. "If you have any more questions, please direct them to Vance Parker, my security manger. There's a matter I need to attend to."

Ian caught the elevator down to the lobby and quickly

looked around. He released a sigh of relief when he saw Tara and Thorn at one of the slot machines. Before he could ask them if they'd seen Brooke, an excited Tara asked, "Is the rumor that we're hearing true? Did your security team actually nab a bunch of jewel thieves?"

"Yes, with Brooke's and Dare's help." Ian glanced around, his gaze anxiously darting around the crowd. "By the way, have either of you seen Brooke lately?"

Tara's smile turned to a frown. "Yes, I saw her a few moments ago. She was leaving."

Ian nodded as he eyed the nearest bank of elevators. "To go up to her room?"

"No, leaving the casino."

He snatched his head back around to Tara and a deep frown creased his forehead. "What do you mean she was leaving the casino?"

Tara narrowed her gaze at him. "Just what I said. She was checking out. She apologized to me for not staying for Delaney's party, but she said that she felt under the circumstances it was best if she left. She then got into her rental car and drove off."

"Damn." Ian rubbed the tension that suddenly appeared at the back of his neck. "Did she say where she was going?"

Tara glared at Ian and placed her hands on her hips. "Maybe. But then why should I tell you anything. You had your chance with her, Ian Westmoreland. Twice."

Ian glared back and then he looked at Thorn for help. His cousin merely laughed and said, "Hey, don't look at me. That's the same look she gives me before telling me to go sleep on the couch."

Ian bit back a retort that, considering Tara's condition, it seemed Thorn hadn't spent too many nights on the couch. He shook his head. He knew how loyal the women in the Westmoreland family were to each other, and there was no doubt in his mind that they had now included Brooke in their little network. That was fine with him because he intended to make a Westmoreland woman out of her—however, he had to find her to do so.

But first he had to convince Tara that he was worthy of Brooke's affections. "Okay, Tara, I blew it. I know that now. I owe Brooke a big apology."

She rolled her eyes and cross her arms over her chest. "That's all you think you owe her?"

He drew in a deep breath in desperation. "And what else do you have in mind?"

"A huge diamond would be nice."

Ian thought about strangling her but knew he would have to deal with Thorn. Although Ian would be the first to admit that Thorn had mellowed some since he'd gotten married, nobody in their right mind would intentionally get on Thorn's bad side.

"A huge diamond is no problem. She deserves a lot more than that."

Tara studied him as if she was considering his words. Then she asked, "And do you love her?"

"Yes." He didn't hesitate in answering. "More than life itself, and I just hope she'll forgive me for being such a fool."

Tara shrugged. "I hope she will, too. She looked pretty sad when she left here tonight and nothing I said could convince her to stay."

Ian nodded and thought he'd try his luck again by asking, "And where did she go?"

Tara looked at him for a long moment before saying, "To Reno. She couldn't get a flight out tonight so she's going to stay at a hotel in Reno and fly out sometime tomorrow."

Panic gripped Ian. He was beginning to come completely unraveled. "Do you happen to know which hotel?"

Tara took her sweet little time in answering. "The Reno Hilton."

With that knowledge in hand, Ian was out of the casino in a flash.

"Yes, Malcolm, I'm fine," Brooke said, biting down on her bottom lip to keep from crying. "No, I'm not at the casino. I'm at a hotel in Reno," she added when he asked her whereabouts. "I'll be flying home tomorrow."

Moments later she said, "It's a long story, Malcolm, and I don't want to go into details tonight. I'll call you when I'm back in town and we'll talk then."

Brooke hung up the phone. According to Malcolm, everyone at national headquarters was blissfully enjoying the news of the capture of the Waterloo Gang. The director wanted to meet with her to express his special thanks. Everyone was celebrating. That is, everyone but Walter Thurgood. From what Malcolm had said, the man was pretty pissed off that he wasn't able to get the credit. In a way, she was glad things had worked out the way they did. Had Thurgood shown up he would have tried to throw his weight around. But she, Dare and Vance had proven to be a rather good team. And then there was Ian.

Ian.

Just thinking his name brought a deep pain to her

heart. During the course of the night, she had felt his eyes on her, and each time when she imagined what he thought of her, her heart would break that much more. As she'd tried explaining to Tara, who'd tried to talk her out of leaving the Rolling Cascade, there was no way she could stay there any longer with Ian thinking the worst of her.

She glanced up when she heard a knock on her hotel room door. She crossed the room wondering who it could be at this hour. It was past three in the morning. "Yes?"

"It's Ian, Brooke."

Her heart began pounding hard in her chest. Ian? What was he doing here? Had he followed her all the way to Reno just to let her know, again, how little he trusted her? Well, she had news for him. Whether he wanted to believe it or not, she hadn't done anything wrong and she refused to put up with his attitude any longer.

After removing the security lock she angrily snatched open the door. "What are you doing—"

Before she could finish getting the words out, a single white rose was placed in her face, followed by a red one. When he lowered the roses she saw him standing there. She had to take a full minute to catch her breath.

"I'm here to ask your forgiveness, Brooke, for a lot of things. May I come in?"

She didn't answer. Instead, after a couple of moments she stepped aside. When he walked passed her, her body began humming the moment she caught his masculine scent. Once he stood in the middle of her room, she closed the door and turned to face him. He looked as tired as she felt, but even with exhaustion lining his features, he looked extremely good to her.

"Is the media still at the casino?" she decided to ask when it appeared he was trying to get his thoughts together.

"Yes, they're still there. I left them in Vance's capable hands."

She nodded. "I would offer you something to drink but…"

"That's fine. There's a lot I have to say, but I don't know where to start. I guess the first thing I should say is that I'm sorry for being so quick to jump to conclusions. I'm sorry for not trusting you, not believing in you. My only excuse, and it's really not one, is that I love you so much, Brooke, and I was scared to place that degree of love into your hands again. I hurt so badly the last time."

"Don't you think I was hurting as well, Ian?" she asked quietly. "It wasn't all about you. It was about us. I loved you enough to do anything to protect you. And over the years, nothing changed. If I hadn't still loved you as much as I did, I would not have cared if the Bureau sent someone to prove what I already know. You're an honest man who wouldn't do anything illegal."

She breathed in deeply before she continued, "This week has been real. My feelings and my emotions were genuine. I wasn't using you to find out information. The very idea that you thought I had…"

Ian crossed the room and cupped her face in his hands. "I admit I was wrong, sweetheart. Call me stupid. Call me a fool. Call me overly cautious. But I'm here asking, begging for you to give me, us, another chance. My life is nothing without you in it. I've seen that for four years. I love you, Brooke. I believe in you. I made a huge mistake, one I plan to make up for during the rest of my life. Please say you forgive me and that you still love me."

She looked deeply into his eyes. Placing the roses on the table she reached up and covered his hands with hers. "I love you, Ian, and I forgive you."

A rush of relief flooded from him just seconds before he lowered his face to hers and captured her lips. He kissed her long, hard, deep, needing the connection, the affection, and the realization that she was giving him, giving them, another chance. Coming here had been his ultimate gamble. But it had paid off.

When she wrapped her arms around his shoulders he picked her up into his arms. He needed to touch her, taste her, make love to her. He needed to forge a new beginning for them that included a life together that would last forever. Knowing there was only one way to get the closeness, that special connection that he craved, he walked over to the bed and placed her on it. Love combined with hunger drove him. He knew he had to show her just how much she meant to him. How much he loved her.

Pulling back slightly, he began trailing kisses along her neck and shoulders as he began removing the clothes from her body. Moments later he dragged in a deep breath when he had her completely undressed. He stood away from the bed and stared at her, absorbing into his physical being every aspect of her that he loved and cherished.

After removing his clothes he returned to the bed and pulled her closer to him. "I love you, Brooke. I didn't realize how much until I spent time with you these past two weeks. And I knew then that we were meant to be together."

"And I love you, too," she whispered when he cupped her butt and pulled her against the throbbing heat of his erection. And then he was kissing her again, putting into action what he'd said earlier in words. Love was driving him, propelling him to taste every inch of her, feel her moaning and writhing and whimpering under his lips. And when he knew she couldn't take any more, he stretched his body over hers, ran his fingertips down her cheek and whispered, "I love you," just seconds before he drove into her, connecting their bodies as one. And then he began moving, rocking, pushing her toward a climax so powerful he had to fight back the spasms that wanted to overtake him in the process.

Meticulously, methodically and with as much precision and love as any one man could have for any woman, Ian made love to her, igniting urges and cravings to explosive degrees. He took his time, wanting her to feel the love he was expressing. He wanted to show her that she was the only woman he wanted, the only one he could and would ever love.

"Ian!"

And when the explosion hit, skyrocketed them into another world, he held on and groaned when his release shot deep into her body. And when she bucked and tightened her legs around him he knew he was where he would always belong.

When they came back down to earth he pulled her into his arms, needing to hold her. He closed his eyes briefly, knowing this was paradise and heaven all rolled into one. Then he opened his eyes, knowing there was one other thing he had to do to make his life complete.

Rising up over her, he looked into the eyes of the woman he loved. "Will you marry me, Brooke? Will you share your life with me forever?"

He saw the tears that formed in her eyes, saw the trembling of her lips and heard the emotion in her voice when she whispered, "Yes. I'll marry you."

Smiling, he leaned down and rubbed his bearded face against her neck, knowing he was the happiest man in the world. He pulled back and, still smiling deeply, he said, "Come here, sweetheart."

And then he was pulling her into his arms again, intent on making love to his very special lady until daybreak and even beyond that.

Epilogue

Delaney's surprise birthday party was a huge success. Tears had sprung into her eyes when she had walked into the darkened ballroom and the lights flashed on and she was suddenly surrounded by family and friends. Even the secretary of state had made an appearance.

And with pure happiness on her face and love shining in her eyes, Delaney had turned to her husband and had given His Highness a thank-you kiss that to Brooke's way of thinking was as passionate as it was priceless.

She had always thought Prince Jamal Ari Yasir was an extremely handsome man and she still thought so, and tonight, dressed in his native Middle Eastern attire, he looked every bit a dashing sheikh. And it was evident that he was deeply in love with his wife. But nothing was more touching than the moment the prince presented his princess with that case of diamonds. She quickly became the envy of every woman in the room. Except one....

Brooke smiled, glancing at the tall, dashing, handsome man at her side. Of course, when Ian's family had seen them together they had begun asking questions. Ian and Brooke hadn't stated the response they had agreed to give earlier. Instead they truthfully and most happily said, "Yes, we're back together and we are planning a June wedding here at the Rolling Cascade."

No one seemed more thrilled with the news than Ian's mom. She had taken Brooke into her arms in a huge hug and whispered into her ear, "I knew he would eventually come to his senses. Welcome to the family, dear."

And speaking of family...

Brooke finally got to meet Uncle Corey's triplets and found that Clint and Cole were two extremely handsome men; typical Westmoreland males. And with her awe-inspiring beauty, Casey Westmoreland was grabbing a lot of male attention.

Brooke also got to meet all the Westmoreland wives. The Claiborne sisters, Jessica and Savannah, married to Chase and Durango. She met Storm's wife, Jayla; and Stone's wife, Madison. Uncle Corey had gripped her in a huge bear hug before introducing her to his new wife, Abby, who was also Madison's mother. Brooke smiled. Talk about keeping things in the family.

After Delaney's party, Ian whisked Brooke off to his conservatory and there on bended knees and under the moon and the stars, he again asked her to be his wife and presented her with a huge diamond engagement ring.

Tears flowed down her face when he slipped the ring on her finger. When he stood up, she looked at him with complete love shining in her eyes. He pulled her into his arms. "I want to kiss you beneath a shooting star," he whispered before trailing kisses along her jaw and neck.

"Do you think we can handle any more passion?" she asked, smiling.

"Oh, I think so. I think that together the two of us can handle just about anything."

And when he leaned down and kissed her, she believed him. Considering all they had been through, they *could* handle just about anything.

* * * * *

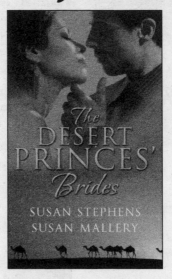

FREE!

2 Books
and a surprise gift!

We would like to take this opportunity to thank you for reading this Mills & Boon® book by offering you the chance to take TWO more specially selected titles from the Desire™ series absolutely FREE! We're also making this offer to introduce you to the benefits of the Mills & Boon® Book Club™—

- ★ **FREE home delivery**
- ★ **FREE gifts and competitions**
- ★ **FREE monthly Newsletter**
- ★ **Exclusive Mills & Boon Book Club offers**
- ★ **Books available before they're in the shops**

Accepting these FREE books and gift places you under no obligation to buy. you may cancel at any time, even after receiving your free shipment. Simply complete your details below and return the entire page to the address below. You don't even need a stamp!

YES! Please send me 2 free Desire books and a surprise gift. I understand that unless you hear from me. I will receive 3 superb new titles every month for just £5.25 each, postage and packing free. I am under no obligation to purchase any books and may cancel my subscription at any time. The free books and gift will be mine to keep in any case.

D8ZEF

Ms/Mrs/Miss/Mr .... Initials ....

BLOCK CAPITALS PLEASE

Surname ....

Address ....

....

.... Postcode ....

Send this whole page to:
UK: FREEPOST CN81, Croydon, CR9 3WZ